THE FARMER

For Elijah,

Enjoy my book!

Other fiction by I. Alexander Olchowski:

The Karma of Butterflies *(Unpublished)*

The Relevance of Men

THE FARMER

I. Alexander Olchowski

Cover design by Rose Tannenbaum
Author photo by John Eldridge
Book design by Melissa Mykal Batalin

To order additional copies of this title, contact your favorite local
bookstore or visit www.tbmbooks.com

ISBN: 978-1-935534-167

Special thanks to the ladies of the New Lebanon Writing group for all their helpful feedback. And to my readers; Dan, Tim, Sky, Regina, Vicki and Barkat. Thank you Rose, for the cover, and Melissa, for your patience. And thanks, of course, to my family.

Dear Reader,

The seed of inspiration for this book came from Ioka Valley Farm, located in Hancock, Massachusetts. I initially met with the owner, a tall, strong man in his sixties named Don, to pick his brain on the best livestock to raise in my situation. At the time I was living on a one-hundred acre former cattle farm, and feeling the urge to reinstate some animals to the land. Don steered me in the direction of meat goats. A year and a half later I had a herd of eleven kiko goats, and a new novel.

The Farmer is dedicated to every small-scale farmer in America. Ten percent of the book's final profits will be donated to a fund dedicated to helping small farmers in Columbia County, New York. And, as part of an Independent Bookstore Tour across the nation, my aim is to sow the seeds for a movement dedicated to strengthening the craft of literature, what has become a threatened art form.

This is the kind of book meant to be held in your hands, to linger on the bed stand for a few nights. Its pages will acquire that unique aroma of a worn, well-read book. And, hopefully, it will sweep you away from life for long stretches of time. To truly read a book is to inhabit it. And to do this we must slow down, detach from the breakneck speed of modern life. We need a return to books in the same way we are returning to good food. Inspired by the Slow Food Movement, this novel will mark the foundation of a Slow Book Movement. Join the cause. Help support the rebirth of modern American literature, and the publishers and bookstores that make it available to us all.

Thanks for reading my story.
www.slowbookmovement.com

I

SUNSET VALLEY

ONE

His small dairy farm was all he'd ever known, all he ever wanted to know, at least when it came to his place in the world. His home. Ed Brown knew other things beyond his home-is-where-the-heart-is-philosophy. Like the freckle just behind his wife's left ear. He knew that brown speck hadn't changed at all in thirty-two years. He still loved to kiss it right before turning out the bedroom light. And Ed knew his two sons as well as a father might expect to. Marvin, the oldest, wasn't going to be a farmer. With a law degree from Columbia, he was working for a firm in the city. In high school Marvin had played every sport, had joined every club he could in order to avoid the chores around the farm. And then there was Jack. The kid lacked academic or athletic prowess of any kind. But he had a natural way with the cows, thrived on hard work, and the farthest he ventured on a weekend night was to stroll down the road a couple miles to visit Katie Smignatelli, the girl he was sweet on. One thing Ed didn't know much about was hope. Having had no real use for it, he preferred more grounded, practical notions. Hope was a luxury, like day-dreams, one a serious farmer just didn't have time for. But he was beginning to make time for it. As his body bent over a little more every day, as his stiffening joints made it harder and harder to get out of bed at five o'clock in the morning, Ed began to hope for one thing beyond any other. He hoped Jack would stay and take over the farm.

Ed woke up well before his wife Susan. He never held it against her that she always slept later than he did. She'd never planned on being a dairy farmer's wife. After kissing her on the back of her head, eliciting a soft sleepy moan, he dressed himself in the cold darkness of their bedroom. Moving carefully to avoid the floorboards that squeaked, pulling on his one piece long underwear jumpsuit, Ed relished the fact that his wife was still sleeping, that he could give her this extra time in bed. She deserved it. Downstairs in the kitchen he turned on a couple lights. The rustic space was defined by old wooden beams, a chopping block fashioned out of a giant tree trunk, and a soapstone sink. He reached into a cabinet and pulled out the can of Folgers. Got a pot of coffee brewing. From the fridge, an old G.E. model with a steel, pull down handle, he took out a carton of eggs and a slab of bacon. It was barely six in the morning. Ed knew he wouldn't be eating again until Susan rang the bell for afternoon supper around two-thirty. So he always made sure his breakfasts were big, in order to get him through the meat of the day. While the bacon sizzled on the skillet he stoked the large cast-iron wood stove in one corner. He thought about Jack, still asleep in his downstairs bedroom. His son didn't need much breakfast, just a couple strips of bacon and a big cup of joe and he'd be ready for the morning milk and anything else that had to be done afterwards. Ed had a bundle of kindling stacked atop a mound of deep red coals from the night's fire. He crouched on all fours and blew hard until the sticks caught and yellow flames blazed up. He leaned a few medium-sized logs across the kindling and got up to flip his frying bacon.

It was a normal Saturday. He could hear Jack stirring to life in his bedroom, woken as usual by the combined aromas of coffee and bacon. But Ed knew things would stray from the norm later, when Marvin was planning to show up for the first time since graduating law school. He'd prefaced his visit to the farm with the fact that he had some news to announce to the family. Susan thought he was getting married, but Jack swore his brother didn't even have a steady girlfriend. Ed hadn't given it a whole lot of thought. Marvin was living a life foreign to everything he knew, the reality he counted on every day. He transferred the bacon to a paper towel, drained most of the grease into an old coffee can, and cracked a few fresh eggs into the cast iron pan. Jack stepped into the kitchen. He was rubbing his eyes with his fists. His blue eyes squinted open under the lights. He was dressed entirely in tan Carhart products, including suede work boots and a canvas cap with a green John Deere patch. Ed was all flannel and wool.

"Bacon's up. Coffee's almost done," Ed said.

"Cool."

Jack sat down at the long wooden kitchen table to lace up his boots. His father focused on the eggs. He flipped the eggs out of the pan and onto a plate. He added some bacon to the plate, poured a cup of coffee, and took a seat at the table. Jack got up to fetch his coffee and grab a couple pieces of bacon, then joined his father at the table.

"You really should have a bigger breakfast," Ed said.

"You tell me that every morning, Dad."

"Well, that's because it's true."

"Can't wait to see Marv."

"Me too."

"Can't wait to hear this news of his either," Jack added.

Ed focused on eating. He didn't share Jack's anticipation about Marvin's promised announcement. The path his first son had chosen was so alien to Ed that he had to force himself to celebrate its landmarks. At the farm there was something to revel in everyday. Marvin could have stayed home. There was plenty of eggs and bacon to go around. The men ate and sipped their coffee in silence. Jack fetched a second cup as Ed rose to drop his dishes in the sink.

"C'mon, son, you can bring the joe with ya."

It was the same thing he said every morning on their way out to the barn for the milking. Jack nodded, like he did every morning, and followed his father out the back door.

Susan liked to wake up at dawn. The clear shaft of light striking the floral papered walls of her bedroom was her natural alarm clock. The day's first light never failed to wake her no matter its shade or intensity. The first thing she did this Saturday morning was lean over and breathe in the smell of her husband's pillow. As usual she picked up aromas of hay and sawdust and, although she didn't like to admit it, a hint of manure. She climbed out of bed and began tidying up the room, moving about with a little extra vigor to her steps. Marvin was coming home today. Making one of his rare appearances. As she made the bed and gathered up her husband's clothes, Susan went over her menu for the afternoon supper in her head. When she got downstairs she would need to check that all the necessary ingredients were in the house. With the bedroom tidied she headed for the bathroom across the hall. There she would freshen up swiftly and efficiently.

She viewed extended time in the bathroom as an obscene luxury, one she knew many women indulged in gratuitously. Ten minutes in the morning and another ten before bed was all she ever needed. Except on Sunday. On Sunday she took a long bath before bed. They had a claw foot tub from an old hotel up the road that had burned down more than a hundred years ago. Ed only took a bath once a year, so someone had to use the beautiful tub. Tomorrow, after church and supper and seeing her son off on his way back to work, it would be bath time. Hopefully she'd still be in the mood to relax after hearing Marvin's news.

Downstairs in the kitchen, clean and refreshed, Susan whistled while she scrubbed clean the dishes from her husband's breakfast. She was happy to see he'd poured out the bacon grease into the old coffee can stored in the fridge. Once or twice, his mind likely focused on an upcoming task on the farm, he'd dumped it right down the drain. She poured out the rest of his coffee, preferring the black tea she would soon set to steep on the thick wooden counter. Coffee gave her the jitters. She hadn't had a full cup since her days at Wellesley College. Her initial survey of the kitchen pantry proved that no ingredients for the upcoming supper were missing. She didn't count the two chickens yet to be slaughtered by her husband and Jack. She would be sure to venture out a little later to help pick out two worthy birds. But she wanted no part of the beheading process. That was a man's job. She had potatoes to scrub and peel, turnips to peel and cut, and an apple pie to bake. Every ingredient except the flour came from the farm. The potatoes and turnips had been in the root cellar since the fall. The apples she'd dehydrated and stored in sealed cans. The butter they'd churned a week ago. The maple syrup for the pie came from their grove of sugar maples. And the milk for the mashed potatoes had been the easiest thing of all for her to come by. Her husband and son made a hundred gallons of the rich creamy Jersey milk every day. Before settling into her kitchen tasks she made sure to stoke up the fire with a few good sized logs. It had been cold for early April. The house still needed a fire in the woodstove every day.

When the men came out of the large barn, the cows milked and fed, Ed noticed the smoke billowing out from the chimney of the farmhouse. He smiled, happy to know Susan was busy in the kitchen. He figured she'd be out eventually to help with chicken selections. Ed already had a couple in mind, but he'd make sure to let his wife make the final call.

"What now, pops?" Jack asked, hands on his hips, eyes bright.

"I was thinkin' we'd start in on the electric fence in the upper pasture – gonna be time to turn these girls loose pretty soon, and we've got some serious gaps in the links after that winter blowdown."

Jack was nodding before his father had finished speaking. Ed's eyes shifted from his son to the topmost pasture. Fresh shoots of lime green grass were just starting to pop up. The creek at the bottom rushed full with the late winter runoff from the surrounding hills. The fresh smell of the air set off a twinge deep inside him, a fleeting bodily memory of what spring had felt like in his youth. The same feeling his son was likely infused with day and night.

"Maybe we should kill the birds first, though. Give 'em time to drain. Then we'll be able to see Marvin when he gets here from up in the fields," Jack suggested.

Ed stroked the white scruff of his chin, considering that sequence of events.

"Sounds like a plan," he said eventually.

On perfect cue the back door swung open and Susan stepped out. "You guys havin' some kinda conference or something up there?"

"We were, actually. Conferring about you!" Ed shouted down at her.

"Oh really? Didn't know I was so interesting."

"You're not, Mom," Jack chimed in, and they all laughed.

Susan joined them en route to the chicken yard off on the western edge of the property. She walked between the two men, all three of them slogging their way through thick, early spring mud. Ed's border collie Jill followed close behind his heels, occasionally catching her black and white snout on the back end of one of his rubber boots.

"Are you excited about your brother's visit?" Susan asked her son.

"I am. It's been awhile. Besides, the whole announcement thing should be cool."

"I know, it's so exciting. You're the only one who hasn't made a guess."

They were standing at the wire mesh fence now, watching the hens peck around the leftover hulls of corn from that morning's feeding, which the men had tended to even before the cows. Getting to the chickens early helped quiet the roosters down.

"No, I haven't. I just know the guesses you guys made are wrong."

"Well, if you had to make one, what would it be?" Susan pressed.

Ed cocked his head at his wife. He wondered why she was so interested in this. When the kid showed up they'd hear what he had to say, simple as that.

"If I had to make a guess, well, it would be . . .um . . .that he's coming home to work on the farm," Jack finally said.

Ed coughed in surprise.

"Could that be possible?!" Susan asked, elated by the idea of getting to keep both her sons around the farm. Ed saw deeper into Jack's strange guess. He gave his son a long hard stare. His muscles tightened. They'd never had an outright discussion about him eventually assuming the brunt of the day-to-day operations as Ed got older. It was just something he hoped would happen given the fact that Jack had not gone off to college, nor was he dedicating himself towards gaining any skill other than farming. Jack held his father's eyes.

"Just a wild guess, Dad. Even if that was true, which it won't be, I'm not going anywhere, don't worry. I've got your back around here."

Ed's muscles released their tension as he turned back to face the chicken yard.

"All right then, enough speculation – Ma, how 'bout that old rooster and the hen next to him over there by the side of the coop? Both of 'em are gettin' a little old – she hasn't been layin' much of anything, and his voice is so outta' tune it gives me a headache."

Susan scanned the yard as if she was looking for better choices, but she knew her husband's judgment was sound. They had other roosters. And she'd noticed how these two were inseparable, so killing one without the other would have been downright cruel.

"They look like fine eating, Ed. You agree Jack?" Susan asked.

"I do, Mom. I sure do."

Susan turned and walked back towards the house as Jack and Ed entered the chicken yard. They each grabbed one of the chosen birds by the feet. Jack had the rooster, Ed the old hen. They carried them to a concrete patio off the far side of the barn, an area designated solely for the purpose of chicken slaughtering. There was no other occasion to be on that part of the property. The sharp stench of rotting guts, an indescribably putrid odor that had caused more than one unsuspecting guest to gag, was often overwhelming. Ed got a cauldron of water heating on the propane burner. Jack locked the birds up in a little cage. Their cheerful clucking confirmed his theory that the chickens never caught on to what was about to happen until the final moment. He sat down on a stump and sharpened his machete with a file. Ed peered into the cauldron, watching the water heat up towards a boil. Jack stood up abruptly, remembering he was sitting on the execution stump stained with blood from past killings. He tucked the file into a pocket, and ran his thumb along the silver edge of the machete's blade.

"How's the water coming along pops?"

"Almost there," Ed said without lifting his head.

"Sweet. I'm going for it."

Ed nodded his approval.

Jack had been doing the actual killing for years now, ever since inheriting his father's machete when he turned thirteen. He enjoyed slaughtering the chickens as much as Ed hated it. He took the rooster first, holding it down with one hand while the other brought the wide steel blade slicing through feathers and into the scrawny neck. There was a quick, terrified squawk. Blood squirted out in a narrow stream that Jack angled away so it splashed off the side of the concrete patio onto a pile of sawdust. While its lifeless body convulsed with nerves, Jack pinned the bird up on a steel cable running from the side of the barn to an oak tree, passing over the sawdust pile. He repeated this process with the hen. When both birds were hung to drain the men strolled up through the fields. They knew Susan would be emerging soon to finish the job they'd started. First she would scald the dead chickens in the boiling water before loading them into the spinning, rubberized plucker Ed had fashioned out of an old clothes dryer.

She would gut them right there on the steel table, tossing the innards onto the pile of blood-soaked sawdust, then head back inside with supper's main course tucked under each arm.

As morning gave way to a warm spring afternoon every-thing was as it should be around the farm. Father and son were stringing new electric fence wire along one tree line of the upper field. Susan was opening the oven door to check on her two apple pies, looking for the rich brown color that would tell her they were done. Ed and Jack saw the dust rising above the long dirt driveway before they saw the black sedan, before Susan heard the quiet crunch of gravel outside her kitchen windows. The men dropped their tools and raced down the rock-strewn, muddy field. They splashed through the creek, then scaled the wooden rail fence at the bottom like soldiers at boot camp. Susan stepped out the back door. Marvin, in black slacks and a bright blue button down shirt, stood awkwardly beside his Toyota sedan, staring around as if he'd forgotten what the place looked like. Susan got to him first, her plaid apron covered in flour, a few potato peels stuck on in various places.

"Marvin!" she shouted.

"Hello Mother."

They hugged in the driveway. It was a long, tight hug that hadn't ended by the time Ed and Jack arrived on the scene. Susan released her son so he could exchange one-armed, manly hugs and smacks on the back from his father and his younger brother. Then they all stood in a circle while Marvin recounted his uneventful journey up the Taconic Parkway. Eventually he glanced towards the kitchen.

"Is that apple pie I smell Mom?"

"That would be two apple pies, Marvin, baking in your honor."

"Wow," he said, shaking his head.

"Yeah, that's why we're so happy to see ya," Ed said, elbowing Jack in the ribs. "Only time Ma' does any baking is when you show up!"

Ed winked at his wife as she crossed her arms in mock irritation.

"Jack and I did our part too, Marv – killed a couple chickens for our supper today."

"I'm a lucky guy," Marvin said.

"You sure are," Susan agreed.

Jack kicked the dirt. His smile had faded. "So Marvin, why don't you spill your beans now and get it over with, so this whole guessing game won't keep spoiling our appetites."

Marvin looked from his father to his mother. They both shrugged.

"Well, all right then." He turned, looking to the south, where the valley expanded into the saddle that cradled their town. "I've decided to leave the firm I've been working for in the city and come back here to open my own practice in Springtown."

"Oh honey, how wonderful!" Susan bubbled, hugging him again.

"That's a great idea," Ed said, reaching out to shake his hand. "It'll be good having you close by."

"Yeah, great, you'll be no different from the rest of these citiots swarming around here in their beamers," Jack spouted, locking his brother's eyes with his own.

"How can you say that Jack?"

"Because, you may have grown up on this farm, but you know nothing about this place. Absolutely nothing."

"Maybe your brother's changed a little bit," Susan said, playing nervously with a stray lock of her curly hair. Ed looked sternly back and forth from one son to the other.

"I doubt it," Jack muttered, and stalked off towards the house.

"I thought he might actually be happy about the news," Marvin said to his parents, shaking his head.

"Eh," Ed said, hands on his overall-clad hips, kicking at the dirt. "You may have changed a bit, Marv. But Jack sure hasn't."

Marvin tried to sound more pissed off than he really was. "So in other words he's still going to act as if he's the older brother?"

"Exactly," Ed confirmed.

Susan cracked a smile. The natural sparkle in her eyes was slowly returning.

Ed put a palm on his stomach. "Anybody else hear these rumblings inside my belly? We can talk more over supper. Let's get down to business, Ma. Smells like those pies are almost done anyway!"

"Oh, I almost forgot all about them!" Susan hurried into the house through the back door.

Ed laid a hand on Marvin's shoulder. "C'mon Marv, let me help you with your bags."

"Thanks Dad."

With the pies cooling and the chickens loaded into the oven for baking, the men sat around the oval maple table by the wood stove while Susan put the finishing touches on the meal. This didn't mean she was left out of the conversation. She made sure to stay involved from her side of the kitchen while she moved between the chopping block, the stove, and the sink. At one point the floor shook with a heavy vibration. Dishes clattered on the shelves.

"What was that?" Marvin asked, clutching the table as if to steady it. "A tank?"

"Another dump truck," Ed muttered.

Marvin looked at his brother for further explanation. But Jack was trying to give him the silent treatment, so Ed filled him in on this local current event. "You didn't hear how the old Wilson farm was sold last year to a developer from the city?"

"No."

"Yeah, the guy bought all five hundred acres, and now he's building a hundred houses up there."

"Holy shit," Marvin said. "Old man Wilson must be rolling over in his grave right now. Literally. I think he was buried on the property. Those bulldozers might turn up a nasty surprise."

"For sure," Ed said, clasping one weathered, deeply veined hand over the other.

Pete Wilson had been the only other dairy farmer in the county while Marvin and Jack were growing up, outlasting all the farmers that used to line their road. All those farms, and so many others like them around Springtown, had been replaced by houses that looked like they'd been plucked out of suburban Westchester and replanted on a little parcel of former pasture. Old Man Wilson, as he was known around town, had blown his head off with a shotgun when milk prices hit rock bottom in the late nineties. Marvin remembered the terrified grief permanently etched onto Chris Wilson's face all through their remaining years in school together.

"But I thought Chris went to college for agriculture and then came back home to try and make the farm work?" he asked his parents.

"He did," Susan clarified. "But he failed."

Another dump truck rumbled past the farmhouse. The walls shook as if from the aftershock of a miniature earthquake.

"Wow. One hundred houses," Marvin said, trying to visualize the great farm up the road, where he had frolicked as a young boy with his childhood best friend, transformed into a subdivision. "What do you think about it, Dad?"

"Eh, those houses ain't gonna affect us, aside from more traffic going up the road. So what. Maybe I'll build a roadside stand and sell our extra vegetables. We'll be fine. No problem."

Susan was putting all her weight into mashing a bowl of steaming potatoes. Her next question came out between a series of grunts. "And will you be living here at the farm when you come back?"

Ed and Jack both looked intently at Marvin. Susan halted her mashing. The whole room seemed to hang on his answer. Susan hoped for a yes. Jack, having been upstaged by his brother all during his childhood, wanted to hear a no. Ed didn't know what answer to wish for. Marvin shook his head.

"Maybe you can get one of them new houses on the old Wilson farm," Jack stabbed.

His voice startled all three of them.

"Listen, Jack," Marvin shot back. "If you have a problem with me moving back to Springtown, just say so."

Jack kept his lips pressed tightly together. His father looked at him as if he was daring him to speak out. His mother looked out the window above her sink, waiting for the moment to pass.

Marvin spoke with a calm, measured voice, putting the issue to rest. "I want to live in town, on a quiet street, and walk to my office. A simple life. That's all."

Jack stayed silent, and the tension gradually receded from the table.

"How nice," Susan said, trying hard to hide her hint of motherly disappointment, the irrational fantasy that her first son might have asked to move back into the farmhouse.

"Yeah, besides, if I did move back in here I might end up doing all Jack's chores on my days off!"

Marvin reached out to slap his brother playfully on the shoulder. Jack caught his arm by the wrist and twisted it towards the ground. Marvin shouted in pain. Ed lunged at Jack, squeezing his bicep with both hands until he released his brother's wrist.

Susan, masher in hand, rushed over to the table. "What's going on?!"

"Nothing, Ma," Jack said. "Just felt like four-eyes over there was makin' fun of me for choosing to help dad run the farm instead of becoming some nerdy lawyer. Like you ever did any chores anyway," he snapped at his brother.

Marvin bristled, sitting up in his chair. Ed stood between them, ushering Susan back toward the opposite side of the kitchen.

"Please, boys, let's not go down this road. We haven't all been together since Christmas. It's a special time. And I'm proud of both of you. You're each a different kind of man. The world needs different kinds of men." He laid a hand on a shoulder of each son. "So can we have a peaceful supper here today?"

Jack and Marvin nodded obediently.

"Good, 'cause my nose is telling me them birds have finished roasting. What's the word, Ma?"

No one brought up the subject of Marvin's decision for the rest of his visit. That evening the family played board games until midnight, rekindling a ritual from days past, culminating in a marathon game of Monopoly won by Marvin. Ed made jokes about politics. Susan asked Marvin about his apartment, and whether he was getting enough to eat. They all teased Jack about his evening visits to his girlfriend Katie's house down the road.

"At least I have a girlfriend," Jack fired back at his brother.

"You sure she's not related to the family?" Marvin jabbed. "Isn't that how the farm boys do it?"

Jack launched a red plastic hotel at his brother's head.

"Hey now!" Susan said, trying to hide a smile while connecting eyes with her husband. They were both taking a little comfort from hearing their boys squabble again. For a moment it felt like time had stopped ten years ago and was holding still for them, that if they could just make the board game last forever nothing would ever change again.

The next morning Marvin joined his father and brother for breakfast, accepting a plate full of eggs and bacon but turning down Ed's coffee. "I can't do that Folger's stuff anymore, Dad."

Jack frowned at him. "Yeah, 'cause you got hooked on that Starbuck's junk down there at law school," Ed said.

Marvin smiled. "I have grown accustomed to a certain level of quality. No offense to Folgers."

"None taken."

Jack slurped at his mug of coffee and shook his head in mock disgust. "Least you brought your milkin' clothes," Jack said, nodding at Marvin's old overalls with patches their mother had sewn on in years past.

"Of course I did," Marvin said, winking at his father. "So are we about ready to head out to the girls?"

"Sure thing. Hey Jack, you can bring the joe with ya.'"

"I know, Dad."

In the great barn the three of them moved as a fluid unit from stall to stall, working together to position and attach the mechanized milker to each cow's set of teats. Marvin winced from time to time at the sharp smell of ammonia rising up from the damp concrete, an aroma his nose wasn't conditioned to anymore. He was much more familiar with the smell of thick books and courthouses.

"Remember that time we lost power for three days or something, and had to do all the milking by hand?" he asked both of them.

"Who could forget that," Ed said as they slid the mechanized milker along the track above the stalls. "In a way I kind of enjoyed it. Wouldn't want to do it again, though. My hands ached for weeks!"

They all bent down under another cow to attach the black suction cups to an udder.

"I remember you usually managed to find some nice excuses for not making it out for one or two of those hand-milkings," Jack said.

Marvin stood up. "What are you trying to say Jack?! Just 'cause I had a life doesn't mean I didn't care about - "

"All right, Marv, leave it alone," Ed said sternly, rising to his feet. "Jack, please, no more comments like that while your brother's home. Both of you are different people. And I love ya' both with all my heart – now let's finish the milking in peace. Okay? It's my favorite time of the day."

They waited for the machine to finish its job, watching the white liquid jerk its way up the clear plastic tubes.

"What about supper?" Marvin asked his father. "I would have thought that was your favorite time of day."

"Eh. You got me. This is my second favorite, then."

Marvin checked for a smile on his brother's face that wasn't there.

After the milking the men ventured across the fields towards the upper pasture, where they would continue repairing the damaged electric fence. On their way they stopped and stood below the spring-fed pond in the middle of the lowest field. It was the cows' only water source, pumped into the barn for the morning, evening, and winter drinking requirements of the herd. There was a separate well supplying the house with water.

"So is that the same creek flowing under Main Street down in town?" Marvin asked, his adult eyes finally making a connection between the small brook born from the overflow of their pond and the rushing creek a few miles down the valley in town.

"Flows into that crick about a mile from here," Ed clarified. "Above town a bit."

"I never realized that."

"Yeah, you can go sit by it on your lunch break and think of us up here making milk," Jack snipped.

"Maybe I will."

Ed bent down just below the outlet, cupped a handful of water, and lifted it to his mouth for a sip. "Still clean enough to drink this time of year, before the cows get out here. Always been that way, ever since my father first settled here. Wouldn't want that to change."

"Me neither," Jack said, bending down for his own sample of the fresh water.

Ed and Jack splashed across the little brook. Marvin moved slowly towards the other side, picking his way over on the rocks sticking up out of the rushing water. The men worked along the upper fence lines through the rest of the morning and into early afternoon, right up until the sound of Susan's two-fingered whistle called their stomachs to attention. Walking briskly down the field they each made guesses about the upcoming supper.

"You can count on chicken soup," Ed said, certain about the fate of the carcasses from yesterday's meal.

"I'll bet she'll mash the leftover turnips with some sweet potatoes," Marvin said.

"And don't forget there's a whole pie we didn't get to," Jack chimed in.

The men stepped into the warm, fragrant kitchen. Ed approached his wife and kissed her on the cheek as Marvin and Jack took turns washing their hands before taking their seats at the kitchen table. By the time they were all seated everyone had noticed the glint in Jack's eyes, like he was holding on to some kind of secret.

"All right, Jack. Out with it," Marvin finally demanded.

Jack leaned back in his wooden chair, clearing his throat. "Well, I've got a little announcement of my own to make, in keeping with the spirit of the weekend." He paused for dramatic effect. The family hung on his words. "It seems, based on a few prints I stumbled on in the backyard, that there's a wolf in the neighborhood!"

Ed stood up and stared sharply down at his son. Susan lowered her eyes. Marvin fidgeted with his piece of pie. Ed's voice boomed. "You sound like you actually think a wolf roaming around our farm is exciting. Is that true?"

"Well," Jack started, wishing now he'd just kept the whole thing to himself. When he first noticed the prints, paws bigger than his fist with claws extending half an inch into the surrounding mud, he'd been wise enough to cover them with his boot before his father had a chance to stumble upon evidence Jack knew would upset him. But here he was announcing the discovery with pride, hoping to garner more attention than his brother in this final hour of his visit.

"There's always been coyotes around," Susan said softly.

"A pack of coyotes will have one hell of a time bringing down a cow – they won't even try," Ed said. "But one wolf would have a good shot, and a few, forget it, they could slaughter three or four of the girls in one shot!"

Ed was pacing heavily about the kitchen. He was visibly disturbed by Jack's discovery.

"D – don't you want to finish your pie, honey?" Susan ventured.

"No." He reached for the can of Folgers in the cabinet.

"We could get some donkeys, Dad. They'll defend cows against anything," Jack spoke up, trying to wiggle out of the situation he'd created. No one could tell if Ed was considering the donkey idea as he scooped out the rich black grounds. His tensed shoulders relaxed slightly while he breathed in the aroma of ground coffee.

"I've heard llamas work too," Marvin added.

"Yeah, but donkeys are better," Jack whispered to his brother. "They don't spit, and they eat less."

"Donkeys are better," Ed said, as if he was talking to the coffee maker.

"So, we'll get some donkeys!" Susan said, finally lifting her head. "Problem solved. Right?"

Ed shook his head. "Only real way to solve a wolf problem is with a rifle. But knowing this state I'd be sittin' in prison for five years if I shot a wolf – they haven't been down this way in a century. Those conservationists'll be running around all over these hills pretty soon. Eh. Whatta' they care about us? We're the last dairy farm in fifty square miles. They get their goddamn milk from the supermarket shelf without any clue where it came from. Whether it's mine or the stuff from Nebraska doesn't matter one bit. Stuff from Nebraska's probly' cheaper anyway, even with the hormones. The hormones are free."

The coffee machine perking away was the only sound in the kitchen. The three of them rarely heard Ed swear. Calmed by the smell of brewing coffee, remembering his piece of pie, he walked back to the table. His steps were lighter now, his face loosening. "You all gonna finish the pie? Cause if not I will!"

Ed sat down and dug into the rest of his apple pie. The others ate right along with him, while a precarious silence settled in around them.

Marvin left shortly before dark. The family gave him a rousing farewell in the driveway to accompany the eggs and leftover food Susan had packed into a cooler for him. Usually Jack did the evening check on the cows, making sure they had enough hay and water for the night, then closing up the doors to keep any marauders out before wandering down the road to Katie's house. But on this night Ed made it clear that he wanted to handle the evening check. So after Jack left for Katie's, while Susan settled in at her spinning wheel in the living room, Ed walked out to the barn with his border collie Jill close by his side. He took note of the stars, finding the big dipper where it hung upside down above his fields. White light spilled out of the little square windows along the front of the barn, casting frames of light on the dark ground.

Ed stepped into the barn and stopped, listening to the comforting sounds of the girls chewing their cuds. He made his way down the aisle, cows on either side of him, moving in no particular rush. Jill scavenged the concrete floor for stray pellets of grain. Some of the cows noticed Ed and showed it, others could have cared less about his presence among them. The ones that were aware were some of his favorites, girls he'd named over the years as they showed him sides of their personalities that set them apart from the rest of the herd. He stopped to visit them, rubbing under their noses, scratching the place between their big brown eyes. There was Daisy, whose patterns of black spots looked like flowers, and who had the habit of snorting like a horse. Julia was the beauty queen, the only cow Ed had ever seen wink on a regular basis. Sandy, the eldest of all, bossed all the young ones around, often pawing at the ground like a bull in heat. And then there was Matilda, possibly his all-time favorite, a cow so gentle and sweet and well-mannered he would have considered inviting her to live in the house if he were a bachelor. He spent time with all these girls that evening, and others too, talking to them in a soft, cooing voice. There was an incredible peace in the barn at night, a feeling he'd forgotten about since Jack had taken on the evening duties. The cows, like any farm animal, seemed to be utterly content with the simple fact they'd made it through another day, looking forward to one last snack before sleep. After doling out the hay and filling up any water troughs that were low he bid them all goodnight, flicked off the lights and secured the doors. Stepping out of the barn he could see the light was on in his bedroom. It was a beacon distracting him from the stars, beckoning him with the promise of soft pillows, and the floral scent of his wife.

"C'mon, Jill, it's bedtime."

The dog followed his heels toward the house.

TWO

SPRING went by in a flash of lime green before any of them had realized it. The summer was always Susan's favorite season. She loved the round fullness of the warmth, the orange moon rise, fireflies flashing in the fields. She lived for the smell of goldenrod in the sun. Night swims under the stars kept her up late. Thunderstorms were her primary form of evening entertainment. Summer on the farm that year began steady and gentle and strong. Marvin was settling into his practice in town and his quaint three-bedroom house on a tree-lined street. The Jerseys were producing great quantities of milk, so even though prices remained just above rock bottom the family could still pay their bills and put food on the table. Ed and Jack had long conversations about ways to diversify. They talked about Angus beef and free range eggs, Christmas trees and hay rides.

"We're a farm, not Disneyland," Jack said when Ed suggested Haunted Pumpkin Night.

"I know, son. But we've still gotta make a buck."

With Marvin making plenty of bucks just a few miles away, while working far fewer hours, the situation grew more evident by the day. Milk could not support the farm anymore. Ed was having trouble affording the taxes, even though he'd re-mortgaged the house the year before. Asking his son for help was not an option. As the fabric of the farm threatened to unravel, Susan was the glue holding the family together, constantly reassuring them at the supper table that everything was going to be all right. Nobody had seen another sign of the wolf. And the dump trucks continued to rumble past on their way to the development site up the road.

Ed sucked it up and went on a campaign to attract the tourists that swarmed across the area during weekends and holidays, sometimes increasing the population in town ten-fold on a given Saturday. To start he ordered a hundred baby fir trees, which he and Jack planted in their least-used pasture. It took them half a day using the hydraulic post hole digger attached to the back of his tractor, an extinct model that Ed estimated to be at least fifty years old.

They ended up with ten even rows, ten trees in each row. While Jack settled down for his customary late afternoon nap after supper, Ed strolled back out to survey their work. The trees were puny little things, all he could afford to invest in a project that would offer no return for at least a decade. He thought the trees looked funny in those rows, that they somehow would never fit in with the rest of the farm. Ed had never cared much for pine forests. They were always so sterile compared to his mixed woods, the stands of shimmering birches, bold oaks, and graceful maples that surrounded his pastures. He kicked at the ground and cocked his head back to look up at the sky. He needed to embark upon the next tourism project, something that would have a more immediate payback than Christmas trees. Summer was almost halfway over. Searching for a way to capitalize on the next season, his mind looked forward to fall.

Fall was all about corn. Their most pressing task in September was harvesting the corn that would feed their cows through the winter. Without a combine, he and Jack spent two weeks hand harvesting ten acres of corn cobs. This left the eight foot high stalks and great, sweeping leaves standing, a towering maze of dried golden plants Jack and Marvin used to have fun getting lost in when they were kids. Before Thanksgiving the dried stalks would be turned into the soil, adding compost to the following year's sewing of oats. Looking past the barn to this field of brilliant green corn, all of it swaying gently in a light breeze, Ed saw his vision of what to do next. Conveniently the idea could easily be combined with a trial run of a dozen Angus beef cattle, which so delighted Jack he didn't even mock the idea, one he otherwise would have considered a much greater sellout than the Christmas tree farm.

That weekend they picked up an old fashioned yoke at a flea market in town. On the following week, while they mostly worked on the wagon that would attach to the yoke, the large black cows arrived by trailer truck from Ohio. The big, confident calves, many of them horned, caused quite a stir among the Jersey milkers, even in their own separate pasture.

"What are we gonna do in the winter?" Jack asked his father on the day of their arrival. "Build a new barn?"

Ed shrugged off the problem. "They'll be fine in a three-sided shelter out there. Angus are tough."

It took them a week to build the hay wagon to be pulled by the two biggest bulls that had just arrived, through trails cut into the dying hay field, a wagon that would hopefully carry large loads of city children whose parents had paid ten bucks a pop for a spot on a bale. The day they finished Ed was on the gravel behind the barn painting a large sign for the wagon. Jack stood over his shoulder and read the bold black lettering out loud. "UNCLE ED'S HAUNTED HAY RIDE?"

"That's right," Ed said, focusing on the witch riding a broom he was carefully painting in one corner.

"You have to be kidding. Uncle Ed?"

"That's me!"

His father's absurd enthusiasm was only making Jack more disturbed about the situation. "What are you gonna do, throw a couple sheets over corn stalks and call 'em ghosts?"

"How'd you know?" Ed looked up with the question.

"Pff," Jack muttered, shuffling back to finish hammering one of the wagon's wheels to an axle just inside the barn. "Sounds just like what a guy named Uncle Ed would think of. It's creepy, Dad. And to think I was excited about these Angus cows. I should have known they would just be pawns in another ridiculous scheme of yours to sell out even more."

Ed stoop up, a paintbrush in one hand dripping black paint on the gravel. His face was set, serious as stone. "We have to sell something besides milk, son."

"Yeah, but does it have to be our pride?"

Jack didn't wait around for his father's answer. He walked off through the barn towards the house, leaving Ed alone with the hay wagon and his half-finished sign. He wondered if leading haunted hay rides through his corn field and calling himself Uncle Ed would really be selling his pride. He decided there was no way to know for sure until he was actually up there holding the reigns of the yoke. Until then it was just another part of survival.

That night in bed, when Ed told his wife how proud he was of the wagon, Susan congratulated him on a job well done and announced she would come take a look at it first thing in the morning.

"Ed?" she asked, her tone shifting dramatically.

"Yes dear?"

"How are you paying for all of this? The trees, that yoke, the new cattle – last I knew we were re-mortgaging the house."

"I've been using a credit card," Ed said softly. "American Express has a new program for small farmers. The first ten thousand you spend is interest free, as long as you start making payments right away."

Susan was silent for so long Ed thought she might have fallen asleep. But her breathing hadn't changed. And when he turned his head on the pillow to look over, her eyes were wide open. "And those Christmas trees will be ready to sell when?"

Ed didn't bother answering a question to which his wife already knew the answer.

"The beef cows will be ready for market next spring," he announced.

What he didn't mention was that he hadn't yet taken into consideration what he was going to feed the new cows through the winter. He'd only planted enough hay and corn and oats for his regular herd of Jerseys. "Either way, Uncle Ed plans on giving a whole lot of haunted hay rides."

"Yes, he'd better. Or Aunt Suzie will have nothing to make him for supper. Not to mention she'll start keeping her clothes on in bed. And that would be a shame for both of us."

Ed thought he saw the flash of her teeth, a quick smile in the darkness, but he couldn't be sure.

One morning in mid-July Jack found his father standing by the bank of the stream below the pond in the lower pasture. His hands were on his hips. His head shook slowly from side to side. Jack walked up and stood next to him.

"Water's low," Ed said.

"It's summer, Dad. The crick's always a little - "

"Never like this."

Ed pointed to the pond. "Ya' ever seen so much mud on the bank? The girls can hardly make it down to the water." There were tracks of slipping hooves all around the bank of the pond. "And look at the crick - so many rocks sticking up. Barely a trickle. Trust me, son, it's never been like this in July. Even August. And it's been rainin' plenty."

Jack nodded, realizing his father was right. Ed turned to look up the road.

"Your mother told me she heard they dug a hundred wells up there. One for each house! Turns out having a private well is a big seller with people these days, ever since serious droughts started popping up all over the country."

"But those houses are like two miles away. They couldn't possibly affect us. Could they?"

"I don't know. I'm sure they've tapped into the same aquifer that feeds this pond, and the well for our house."

"Bastards," Jack said, his eyes narrowing as he followed his father's gaze towards the north, where the valley constricted into a dark hollow. "What should we do?"

"I think I need to take a ride on up there, check out the operation, maybe have a little chat with the head honcho."

"I'm coming too," Jack stated.

Ed turned to face his son. He spoke in a strong, stern voice. "No, son. You'll stay here and watch over things. The water is dangerously low. If it keeps dropping we'll be hauling buckets from the house in no time."

They both looked back down at the meager creek.

"You really think it's going to keep dropping?" Jack asked.

If the pond lowered another foot the creek would stop completely and, worse than that by far, the water pump feeding the barn would no longer be submerged.

"I don't know what to think," Ed said, shaking his head. "Hopefully when I get back I'll have us an answer. Otherwise there's nothing we can really do."

"Except pray," Jack blurted out, surprising them both. Neither man had ever uttered a prayer in his life.

"Can't hurt," Ed muttered, still digesting his shock over his son's sudden religious inclinations.

"It sure can't, pops."

THREE

DAN Cook was not an average developer. He'd been aware of the travesty inherent to the business well before he got in it, and recognized that his fortune had been made partly by ruining landscapes and damaging the earth. So Dan tried to focus on the fact that people needed homes to live in, and if he didn't build them then somebody else would. But beyond this underlying shame brought on by the realities of his career, what mattered above and beyond all else was that being a developer was simply his means to a very specific end. As a Harvard grad, his life could have gone in many different directions of success. But he'd bucked the adamant protests of his family and dove headfirst into homebuilding. As hard-working as he was intelligent, Dan Cook rose quickly through the ranks, owning his own building company by the age of thirty. He hated everything about the business. But he stayed in it with one all-consuming goal, to become a multi-mil-lionaire. Having achieved this end, trying hard not to regret the means that got him there, he was now a free man. After finishing this last project he could go anywhere, and do whatever he wanted once he got there. He would finally possess the ultimate version of the American Dream.

Dan had suspended all his other commitments, both personally and professionally, gearing himself up to spend an indefinite amount of time at the site of his new project upstate. For the past few months he'd been spending only a few days at a time in Springtown, setting up his trailer office at the development, overseeing the early stages of construction. Leaving Manhattan in his Prius, navigating towards the Taconic Parkway, he wondered if he would be able to truly leave the city behind. The towering glass skyscrapers, the honking rush of the cramped streets, the smell rising up through subway grates, all of this was finally beginning to feel like home. It had taken almost twenty years of living in the Big Apple, a daily life he resumed in between each new project, to squeeze some comfort out of the city. If life gave you an apple, he liked to tell people at cocktail parties, even a giant one enveloping eleven million people within its skin, the only thing to do was make apple juice. That's what he'd been trying to do for twenty years, and was just starting to enjoy the flavor.

But here he was driving his hybrid north along the racetrack curves of the Saw Mill, leaving behind this precarious hold he had on a place to call home, exchanging his Madison Avenue penthouse for a room at the Springtown Holiday Inn, trading a five minute stroll to his office with a cup of Starbucks in hand for a ten minute drive past a stinking dairy farm with a cup of Dunkin Donuts in the cup holder. But if his career had taught him one thing it was that success demanded adaptability. A fortune could only be built atop an ability to change. So as the Taconic wound its way through green valleys, as strange smells of plowed earth and goldenrod pollen slipped in through the vents, Dan tried hard to forget Manhattan, to block out its endless possibilities for romance and its bear-hug embrace of those with power. He would have to exchange the city he'd just learned how to love for a small town that only came alive on the weekends, when others like him arrived with money to spend and a cultural sensibility that extended beyond all-night diners and drive-in movies.

When planning out Sunset Valley, the one-hundred home development on the old Wilson track, he considered it to be his pinnacle achievement as a builder. Dan wanted to do this one right, and was sacrificing enormous profits to make all one hundred homes Green Certified. The entire subdivision was to be powered by the three giant windmills along the top of the surrounding ridges, and rows of solar panels across a sloping meadow. And, what had been an easy decision given the renowned quality of the local spring water, filtered by limestone and coursing through a myriad web of under-ground rivers, every house would have its own well, each well capped with an old-fashioned hand pump, a finishing touch that made Dan smile one afternoon as he hovered over the latest blueprints in his on-site office. The plans were being executed by a dazzling array of men and machinery on the other side of the vinyl blinds on his trailer's windows.

Dan Cook didn't have a secretary. So when a loud knock drew his attention from the large blue sheets covered in white ink, he got up from the drafting table and opened the flimsy door of the trailer himself.

"Who's in charge of this operation?" Ed asked forcefully, his black eyes scanning the makeshift office.

"I am. Dan Cook. Who are you?" Dan reached out a hand.

Ed shook it, hard and quick. "Ed Brown. I own the dairy farm down the road."

"Yeah, sure. I've heard about your place. And I've been indulging in your delicious milk. Please, have a seat." The developer motioned for Ed to seat himself in the swivel chair alongside his drafting table.

"No thanks," Ed said.

"Suit yourself."

Dan took a few steps backwards, looking for breathing room, feeling like the space was too small for both of them. And Ed was staring a hole through his chest.

"What can I do for you, Farmer Brown?" Dan asked, supporting himself with one arm propped on his drafting table, wishing he could hold up his other hand to block the piercing stare of this neighbor of his, a potential adversary standing there in the horizontal shafts of daylight streaking through the dusty air.

"My pond's run almost dry, same pond my cows drink from. And I have reason to believe the wells you've been drilling up here are sucking my water."

Dan was flushed with a wave of innocent confidence. His developments had certainly screwed people in the past, something he wrote off as a necessary aspect of turning a profit in the world of business, but drawing from Ed Brown's water source had never been considered during his planning of the project. His reaction was unnaturally cocky.

"I highly doubt my hundred wells are affecting your pond two miles down the road," Dan said, even as one part of his mind told the rest of it this was a definite possibility. Regardless, he'd sparked Ed's temper.

"You'll be hearing from my lawyer," Ed stammered. He spun around, opened the door, and slammed it behind him. The whole trailer shook in a violent spasm. Dan's blueprints cascaded to the floor around him.

Driving home Ed took note of the day, the kind that is mostly sunny or partly cloudy, depending on the mood of the observer. Seeing mostly sun, he was speeding. The last statement he'd boldly made in the double-wide office had shocked him. He wasn't one to pick a fight with some city-slick developer like Dan Cook. And he didn't have a lawyer. Then it hit him, a revelation that made him drive the pedal even closer to the metal. Of course he had a lawyer. His lawyer was his son. Although Marvin had been building up a decent work load of cases during the first few months of his practice in town, mortgages and small business loans and driving infractions, Ed was certain his son would jump all over the chance to take on a lawsuit as dynamic and challenging as this one against Mr. Cook promised to be. Beyond helping to save the family farm, the case had the potential to chart a course for Marvin's career. Nearing eighty on the straightaway approach to his driveway, Ed knew he had to call his son first thing when he got home.

Susan had delayed the afternoon supper, and was busy monitoring food she was keeping warm on the stove top when Ed stormed into the kitchen in a flurry of excitement. He made a beeline towards the cordless phone hanging on the wall.

"Did it go well up there?" she asked him.

"Sort of," Ed said, dialing Marvin's number.

"Who are you calling?"

"Marvin."

"Oh. Why?"

Susan was so perplexed by this hyper version of her normally calm and collected husband that she entirely ignored the pots and pans, took her attention away from the food simmering and steaming on the stove.

"Because," Ed said. "I need a lawyer."

Jack was in his room eagerly awaiting supper. When he heard his dad's voice in the kitchen he jumped off his bed and made his way down the hallway. But he stopped short of entering the kitchen, choosing instead to listen in from the dark anonymity of the hallway. Jack couldn't see his father, sitting now at the kitchen table, but his mom was in clear sight, looking unusually lost in her own kitchen.

"Marv, hey, it's your father. Listen, I was at that new development up the road this afternoon, and I met the owner, some hot shot named Dan Cook."

Jack stayed in the darkness, secretly listening to his father continue.

"Yeah, the asshole denied his wells could affect my water table, but I don't believe him for one second. He's smart enough to know better. So, I got to thinkin on my way back home that I should take the bastard to court. And then I figured you could be my lawyer."

Ed listened to Marvin's response. "What do ya' mean something has to happen?" he asked his son. "You mean some kind of disaster or something?"

Susan started breathing a little easier.

"Oh, I see. Well, I guess I'll just have to deal with the guy for now. But if push does come to shove for some reason, will you be ready for me? Good. All right, then, Marv. See you soon, I hope." Ed hung up the phone.

Jack strode into the kitchen as if he'd been in his room the whole time and hadn't heard a thing. "Hey guys, what's up?" he said cheerfully.

"Nothing," Susan said, cutting Ed off before he'd had a chance to speak. "Just about to put supper on the table."

"Cool."

During the meal Ed filled them both in on his visit to the development, and Marvin's conclusion that they had no case.

It would take some kind of dramatic event, a crisis linked to their water shortage problem, to justify a lawsuit. He told them that he had no idea what such a crisis might be. "I think I want to have Dan Cook over for dinner," Ed concluded abruptly.

"Why?" Susan asked.

"Because," Ed said, taking on his favorite role of family sage. "Your enemies are the best people to befriend. If you can pull it off, that is. Right Jack?"

"Right pops," Jack said, his voice wavering slightly.

"Makes sense, I guess," Susan consented with marked hesitation.

"Of course it does," Ed soldiered on. "Besides, after a few bites of your food, Suzie, he'll be like putty in our hands. Don't you agree, Jack?"

"Sure Dad. Whatever you say."

FOUR

JACK boycotted the meal with Dan Cook, slipping out for a Dairy Queen date with Katie, his quiet way of protesting this move of his father's. Ed forced himself to adjust his eating schedule to accommodate a more standard six o'clock dinner time. Susan devoted hours to preparing a three course meal that showed off many elements of the food they raised and grew there on the farm. Soon after Dan arrived Ed offered him a beer, poured himself a half mug of coffee, and proceeded to give the developer a tour around the farm. This gave Susan the extra time in the kitchen she needed to put the finishing touches on the food. When the men returned they were in the midst of a conversation about the science of rotational grazing, a topic she appreciated but had little to add beyond what her husband knew. With the cooking basically finished, she leaned against the wooden counter and sipped a glass of cranberry juice. Her eyes, so used to taking in the sight of her husband, his over-sized, muscular frame, his bold features, naturally settled on what was foreign. Dan Cook was from another world. He wore white linen and blue jeans and black leather shoes. He was stepping into her world like an actor who was confident on any kind of stage.

While her husband did his best to engage the big-city developer in light conversation at the table, Susan whirled about the kitchen. She was doing things that didn't need to be done, washing already clean plates, drying bowls that weren't wet, rearranging orderly shelves. She could feel Dan's eyes on the back of her neck. She glanced over her shoulder a few times, feeling like an innocent animal being brazenly hunted down. Dan was careful to give Ed the majority of his visible attention, a soft version of his gaze. But he made repeated efforts to include Susan in their conversation even as she pretended not to be listening, casting barbed, fish-hook questions towards her side of the room.

"And what do you think about the future of dairy farms, Mrs. Brown?"

Her usual concise eloquence had vanished the moment he walked in the door.

"Survival of the fittest," was all she could spit out.

"Like everything else," Dan added, throwing her a wink as he and Ed continued their discussion.

When the topic shifted to Marvin and Jack, Dan ensnared her with another question.

"Hard filling your time, Mrs. Brown, now that your boys are all grown up?"

Susan shook her head vehemently while loading up the three plates she'd just pulled from the oven. "Not at all. I have plenty of projects to keep me busy."

Ed pointed out her office beyond the wood stove. "Sometimes it seems she's in there for days on end. Outside of supper time, that is."

Dan raised his eyebrows. Susan forced a chuckle.

"Did you go to college, Mrs. Brown?" Dan asked as she arrived at the table with their plates heaped with steaming food.

"I did. Wellesley. Class of - I left after Junior year."

"And why, may I ask?"

Susan hovered at the table, trying hard to balance on this tightrope thread of conversation. "I married a farmer. That's why." She smiled at Ed, who was staring at Dan, then spun on a heel to go retrieve her own plate of food.

Ed cracked a slow grin. "It's a full-time job."

"Yes. I imagine it is."

Susan joined them at the table.

"This is amazing," Dan said after two bites.

"It's our pleasure to have you, Mr. Cook."

After less than a minute punctuated solely by the clink of silverware on the ceramic plates and the sound of three jaws working away, Dan launched into new topics of conversation. Ed never liked to talk much while he ate, so Susan engaged their guest, eagerly following him down the path of each subject he chose.

Susan wasn't becoming attracted to Dan as a person. For one thing she didn't know him. Rather it was what he represented that was sneaking up on the blind side, enticing her towards the unknown realms he represented. He obviously lived in a separate reality from hers, a lush existence, comfortable and secure. A man like this wasn't yoked to a piece of land and a few hundred hoofed animals, chained like a slave to the rise and fall of milk prices. Dan Cook was fully tapped into the real estate market, and the commodity of land would only continue to rise for as far into the future as anyone could see. This developer also reminded her of the only man besides Ed she'd ever loved, a serious Ph.D. student at MIT, a good Jewish man on a scientific track. Susan had dropped that relationship, along with her senior year of college, in one fell swoop, trading both for a young farmer named Ed. She hadn't looked back since. Until now.

As the evening progressed, tired of the effort involved with avoiding Dan's green eyes, she began eagerly anticipating his departure from her house. Even as Ed was being a gentleman by having the man who was one step away from an enemy over for dinner, Susan couldn't help indulging in her draw to him as the minutes stretched into hours, an irresistible tug born out of his wit and charm and casual sophistication. But what drew her the most was Dan Cook's evident physical strength, his tan sturdy features and well-defined muscles. He was strong like a jaguar, his body holding a built-up reserve of power, able to strike with full force if the moment required it. Ed was the strongest man she'd ever met, an ox able to plow through whatever happened to stand in his way. But, especially lately, he'd been so weary by the end of an average day on the farm that he could hardly make it up the stairs to bed. Although Dan was likely a similar age as Ed, if not older judging by the extent of gray in his hair, he seemed to have a reserve of power that her husband lacked.

Susan was shocked by these hints of infidelity in her thoughts. The man was a developer, squeezing profits out of nature. What had happened to her idealism? Even while she asked herself that question Susan knew the answer. Her idealism had vanished the day she became a mother. Although she did little things to try to make the world a better place, her focus had always been on family, and the stability of hard work. But she and Ed were in their fifties now. Fully aware that one final phase of life was rapidly approaching, she cringed at the thought of the never ending hard work required just to sustain their daily existence. She was also cognizant of Ed's easy contentment with the notion of dying in the saddle, so to speak, passing away while toiling at another one of the endless tasks on the farm. She was different, though, and dreamed of pampering herself just a little bit in her elder years. This had to be the ultimate source of her shocking attraction to Dan Cook, to the freedom afforded by his financial success, his ability to go anywhere at any time and focus on the next adventure rather than the next day of survival.

Dan talked about overseas markets and hedge funds, past projects, and his vision for Sunset Valley. Ed was unusually silent for most of the meal, while Susan asked question after question. Over dessert, blueberry cobbler with homemade ice cream, after Dan finished describing his plans for integrating some the old dairy farm's features into the development, icons like the great silver silo he planned to refurbish and leave standing, Ed asked the developer his first and only question of the night.

"So tell me, Mr. Cook, after you build on a piece of land, and sell it all in little chopped up pieces, what do you have left except money in a bank?"

Dan looked deeply confused. Susan lifted her eyebrows, encouraging him to answer.

"Nothing. Making money is the whole point. Why do you ask this question?"

Ed scooped up his last bite of cobbler. "Well, let's just say for some crazy reason the bank you keep all that money in fails, like 1930 all over again. Then you really have nothing. Right?"

Dan coughed out a laugh. "Are you saying the world's biggest economy could actually slide into another depression? You have to be joking."

"I'm not," Ed said firmly. "All empires collapse when they get too big. Just ask the Romans. Right, Suzie?" Ed threw his wife a playful wink as he got up to refill his coffee.

"I think Jack's home," she said.

Jack's arrival back from his night out with his girlfriend finally ushered Dan towards the door. When Ed introduced the developer to his son, Jack refused to shake the man's hand. Dan nodded.

"All right, then. I'll take that as my cue to head out."

He thanked Ed and Susan as he stepped outside and headed for his Prius parked in the driveway.

After closing the door behind their guest Susan spoke up, shocking both Ed and Jack with her words. Her voice was thin, her tone urgent. "Let's go away, Ed. Just for a night or two, someplace nice we can drive to for a little getaway from all this new stress. Jack can take care of things, right?"

"Sure Mom," Jack said, a strange glint in his eyes that neither parent noticed.

"Well, okay, if you want," Ed said, bewildered. "But only one night. Two at the most."

"Two," Susan said quickly, smiling nervously.

Ed had never been off the farm longer than two nights since he was about Jack's age, and never planned to, as much as he did trust his son to take care of the place.

Later, stretched out in their warm bed, the couple lay there in silence for awhile as the deep of night settled around them. Eventually Ed spoke up. "So where should we go?"

"How about the Adirondacks," Susan proposed, curling into him.

"Why not," Ed said.

The place was special to both of them, the setting of their courtship almost thirty years before. Neither had been back since. A silence fell over them as the collective space above their bed filled with bodily memories of their early lust for one another. After some time had passed, eager to forget the adulterous undertones of the evening, Susan lifted the covers and rolled up on top of her husband. For them, making love had become an almost subconscious act. Their bodies joined with minimal effort, and they rocked together like a small vessel on a gentle sea, the past and the future uniting in the moment.

Jack lay awake in his bedroom downstairs, his wide-open eyes staring at the ceiling. He was thinking about their pond, the development, and Dan Cook's green eyes. A slow and steady rage had been swelling within him, an anger that was now beginning to consume him. Jack tossed and turned, desperate for sleep. There was nothing worse than waking up exhausted for the morning milk. But how could he relax with this new enemy lurking up the road, this developer that was so brazenly threatening their livelihood? And, perhaps worse than that, his older brother had come back home just when Jack had been thinking he was gone for good. He loved Marvin, and always had, but it was a competitive kind of love that could only grow within a certain formula Jack had constructed in his mind. The equation he envisioned would work only if he was at the farm, gradually taking over the operations while his brother was off pursuing his fancy law career, returning home for holidays, for the huge meals and games of Monopoly and the subtle tension that had existed between them since Jack's memory had begun. Giving up on sleep, ignoring the Steinbeck novel on his bed stand, he let his mind wander to thoughts of sabotage. The mini-suburbia up the road was an unwelcome intruder into his world. He would have to kill it. There was no way around this fact. And in doing so he would risk his family's most precious resource. But he was certain he could pull it off without causing any lasting harm. It was just what he had to do, a necessary defense of the place that sustained him. His last thought before falling asleep was that he hoped to see the wolf in his dreams, as he had on many nights of late.

FIVE

JACK saw fear in his father's eyes for the first time in his young life. These glimpses were never long-lasting, and were separated by long stretches of time. But seeing anything resembling weakness in his dad, the man who had always reminded him of a rock, scared the hell out of him. Jack knew that even though he was now officially an adult, he was by no means ready to run the farm. He used all of his inner strength not to let his own fear show through and add to his father's worry. He caught himself staring at the pond often, day-dreaming about what he planned to do while his parents were away. During the milking, and throughout the day, Ed would alternate between utter silence and long-winded speculations about what act of fate might enable Marvin to file a lawsuit against the developer. Jack never gave his opinion one way or the other, because Ed never asked him for it. His only opinion was that he wanted his father back. And if that took an act of his will instead of waiting for fate to one day step in, so be it. He was ready to pull the trigger.

Jack woke up in the blue-gray light before dawn. He cursed, knowing he was late without having to see the clock. The long summer nights on the roof outside Katie's bedroom window had been too seductive over the past few weeks, when he indulged in the peaceful respite from his days spent in the company of his father. But the result had been a string of tardy appearances for the morning milk. True to form Ed hadn't been waking him, choosing instead to get going in the barn alone, raising the guilt factor when his son did show up. So Jack was startled when he looked up to see Ed standing in his doorway. Then he remembered this was the day his parents were leaving on their little two-day getaway.

"Dad, morning, sorry I'm late."

His father turned and walked down the hallway, expecting him to follow. There would be no time for coffee.

In the barn Ed turned his attention to the water pipe coming in the west wall of the barn. Powered by a solar pump, the pipe carried water from the pond outside, dumping it into channels that flowed above the stalls, spilling out to fill individual troughs below at timed intervals. The troughs were lower than ever.

"I've cut down on the flow from the pond in order to conserve, but you need to keep a close eye on the water level out there. If it falls below that pump we're screwed. You'll have to get the troughs filled from the house somehow. I don't expect this to happen, but be aware just in case."

Jack nodded obediently even as his hands shook from the nervous expectation of what he planned to do. After the milking was over Ed packed up the car and they were on the road by ten in the morning. Not wanting to waste any time in executing his scheme, the first thing Jack did was turn on every faucet in the house. He'd been noticing their water pressure declining of late, and was certain it would take hardly any time to drain the house's well dry.

In the barn he emptied out the troughs by hand with a bucket. Then he headed out to the pond, where he set about digging a new, lower outlet connecting to the original stream leaving the pond, a trench he would fill back in perfectly once his goal was achieved. By midday the pond was just a puddle of mud, so when he led the cows back in for the afternoon milk they had no water to drink.

Back inside he prepared his supper using a few gallons of water he'd saved, as the house taps had stopped flowing completely. He would make sure to tell his father that he had tried to fill the troughs from the house but the water had run out quickly. But he would also invent another detail, that when he'd gone to sleep at night the pump had been working, and when he woke up he found the flow had stopped sometime during the night, preserving an image of responsibility. The cows would wither to the brink of severe dehydration before the vet arrived. He'd be sure to call the local newspaper as well, who would no doubt send a reporter to the scene, creating enough of a stir for his father to have a case without losing a single animal. That was the plan.

Preparing supper for himself was hard enough, but finding sleep that night was impossible. Tossing and turning, Jack thought about heading to Katie's house for distraction, but decided he should stay and see things through like a man. So he stayed up all night reading East Of Eden and strumming his used guitar, inventing chords that could never have formed a melody, yet gave him some much needed peace of mind. Getting through the night was a long journey into and out of darkness. The next day, however, was a waking nightmare. He milked the girls as usual, noticing their production had dropped dramatically. He fed them their grain, but some refused to eat. Sandy, the eldest, was the first to go down, joined quickly by a few others, including his favorite cow Julia The Winker. Seeing the peaceful creatures suffer was almost more than he could bear. But for his plan to achieve the serious effect he needed, another long day lay ahead. Jack busied himself by filling in the trench he'd dug to empty the pond. Then he made a few excursions to the neighbors for water, all of whom refused to donate given the fact that their own wells were also being depleted by the developer.

Around mid-morning he placed a frantic call to Mark Ridley, the family vet. He didn't have to fake his tone of urgency in the message he left. Jack hadn't meant to cause the death of any cows, and was terrified that he'd waited too long. His research had told him that two days without water was much different than one, although bovine fatalities from dehydration were not very well documented in the books he'd found at the local library. Needless to say it was the longest day of his young life. He avoided the barn even as strange noises began emanating from inside, the wailing sounds of suffering animals. He didn't bother milking them that afternoon, knowing there would be no production. Finally, late in the afternoon, the vet called him back. He told Doctor Ridley about the situation. The vet tried to calm Jack down by explaining that cows could easily handle twenty-four hours without water.

He was on a long-distance call in the western end of the state, and wouldn't be able to get to the farm and assess the situation until the next morning. Jack's throat clenched up tight, making it hard for him to swallow. He choked out a goodbye and started pacing frantically back and forth inside the barn. In an act of desperation he drove to the supermarket, where he used the little savings he had to purchase some gallon jugs of spring water. Back home, he used a funnel to pour the water into the mouths of the downed cows, hoping they would revive by morning. Inviting a reporter to the house was no longer on his mind. Jack's only thought was to make it through the night with his sanity preserved.

Jack didn't sleep at all that night, allowing Steinbeck's eloquence and the dramatic ending of East Of Eden to distract
him for periods of time. By dawn the wailing from the barn had
grown incessantly loud, but still Jack avoided the scene inside,
waiting instead for the vet to arrive. He paced across the back
porch of the farmhouse, marching in circles, plugging his ears
against the rhythmic cries of suffering cows spilling out in waves
through the barn's open windows. Needing a distraction, hoping
to salvage some kind of positive result from the situation, he dug
out the local newspaper's number from his wallet. After explaining things to the editor, who was familiar with Sunset Valley as
the paper had already run one story on the future development,
Jack was informed that a reporter would be at the farm shortly.
Less than half an hour later a beat up Ford Escort pulled into
the driveway. A balding, middle aged man, with thick glasses
and a substantial belly, climbed out and approached Jack. One
hand clutched both a mini tape recorder and a note pad. The
other reached out to give Jack a hand shake.

"Mike Richards. Springtown Daily."

"Jack Brown."

There was a coffee stain on the front of the reporter's cheap
white dress shirt. A row of pens lined the chest pocket. Jack
was already regretting this newspaper man's presence. He
nodded towards the barn.

"That's where the action is. I have to wait here for the vet,
but go on out if you want."

The reporter nodded. He made his way out to the barn,
waddling awkwardly like a man that rarely walked on anything besides concrete. Jack watched him make his way into
the barn's front door, recoiling repeatedly from the stench
before finding the fortitude to step fully inside.

Mark Ridley arrived a short time later. Jack led him out
to the barn. Shocked into action by the scene in the barn, he

began giving as many fluid IV's to the downed cows that he could. Seven had already died overnight.

"What the hell happened here?" the normally reserved man asked Jack while they bent over Julia the Winker.

The reporter hovered above them, his mini recorder held in a fat hand over their heads. Jack shook his head. The vet, who'd known the cows for years, seemed just as shaken up as he was.

"The pond dried up. And the well for the house. That development up the road has stolen our water. That's what happened."

There was a thinness to Jack's voice as he tried to hide the darker half of this explanation.

Mark nodded slowly. "I hate that place."

"Have you been up there?" Jack asked, relieved for a change of topic.

"No. I'd been to the Wilson farm so many times over the years, I don't think I could bear the sight of it. My imagination, and what I've heard from your father, is bad enough."

They moved on to the next downed, writhing cow. The reporter moved with them.

"Yeah. I haven't gone up there yet either," Jack said.

At one point the cows ceased their moaning all together. Something had shifted inside the barn. Mark and Jack looked up towards the front entrance. Ed stood there in the doorway, his arms lifting, his palms facing up. Back-lit by the late morning sun, to Jack his father cast a long shadow that ran down the entire length of the stalls, cloaking the whole scene in darkness. Mark continued his work while Jack rose up slowly, summoning all his courage to meet his father's blazing black eyes.

"What the hell! I leave you here for thirty-six hours and I come home to this? And who the hell are you?" he snapped at the reporter.

"Mike Richards, sir. Reporter for the Springtown - "

"Get out. Now."

The man clasped his recorder with both hands and stumbled out of the barn.

"Do you have an explanation son?"

Jack stood his ground as his father marched towards him. "We ran out of water," he said forcefully. "Even in the house. I did my best, Dad! I went to the neighbors -"

"Did you call the fire department? Ever think of that?"

Jack shook his head. It was true, he hadn't thought of that. Ed lifted his arm to slap his son across the face, then lowered it as he saw Julia The Winker. Her tongue was hanging out, her eyes vacant. She was lying on her side in the stall. He stumbled over to her, dropped to his knees, and placed his forehead between her eyes. His body convulsed with violent sobs. Jack wanted more than anything to flee the barn and hide out in his room, behind his mother's protection. But instead he walked over and placed a trembling hand on his father's back, and held it there as long as he could.

Marvin showed up that evening to help. By then the main job was burying the dead cows. Jack wanted to burn the seven carcasses, but everyone else managed to convince him that was a bad idea. So the men worked straight through usual supper time and into the night digging a mass grave in the patch of scruffy woods behind the chicken coop. The brothers took turns operating the tractor while Ed choreographed the dimensions of the grave. He had them make it big enough for at least twenty head. In the barn there were still ten more stricken ones on the verge of death, where the vet was tending to them as best he could. By the time the burial pit was ready and all the bodies had been hauled out to the spot, darkness had set in. Jack sprinted to the house, where Susan had a meal percolating, to retrieve the Tiki Torches off the back porch. The towering candles gave the burial a ritualistic atmosphere. The three men, silhouetted against the surrounding brush, worked in reverent silence, carefully lowering one cow at a time with a chain of six hands. Jack, the first link, looked down at his father in the bottom of the pit as he arranged the last carcass gently on top of another, tucking in the sheet that wrapped around it. Watching the scene from above Jack felt the urge to pray, but he wasn't sure how the others would handle it. So as his brother helped Ed up and out of the pit, he vowed to come back out later that night and offer a blessing for the dead cows. Not wanting to share his newborn belief in a higher power with either of his parents, he didn't defend himself when Ed snapped at the sight of him leaving the house at his usual hour.

"Where do you think you're going?"

"Just for a quick visit with Katie," Jack stammered.

Susan placed her hand on Ed's knee. "Let him go, dear. He probably needs to talk to her about it. Right Jack?"

"That's right, Mom. I have to tell her."

After Jack stepped out the back door of the kitchen Ed turned his attention to Marvin. It took him a great amount of effort to speak. "So. I guess we got what we needed to sue that developer up there. It's obvious his wells caused this tragedy. Do you think we have a case now?"

Marvin took off his glasses and polished them with his shirt. "I think you have a case, Dad. And it would be my honor to represent you. Should we go for the jugular?"

"Well, I'll have to get new cows, and dig two new wells, deep ones, and that'll set me back at least thirty grand."

At this point Susan drifted in from the living room, where she'd been at her spinning wheel in an attempt to calm her nerves.

Marvin looked up at her from the table. "What do you think, Mom?"

"I say take him for all you can."

Ed and Marvin exchanged a surprised glance.

"I'm thinking we might be able to get at least a million out of him, to be honest," Marvin ventured. "He'll want to settle out of court to avoid any media coverage beyond whatever article that newspaper man comes out with. I could start at two million, with the goal of not going under one."

Ed's eyes swelled wide open.

Susan nodded down once, sharply. "Sounds good," she said, turning to head back into the living room.

Marching up the hill towards the burial spot, Jack thought about the irony of his white lie about going to talk to Katie. He was going to talk to someone. Or something. At that point Jack thought of his god more as a thing than a someone, mostly because he couldn't picture a holy figure being responsible for the shooting stars he'd been seeing every night with Katie on her rooftop. The catalyst of those long streaks of sparkling light was an entity he had trouble imagining. The fact that the comets were always timed for both their eyes to see was making Jack a believer in something beyond every day reality. He believed in a god that was the force behind nature, present in the infinite beauty but revealing itself only in flashing moments, most of which happened on his girl-friend's rooftop. Until tonight. Tonight God was more in the gravity. Jack didn't bother looking up at the stars as he stood praying on the edge of the grave. God wasn't up there. Tonight was the opposite of his nights outside Katie's bedroom. God was death tonight. There was no other way around it.

"Please, God, take the spirits of these fine animals into your kingdom. They served us well, and should be honored in death as they were in life. And please, God, forgive me for this mistake. It was the act of a fool. We can't afford to lose any more girls. I think I would survive if this farm died, but my father . . .I can't see that look in his eyes anymore. God, please make it end. Make Dan Cook go away. I'll give you whatever must be taken in exchange for this to happen."

Jack dropped to his knees. He pressed his palms together at his chest and peered down into the pit of carcasses. "Make it end," he whispered, still unsure exactly to what, or whom, he was speaking.

SIX

ED, deeply saddened by the loss of his seven cows, was not himself for many weeks. He hardly spoke to anyone, nor did he hang his head. Instead he chose to work harder than normal, gritting his teeth and grinding through the hours of the day. It helped that there was more work to do now than they'd had in many years, beginning with the massive task of digging a new well while keeping the cows supplied with water. Although Marvin was practically guaranteeing a victorious lawsuit worth at least a million dollars, Ed wasn't one to count unhatched eggs. One thing Marvin had learned about lawsuits during his brief career was that each case took more time than one would think, a point he repeatedly stressed to his father. So with an Amex card filling up, mortgage and equipment loan payments totaling over five grand a month, and utility bills that would shock the average person buying a gallon of milk, creating a temporary water source for the cows would have to be accomplished with no budget at all.

As for getting the water to the cows immediately, both Ed and Jack were amazed by a decent outpouring of assistance offered by some locals, mostly old timers still lingering in the area who'd caught wind of the tragedy at the legendary Brown Farm. One hundred people signed a petition calling for an emergency meeting of the town board, which quickly granted the request to open a privately owned spring on one of the back roads. It was an historic source of water once used by Native Americans in healing rituals but had been closed off to the public for a generation, controlled by an eighty-year old widow who vigilantly maintained many NO TRESPASSING signs. So Jack made multiple runs a day with the huge plastic tank loaded in the bed of his truck, siphoning the water through a hose and into the troughs. The crystal clear mineral water, along with a careful ration of corn feed Ed had been saving for an emergency, helped the surviving girls make quick recoveries.

To create a well that might provide water for both the house and the barn, until Ed had the money he needed to dig a new, professional one, the men came up with a technique that could utilize the maximum abilities of their tractor. Using the mechanical post-hole digger attached to the back of the tractor they drilled down a few feet. Then the front loading bucket was used to scrape the surrounding earth down to an equal depth, a level from which they would drill again. They figured eventually the post-hole drill would strike one of the underground rivers they knew to be coursing under the property. Thirty feet down, however, they hit solid bedrock. Ed cursed, knowing his giant fence-hole sized drill bit was no use for penetrating such a thick layer of rock. He cut off the old tractor and peered up until his eyes reached Jack, standing thirty feet above.

"We're fucked," Jack stated, eying the solid white rock underneath the tractor's wheels.

"I think so," Ed said. He threw up his hands and started cackling with a dark kind of laughter.

"What's so funny?" Jack shouted down at him.

"How the hell are we going to get this beast out of here?!" Ed shouted back, throwing his arms at the mounds of dirt and roots surrounding him. Neither of them had stopped to think about this scenario, as they'd been entirely focused on finding water with the means at hand, and had piled the earth they'd been excavating in a way that blocked the tractor's path back out.

Jack shook his head. "Like I said, we're fucked."

Ed climbed down off the tractor and scaled the rope ladder hanging down one side of the deep pit. When he reached the top Jack was already glowing with a fresh idea.

"I got it," he said, "Katie's father uses dynamite to excavate limestone at his quarry. I'd have no trouble getting us some sticks that'll blow us down twice this deep, to a level we know will have water, since the table is forty feet and we're already down thirty."

Ed peered into the giant hole, pondering his son's idea. "What about the tractor?" he asked. "We'll have to dig it out first. I need to call some people."

Jack was quick to respond. "Let's drown that old beast. That'll give us a good excuse to buy a new one."

"You're kidding, right?"

Jack shook his head. "Once Marvin finds out what we had to do he'll make sure you win the lawsuit. There isn't the time, or the money, to get a backhoe in here right now."

"But there is time," Ed protested. "We have the use of that spring indefinitely."

"Listen, Dad," Jack stammered, raising his voice. "If you expect me to take over here one day, you have to let me start making a decision every now and then. I say drown that damn tractor. The thing doesn't start most winter mornings anyway. We'll buy a new one on credit, and pay it back when Marvin wins the settlement."

"If Marvin wins," Ed said, shaking his head.

"If he doesn't win I'll work odd jobs in town until I pay the new one off myself. Deal?"

Ed cracked a half smile. He appreciated Jack's stubborn persistence, what was a necessary trait of a good farmer. But so was practicality. An old tractor was valuable to have around for spare parts. He let out a long sigh, a gulp of breath he'd been holding onto for some time. Having already turned down Marvin's offer of a loan to dig a real well, Ed was literally in a hole with no other way out, assuming he wanted to save his pride along with his cows. Pride was the only thing besides his land and his family that mattered to him in the end. So he agreed to drown the old tractor, making a leap of a magnitude he never had before, deciding to fully trust Marvin's ability to win the case against Dan Cook. Ed knew the significance of what he was agreeing to. He could feel it collecting on his skin in the form of a cold sweat as Jack bounded towards the house to call his girlfriend's father. The kid was visibly excited by the prospects of a large explosion. Ed was thinking mostly about what his grandfather, who had grown up farming with horses in rural England, had told him so many times, that in America a farmer without a tractor will likely become a beggar in no time. All of a sudden Ed was standing face to face with these words recorded firmly in his memory. He stood, and held his ground, because there was nothing else to do. Because his son did have to start making a few decisions, even if they were the wrong ones.

Katie's father, a stout, jovial man named Smitty, made it to the farm late that afternoon. Jack was happy to assist him with placing the thick sticks of explosives in strategic locations at the bottom of the pit, and with wiring the dynamite to an ignition box a hundred feet from the hole's edge. His jubilation stemmed not only from the fact that now his father was forced to make that evening's run to the spring, but also because he knew Katie was watching closely, studying how he was interacting with her father. Jack had little contact with Smitty, and privately craved his acceptance. Katie would insist that her father approved of him, but Jack had been eagerly anticipating an opportunity to show the man how well he could work. So he scrambled under the tractor and all over the base of the pit chipping out holes in the bedrock with a special chisel, making slots for the sticks of dynamite. He worked furiously, outpacing Smitty substantially. Sweat poured down from his temples. Blisters sprang out on his hands. After Smitty had shown Jack what he wanted him to do they worked along in silence. When Jack had the main fuse running up a wall and out of the pit, the big man joined him and Katie on the edge.

"You're a damn good worker, Jack Brown," he said, then abruptly marched off towards the ignition box. Being the one with the fuse head, Jack knew he was supposed to follow. He lingered just long enough for Katie to see the pride radiate across his face.

"I told you he liked you," she said, squeezing him around his waist.

Jack kissed the top of her head, burying his lips into her brown curls. "Now I finally believe you," he said.

They waited for Ed to return with the water before proceeding. Once he had the siphon flowing into the troughs, all four of them gathered behind the push-button detonator Smitty had set up behind a substantial boulder. Ed was trying hard not to show his deep-seeded dread about the act he'd agreed to set in motion. Susan, wanting to be absent for the death of their precious tractor, had taken a ride into town for a few staples from the grocery store. While they all crouched behind the boulder, Smitty let Jack push the blinking red button on top of a small box. Unlike in the Road Runner cartoons the electric fuse traveled fast and invisible. The explosion rocked the ground, knocking everyone except Smitty backwards amidst a hailstorm of tiny pieces of metal, dirt pellets, and broken stone.

"Yahoo!" Jack shouted out towards the sky.

A cloud of dusty smoke hung in the air as they gathered themselves, checking for cuts or bruises. Everyone was unscathed, proving Smitty's calculations to be correct. Jack and Katie held hands, walking behind his father, Smitty following after them. When Ed reached the ragged edge of a pit that was now twice as wide, he dropped down to his knees and raised his open hands high above his head in a kind of victory salute. He shook his head back and forth, grinning like a madman. He was a madman in that instant, crazy to be happy after submerging the tractor that was so dear to him. But at the same time Ed knew it was completely rational to prize water over anything else. After land, without water a farmer had nothing. These were not his grandfather's words. They were his own.

Jack stepped up to the edge of the hole. He placed a hand on Ed's shoulder and peered down. Whatever was left of the tractor was nowhere to be seen, already hidden by the water gushing in from all angles, bubbling from below, rising steadily up the dirt walls. Ed lowered his hands at his son's touch, revealing a look of shocked disbelief.

"Looks like we've got ourselves a new pond," Jack said.

"Sure does," Ed said, standing up, gazing towards the lower pasture and the dried out depression that had been the barn's water source since the first days of the farm. "Well, ain't no time to waste. Maybe Katie can help us move the pump down here. I'd like to have this water feeding into the barn by nightfall. We can worry about the house later."

Jack looked over at Katie, standing now beside them. He lifted his eyebrows. She smiled.

"I'm in," she said happily.

"You're always in," Jack said.

"I am. There's no other way to be, right?"

"Right."

SEVEN

W H   Susan drove off from the farm that afternoon, just after her husband had returned with the load of water, she hoped they'd all be so engrossed with the project at hand that no one would notice her turning left at the end of the driveway, heading away from town and towards only one possible destination. The idea to confront Dan Cook had come to her out of the clear Adirondack mountain air. Like all ideas, thinking it up had been the easy part. Susan had butterflies up into the back of her throat as she pulled into Sunset Valley. She noticed that one of the Wilson's great silos had been left standing, freshly painted in shining silver. It rose up like an artifact of some former civilization, preserved intact for the future inhabitants of these neighborhoods to contemplate in their spare time. There were towering piles of gravel and dirt, a web of paved streets without names, concrete foundations surrounded by spray-on grass. And each lot was garnished with an old-fashioned, hand-powered water pump.

Susan remembered Ed's description of the trailer vividly, and found it right away. She parked her station wagon between a mud-cloaked bulldozer and Dan's shiny silver hybrid. Everyone else seemed to have left the site for the day, giving the scene an apocalyptic feel. As Susan approached the single step leading up to the trailer door she was trying hard to calm her heartbeat with long, slow breaths. Standing on the rickety wooden stair she paused before knocking. Momentarily amnesic about her reason for being there, she searched through her scattered brain for the motivation behind this visit. It took only a moment for her to remember with full clarity the reason she'd come. She had to speak with Dan face to face, and set the record straight.

Lethargic after a long day of bureaucratic nightmares, Dan opened the trailer door slowly. When he saw who was standing there he caught his breath, then collected himself.

"Mrs. Brown."

"Mr. Cook."

"Please, come in."

"Why don't you come out."

His face lifted with surprise. "Sure, why not."

She backed off the step. Dan climbed down obediently and stood facing her. He wore the same basic outfit as he'd had that night during dinner - blue jeans, black loafers, and a white linen shirt.

"I have to say I'm a little surprised to see you here," Dan said.

"I'm surprised that I came."

Dan looked straight into her eyes. Susan wasn't used to this kind of boldness in men she'd only recently met. His confident attitude, even as he moved down a step to stand below her line of sight, made her wary. She was still trying to remember what she had come there to say.

"Well, it seems like I wasn't the only one who felt a spark the other night," Dan said.

After this remark of his the monologue she'd practiced in front of the mirror over and over the night before, while her husband had been sound asleep, rose up in full clarity.

"You were the only one," she lied, stepping down onto solid ground for a sturdy footing from which to attack. "I'm a married woman, Mr. Cook. I have to say I admire your bravery in flirting behind my husband's substantial back. You got away with it, that time. And I let you, for reasons I'm still not sure of. But the bottom line is that I love my husband, and will never stray from his side. That's what I came here to say."

Dan met her intense stare with one of his own, the fierce look of a successful man trying to grab something he'd grown accustomed to having over the years, love and lust intertwined as one. This time Susan saw him much more for what he actually was, a successful man over the hill of his prime, striving to experience what he used to obtain with relative ease.

"Fair enough," Dan said, hands on his hips. He didn't seem the least bit fazed by her words, like he still believed the ball was in his court. "So since you went through the trouble to come all the way up here, the least I could do is take you out for dinner, to the nicest place in town. What do you say, Susan?"

She let the shock of his proposal, and the way he'd said her name, settle in before replying. "I can't believe you have the nerve to ask me, a married woman, out on a date after what happened to our cows thanks to this wretched place - "

"First of all, I object to letting you use a word like wretched to describe something that's barely a tenth complete. And, second, my hydrologist agrees with me that although my wells here have reduced the water table, the pace of your farm's depletion was unrealistic, even suspicious. I would venture to guess your brooding son Jack there has it in for me, and likely had something to do with the timely tragedy you folks just went through." Dan shook his head. "He'll grow up sooner or later," he added, as if he knew Jack as well as she did, which was actually not so very well at all these days.

Even with this absurd accusation being slung at her, Susan held her ground. "I won't be going out to dinner with you, Mr. Cook. Also, this is the last time I'll be coming here. And don't dare step foot on our farm again. If you do, I will tell my husband to shoot you."

She spun around and walked deliberately to her car. She climbed in and drove off. Moisture filled the corners of her eyes. These dewy precursors of tears arose not out of sadness, necessarily, but were born out of the wistful recognition that life was like a river, sometimes bending into eddies, other times coursing in rapids, but always moving forward. Her meandering youth had allowed for a few little pools of romantic connection, places she'd lingered in briefly before the current had pushed her onward. Loving Ed had since become her banks, defining the flow of her life without constricting it. She couldn't wait to be back on the farm, and barely remembered to head past their driveway and into town for the groceries she'd supposedly been getting this whole time.

EIGHT

WITHI a few days after the dynamite event Marvin had filed a civil suit at the county court, a date for a hearing had been set, and Dan Cook had been notified. Marvin realized he and Ed would need to have a series of meetings leading up to the court date in order to get on the same page, preferably at a location other than the farm, where Ed had a hard time sitting still during the daylight hours. So it quickly came to the family's attention that another pair of hands would be needed, at least temporarily. Jack, knowing the absence of his father would only mean an increased burden on his already sore shoulders, brought this notion up over coffee one morning before dawn.

"You know how we've been talkin' about hiring an extra set of hands around here?" he asked his father.

"You found us a Mexican?" Ed's face brightened for the first time in weeks. Having heard the stories from restaurant owners and construction companies in the area for years, the reputation of Mexican help had reached near mythic proportion in both of their minds.

"I found us something even better," Jack announced. "A Brazilian."

On Monday nights Jack played basketball at the high school gym. A number of Hispanics showed up, including two Colombians employed as cooks at the fanciest restaurant in town. They'd told him about the dishwasher they worked with, a fifty-year old Brazilian named Javier. They told Jack they'd never seen anyone work so hard. His nickname at the restaurant was The Mule. Even though he worked ten-hour shifts washing dishes and prepping half the menu, they said Javier was always looking to pickup daytime work. Jack had been storing this information for months, waiting for the time to come when they needed help at the farm. So later that day Jack stepped out into the driveway and called the number the Colombians had given him. Stumbling around the man's broken English and heavy accent, Jack managed to hire him, convey directions to the farm, and invite him to show up as soon as he could the next morning.

"Sim," said the gravelly voice. "I ride bike. Obrigado, senhor."

Before Jack could offer him a lift Javier hung up.

The next morning Jack found his father brewing a second pot of coffee. Ed poured water into the back of the machine and clicked on the brew button.

"Did you get a hold of that Brazilian yesterday?" he asked.

"I did. He took the job. His name is Javier."

Ed reached his hand up and they slapped a high five.

"When does he start?" Ed asked.

Jack glanced at the clock above the table. "In about twenty minutes."

The two men drank their coffee at the counter, checking the driveway for any sign of Javier's arrival. It was a big moment for both of them, at a time when they needed a boost. He would be the farm's first true employee, a milestone that might not have meant so much if everything was fine around the farm. Everything was not fine.

"There he is!" Jack said, pointing out the window where the short man with long black and gray hair tied into a pony tail was leaning his little BMX bicycle against an oak tree beside the driveway. He was dressed in jean shorts, a tank top, and work boots. His calf muscles bulged out above his white socks. His arms were deeply veined. They could see all this from the kitchen window. And when he turned to face the house they could also see a long, deep scar running down the length of one cheek. He wasn't smiling. His eyes were dark and narrow. Ed and Jack exchanged a look, each deciding to accept this man without reservation, not because they were desperate, but because they each believed in the basic goodness of people.

They also believed in hard work. By the end of the day not only had the rumors of the Colombians been proven true, Ed and Jack were also practically speechless as Javier bid them farewell to peddle off towards his night job in town. He'd embarrassed them in the barn by cleaning at a pace that eclipsed both of them combined. He shoveled more manure, swept away more urine, scrubbed with bleach on his hands and knees longer and with more diligence. And he scraped algae out of the troughs with razor blades after insisting Ed's method with wire brushes was not efficient, completing the grueling tasks assigned as a test of his capabilities. He refused their offer of supper, continuing to clean while Ed and Jack shamefully went inside to eat a quick meal. They brought him back a plate and he paused to shovel a few bites in his mouth before returning to the task at hand. He was an hour late for his restaurant job because he didn't want to leave the barn before the work was finished.

Ed got up the next day before dawn and began by doing the same things he always did. He left Susan sleeping in bed and went downstairs. He made a big pot of coffee followed by an egg and bacon breakfast followed by the arrival of his son. After Jack had finished his bacon and first cup of coffee, Ed followed him towards the back door.

"Dad, we've got the milking," Jack said, holding out an arm to stop his father. "Me and Javier. Look, here he is."

Ed glanced out the window to see the long-haired man leaning his little bike against the tree. He'd almost completely forgotten about the addition of their new employee. A wave of panic coursed through him. "What am I supposed to do?" He wasn't asking his son as much as himself.

"You'll think of something, pops. The lawsuit will be happening before you know it, and you'll need all your energy for that."

Ed moved to the coffee maker to pour himself another cup. "I guess you're right," he muttered. "See you later."

Ed watched his son out the window throw an arm around the short man as they walked together to the barn. He started pacing around the kitchen. The morning light was growing brighter, urging him to figure out something to work on. He moved to the phone. It was very early, but he called his vet anyway. The cows that had survived should be checked out just in case there were any lingering problems. While dialing the number the thought of another steep fee rose up in his mind but he snubbed it out quickly, reminding himself about the lawsuit, entrenching himself further in the absolute faith that Marvin would succeed. Ed had no choice but to go out on this limb. If his son failed they would lose the farm.

Late that afternoon, after examining the cows and declaring them all healthy, Mark Ridley sat at the kitchen table with Ed while Susan was working on supper.

"What is that developer doing up there anyway?" Mark asked.

The vet was a young man who resembled a pro football linebacker, with burly shoulders and a thick neck.

"Building houses. Digging a hundred wells. The usual crap they do. Maybe I'll find out more during this lawsuit," Ed huffed.

"Eh, I doubt it. He'll be keepin' his secrets to himself, I'm sure."

"Yeah, you're probably right." Ed shook his head. "Marvin thinks the guy might throw a lot of money at me to avoid a trial . . . but he says the only way to stop the development is to take it to court. The whole process is already making me nauseous, and it hasn't even started."

"Why would you want to stop him?" Mark asked. "I mean, now that you have water again and he pays you a healthy settlement, more than enough to dig new wells and replace the cows you lost. Is your son one of those tree-huggers?"

"Not really," Ed said.

"He's always loved nature," Susan said from across the room, not lifting her head from the chopping task at hand.

"Well, he does have a shot at makin' a splash on this case, I'd say."

"I'd say you're right," Ed grumbled. "Just as long as the splash doesn't hit me I'll be fine. Although keeping it simple would surely be ideal."

Ed turned to watch Susan move about the kitchen. He was enjoying the easy slide into the best part of the day, even though his body was wound up tight from not working. "You should stick around for supper, Mark. From the smell of things it should be ready soon," he proposed.

"'Bout twenty minutes, dear," Susan said.

"It does smell awfully good in here," Mark said.

Ed knew the young man was a bachelor, and had nothing in the way of home cooking to look forward to after his days of tending to the health of large farm animals.

"Then stay," Ed prodded.

"All right. If you insist."

"I do. And I won't even deduct it from your bill!"

The two men had a good laugh.

"Can I do anything for you over there, Mrs. Brown?" Mark asked.

"You can do the most by staying at the table keeping my husband occupied with conversation so he doesn't get in my way like he tends to right about now, dipping his dirty fingers in my sauces - "

"All right Ma', leave the poor doctor alone."

"Can do, Ma'am," Mark stated.

The men resumed talking. Their conversation stayed away from the dark topics of dead cows and the development, drifting easily from local town politics to the baseball season to, eventually, wolves. Ed, curious about the vet's take on the situation, shared Jack's discovery of the predator's prints.

"You seen it?" he asked the vet.

"Can't say I have," Mark admitted. "Haven't even heard anyone else mention a wolf in these parts, and I talk to pretty much everyone."

Susan and Ed exchanged looks.

"I'm not sayin' your son is making it up. Don't think that."

"I don't," Ed said.

"Good. Well, I'm not sure what to think. There hasn't been a wolf sighting around here in over a century, I believe."

"You're right. My grandfather, man who bought this land, shot one of the last. I remember stroking the pelt when I was a tiny kid. Beautiful animal."

Mark flinched ever so slightly. "If a dead one is beautiful can you imagine what seeing a living one must be like?"

Ed coughed into his fist. The two men locked eyes.

"You a tree-hugger too?" Ed asked.

The corners of Mark's mouth twitched, as if he wanted to smile. He looked down at the table instead, unable to hold Ed's stare any longer. "I have to admit – farmer versus developer, I'm with the farmer all the way. Farmer versus wolf, well, I'd have trouble takin' either side, but I'd lean toward the wolf."

Ed nodded slowly, pursing his lips. "You hear that, Ma?" he said over his shoulder.

"Hear what," Susan said.

It wasn't a question. Both men knew she'd heard them but didn't want to get involved. Ed wondered if she agreed with the vet. He decided it was something best left for their bed-time conversation later on. Susan pulled plates down from a cabinet.

"Jack!" she shouted down the hallway. "Supper's ready."

"Great," Ed grumbled, getting up to set the table as Mark shuffled awkwardly into the corner, trying his best to stay out of the man's way. Susan knew that once her husband had a little food in his belly he'd forget all about the politics of tree hugging, and the conservation of wolves. The love she'd just mashed into the potatoes would bring him back down to the ground, and close to the things that really mattered.

NINE

THAT summer Jack began scanning the perimeter of the fields at all hours of the day, and on moonlit nights, hoping to spot the wolf. He was motivated not by a fear for the safety of the cows, as he thought maybe he should be, but instead by a deep-running desire to connect with this wild creature, an animal living in a completely different realm than the placid domesticity of the farm. This wolf had marched right through their backyard as if it owned the place, taking nothing even though it could have taken anything. So he watched, day after day after day. And then he saw it, working late one October evening building a bridge across the ditch that used to be the creek running out of their pond and through the lower pasture. The animal, all hunkered, with piercing yellow eyes and a bushy gray mane, emerged from the woods and loped through the field at a steady trot. Jack followed it the entire way. Every molecule of his being was charged, on alert for what his brain would tell him to feel, how to act, whether to stay or run. He stayed, transfixed, heart pounding in his ears.

The wolf stopped halfway across the field, turning its great head to stare Jack directly in the eyes. In that moment, locking eyes with a timber wolf, two things happened to Jack, not in order but simultaneously. He became aware of what his god looked like, and he knew, also with total certainty, that he would one day leave the farm. Later on, thinking back on that moment, he decided the wolf had been the messenger of these two pearls of wisdom, because when the animal abruptly turned to saunter across the rest of the pasture and into the woods, Jack was flooded with questions. How did he pray to a god contained in the eyes of a wolf? Where was a church for such a believer? When would he leave the farm? Where would he go? Why? All these questions where too much. He tipped his head back and did the one thing that felt right in that moment. He howled. It was a long, drawn out bellow that came from below his belly button, vibrating his ribcage as it echoed off the surrounding ridges.

Marvin took the suit against Dan Cook very seriously. Not only was it the biggest case of his young career, but the future of his own father's farm was dependent on him winning. The temporary well was already leaking into the surrounding soil, and what little profit Ed was turning was being lost due to the drop in the size of his herd. Marvin had Ed meet him at the town park every morning for a week. Seated at a red picnic table, they focused primarily on a strategy for winning a settlement. Marvin taught his father about posture and body language, when to show emotion and when to use a poker face.

"I'm expecting a lot of back and forth with this guy. As successful as he is, he's gotta be smart. There'll come a time when I'll be shooting from the hip, I'm sure," Marvin coached. "All you have to do is follow my lead."

Marvin researched the case every afternoon and evening, bringing what he'd discovered to the park the next morning. They studied up on water rights cases involving farmers versus corporations and developers, ninety percent of which were ruled in favor of the farmer. Marvin planned to use these kinds of facts to encourage a settlement.

"But if he tries to go under a million I say we take him to court, where I think you'd win even more, especially when we throw in emotional suffering. Not to mention the outside chance we could shut the whole project down completely. But that's a long shot."

So at the end of the week, armed with statistics and a strategy, they called Dan Cook from Marvin's office in town, located in the downstairs floor of a refurbished colonial house tucked behind Main Street. Information already had a number listed for Sunset Valley. Marvin was all business on the phone, while Ed paced back and forth in front of his desk.

"Yeah, hi, is this Mr. Cook? Great. I'm Marvin Brown, Ed Brown's son. And his attorney. As I'm sure you're aware, we filed a suit against your company in civil court last week. The purpose of my call today is to see if you might be interested in meeting my client for a possible settlement agreement so we can all stay out of court and not waste more time than we have to."

Ed stopped and leaned over the desk, trying unsuccessfully to catch the developer's voice through the receiver. Marvin was nodding, smiling up at his father.

"Yes, we'd like to get it over with too. My father wants to meet in the park here in town, if that's okay with you. He hates being inside."

Ed winked at his son and resumed pacing.

"Great. Four o'clock it is."

Father, the client, and son, his attorney, waited at the red picnic table in Laurel Park. Sounds from a nearby little league game mingled with the scent of leftover charcoal in the grills. Feeling more than prepared, neither of them spoke, each quietly contemplating his own thoughts. Marvin was wound up tight with a pressure to perform unlike any he'd ever experienced before. The professional aspiration and filial duty contained within the moment at hand combined to weigh down heavily on his frame. Meanwhile Ed's conscience was waging an internal war with itself. Never before could he have imagined himself in such a position, seeking any amount of money from a lawsuit. It didn't fit with the way he'd lived his life. He'd paid for everything with milk. What milk couldn't buy they'd always gone without. So he was struggling to justify this action he'd chosen to take, engaging an enemy in battle with the hope of a monetary reward. His mind's eye focused itself on one word, one that had been interchangeable with the word milk throughout his life. Survival. Sunset Valley, and Mr. Cook, threatened the survival of his farm, a place he would fight for to the death if it came down to it. He just never thought the battlefield would be a court room, the weapons a pile of documents and witness testimony, and the general in charge his first born son.

Before long Dan approached them, his Armani suit outshining Marvin's three-piece from J.C. Penney, both outfits contrasting sharply with Ed's worn overalls over a white t-shirt. Dan took a seat across from them at the picnic table. There were no briefcases or fancy notepads, only three pairs of hands ready to shake. Dan focused most of his attention on Ed as Marvin delivered his monologue.

"So, Mr. Cook, you know why you're here. My father lost seven cows, all dying from intense thirst thanks to the wells of your development. We have a veterinarian and a hydrologist ready to testify in court, along with hundreds of local character witnesses who've declared they will vouch for my dad here. A developer against a farmer in a case like this barely has any chance. A developer who isn't from around here has none. That's just the facts. Although you bought what had been the only other dairy farm left besides my father's, the old timers, and many of their children and grandchildren, are the ones that populate this area year round. To these folks, even if they now might get by working at Wal-Mart, memory and loyalty run as deep as the new well my dad needs to drill thanks to Sunset Valley. In other words, the jury will not be on your side."

Marvin paused, giving the developer an opening to speak. Dan and Ed were staring each other down like two gunslingers about to have a draw. Their concentrations were so focused that Marvin wondered if they'd heard any of the words he'd just uttered so passionately. Dan reached into the inside pocket of his suit jacket, pulling out a checkbook and a ball point pen. He clicked the pen a few times with his thumb.

"How much do you want," he stated, his voice like steel, his eyes still fixed on Ed.

"Two million," Marvin said quickly, trying not to glance down at the checkbook.

Dan's expression remained unchanged. With one finger he pushed his sunglasses back on top of his head. "Is that all?" he asked, lifting his eyebrows.

Marvin flinched. He felt like a helpless mouse being toyed with by a tomcat.

"I thought you folks were going to ask for more. It's not often a farmer has a shot at being a multi-millionaire. But I have a settlement of my own to score here today." Finally Dan turned his bright green eyes completely on Marvin. "Are you ready to play ball?"

The shouts coming from the Little League field lent a strange undertone to his analogy for their bargaining session. Marvin raised his voice. "I don't know what you're talking about, Mr. Cook. You're not exactly in a position to bargain right now. When it comes to the emotional suffering of farmers around here, any judge you get will take you for all he can. Especially someone with your kind of money."

"What do you know about my money?" Dan asked, tensing slightly before relaxing again into the posture of confidence he'd been maintaining.

Marvin stayed quiet, letting the developer guess what he might know about his personal worth, which was nothing.

"Seems like your son's going to be one hell of a lawyer, Farmer Brown." Dan was looking back and forth between them now. "But I didn't bring my checkbook here today hoping to avoid court. I have a great lawyer, and that nice courthouse in town beats sitting in my dusty trailer any day. So if I write you a check not for two million, as you requested, but for ten, right here and now without so much as a blink, it won't be to buy myself out of a nasty trial that I'll likely lose."

Father and son exchanged a confused glance.

"Continue," Marvin said, guessing the direction Dan planned to take the conversation, certain his father would never consider selling the farm, no matter the price. Dan Cook's features shifted into an alternate version of himself. His eyes grew hooded and dark, his back curved forward. He was an animal about to pounce.

"You can't buy my farm," Ed stated, his fists clenching under the table in visceral defense of his land. "It's not for sale. And never will be."

"It's not your farm I want. It's your wife."

Ed jolted up and over the table, bellowing a kind of primal war cry while his hands clenched around the developer's neck. They fell to the ground where Ed straddled him, already beginning to choke the life out of him.

Marvin couldn't pull his father off, and resorted to shouting for help. "He's gonna kill him!"

A group of little league dads came flying across the grass. Ed leaned down, his nose less than an inch from Dan's forehead. "Keep your ten million dollars, you fucking bastard," he hissed. "You're gonna need every penny of it in the bank when we take you to court."

Noticing the stream of big men running towards them Ed spat right into Dan's wide open eyes just as the baseball fathers tackled him. Gasping for air Dan jumped up, retrieved his checkbook, and bolted off towards the parking lot.

TEN

Ed Brown was not prone to jealousy, as anyone who knew him would have attested. On the rare occasion that this emotion did rise up, when he noticed a male tourist scoping out his wife in town, or when a local husband left his eyes on Susan's breasts a few seconds longer than the average random glance of appreciation, Ed was quick to squelch any jealous notions as fast as they came up. These were the only times he dabbled in employing what his wife had shared with him about Buddhist meditation, how to practice dropping a thought as soon as it arose. He'd long ago vowed never to lose his otherwise hair-trigger temper because of jealousy, which he considered the lowest of human emotions. So there in the park, after Marvin shuffled the little league dads back towards the halted game, Ed worked hard to maintain a calm dignity in front of his son.

"Holy shit!" Marvin exclaimed, shaking his head. "What was that?"

Ed pulled at his chin, still trying to digest what the developer had said, and to gauge the effectiveness of his reaction.

Forcing any hint of rage down into his bowels, he knew there was nothing to say until he talked with Susan.

"I have to go home, son."

"I know, Dad."

When Ed got back to the farm he could hear the whir of the machine in the barn, signaling that Jack and Javier were in the midst of the afternoon milking. Stepping inside the back door, he saw that Susan was in her office off the kitchen. The door was cracked. A Vivaldi string concerto leaked out.

"Honey?" Ed said, knocking gently on the door frame. The music stopped.

"Yes dear?"

"We have to talk."

Ed took a seat at the kitchen table. Susan emerged, and sat across from him. Her face was tense with concerned anticipation.

"How did it go with Mr. Cook?"

Ed couldn't help cracking a sardonic smile, trying hard to trust the innocence in her voice. "Susan?" His voice had gravity. "Tell me about you and Dan Cook."

She closed her eyes, took in a deep breath. Exhaling and speaking at the same time, she defended herself with confidence. Rather than admit to her own fleeting attraction to the developer, a confession that would have likely made the situation worse, she explained how she'd picked up on his subtle flirtations that night he came over for dinner. Then she described her clandestine visit to his trailer in order to set things straight. "The last thing I said to him was that if he ever stepped foot on our farm you'd shoot him."

Ed nodded, his body relaxing slightly, his anger slowly releasing like sweat passing out through the pores of his skin. "And I would," he boasted.

"I know you would, honey. That's why I said it."

"Well, you're not going to believe what he said at our meeting today. You might want to sit down."

Susan sat down. Ed told her about Dan's ten million dollar offer.

"You should have taken it," Susan teased. "Then I could have divorced him the next day, and we'd be rich."

"Not a snowball's chance in hell would I let that slimy bastard put one finger on you, not to mention have you for one night. Please tell me you were kidding."

Susan beamed, attracted to this urgent defense of what was his. "Of course I was," she said. "Now come over here and kiss me."

The sparkle in her eyes told him it was okay to be proud that he'd won her love during that Adirondack summer all those years ago, and that he could be certain she wouldn't make him fight for it all over again.

Catching bits and pieces of his parents' intense conversation while lying on his bed, Jack slipped out the window and jogged down the road to his girlfriend's house. He was spending many more long nights at Katie's than ever before. These late summer nights on her rooftop were becoming his church. Even if Jack had hated dairy farming, which was the opposite of the truth, he would have found another reason to stay home in order to be with her. Katie Smignatelli was everything he loved about the country, all freckles and brown curly hair. She'd belonged to the 4H Club since middle school, raised pigs and sheep, and worked part time as a caregiver in the nursing home in town. She could bake a cherry pie, and any other flavor too. She rode horses, loved pickup trucks and country music, and often smelled like sweet alfalfa hay. Sometimes, stargazing with her on the rooftop after slow, hushed sex in her bedroom, Jack caught himself getting stressed about the likelihood that he'd already found the woman of his life. He tried to tell himself he was a lucky man, because many men never found what he had, so he should step up and accept it.

Jack was being unusually silent this evening, and Katie was letting him. He wanted to talk to her about things, but didn't know what to say. All he knew was that this developer was causing havoc at the farm. He sipped on his cheap beer. She took a few hits off a joint. They each had their post-coital substance of choice. His was a six-pack, the cheaper the better. Schlitz and Genessee were at the top of his list. She preferred a hand-rolled joint of the wet local pot that her cousin grew.

"I don't know what'll happen if Marvin wins us a lot of money from this guy."

Jack kept his focus pointed up on the emerging stars, hoping he'd see a shooting one to confirm that this simple rooftop world with his girlfriend still existed.

"Why wouldn't it be anything but wonderful?" she asked, putting out the half-finished joint on a shingle.

"Farmers are supposed to be poor. Keeps us honest," Jack muttered.

"I thought farming kept you honest."

Jack had no reply. He knew she was right. The money shouldn't change much except give them a well and a new tractor and some peace of mind.

"I guess some part of me wants more than dough. I want him to get shut down. There's something more going on now than just the water issue, something between my parents because of this guy. The whole situation stinks."

Katie sat up. "But what can you do to change it?"

Jack hadn't dared to tell her about his role in the death of the cows, so he couldn't share his certainty that since his own actions had caused the problem, he had to step in again to restore the balance of things.

"Look at me," she said finally.

"I'm waiting for a shooting star. C'mon, lie down in my lap like you always do, so we can watch together."

"First tell me what you're thinking."

Jack looked at her. "I'm thinking I love you. And that I hate Dan Cook."

Katie lowered her head down onto his lap. They gazed up at the stars.

"Well, you have good reason for both of those thoughts."

Jack smiled. "I don't even know the guy, though."

"Yeah, but it's so much easier to hate than to love, don't you think?"

"I do. And I loved those cows that died as much as my dad did," he said, unsure why he was bringing that up.

Katie leaned up to kiss the bottom of his chin as a meteor flashed across the western sky. Jack's whole body jerked. She pulled away.

"Did you see that?" he asked her.

"I missed it. I was too busy kissing you."

Jack hugged her into his chest, his eyes following the train the comet had taken, east to west across the big dipper. The shooting star had indeed confirmed that this world with Katie still existed. At the same time, because of its westerly direction and the state of Jack's mind ever since his encounter with the wolf, the comet had also hinted that a manifest sort of destiny might be lurking in his near future, a westward expansion of his spirit that could only be pursued alone. That's what he told himself, anyway. If a god could speak only in signs, then it was up to him to put them into words.

Their relationship had changed little in the two years since high school. Sometimes Jack worried about this fact. Usually he didn't. They spent most of their time at her house, sneaking in sex whenever they could, Jack remaining in constant fear of being caught by Smitty, a man with arms the size of his legs. Smitty Smignatelli worked as hard as any man Jack knew, including his own father, and was likely aware that he'd taken Katie's virginity. Indulging in their minor vices was much less stressful than the secretive sex, with the music loud but not too loud, Jack moving in and out of her in slow, gentle strokes. His efforts to keep the bed from squeaking led Katie into regular orgasms, something she didn't know to appreciate, since Jack was her first lover.

In the winter they traded the rooftop outside Katie's bedroom window for the attic above it, a space they'd converted into a hangout lounge where they sometimes entertained small groups of friends. A mini fridge held Jack's six packs. Katie blew her pot smoke into the fan venting to the outside. Her visits to the Brown farm were more defined, usually for supper followed by a board game of some kind. Later they might climb up through the pastures to take in the moon or the stars before Jack walked her home down the road. They were high school sweethearts determined to preserve the sweetness of what they had beyond graduation, unconcerned by the migration of so many peers, all the ones that had fled the area right after school, leaving for college or the city. This mass exodus had led to the termination of every couple they'd hung out with in high school. They never spoke of engagement, or children, content for now to bask in the pleasures of a youth shared.

Although he sometimes missed the bacon and coffee due to his late night romance, Jack always made it to the morning milk on time. Stressed by the imminent trial, Ed was snapping easily. One morning when Jack sauntered into the barn fifteen minutes later than normal, whistling a Johnny Cash tune, he was surprised to see his father working alongside Javier.

Ed's words hissed out of his mouth. "Quit your whistlin' and start milkin' – you're late. I had to take your place out here."

Jack kneeled quickly beside him and manned his half of the milker. "Sorry, pops."

"You should be." Ed hung his head. "I'm just stressed out. That's all. I'm all bent out of shape thinking about going to court and all that. And I miss milking."

Jack laid a hand on his father's flannel-clad shoulder. "You guys will take him for all you can, Dad. I know that. And you're going to win. Then we'll buy more Jerseys, and you can start milking again, 'cause we'll need the help."

And if you don't win, Jack said to himself, he would take matters even further into his own hands.

A week before the trial was set to start a check arrived in the mail, made out to Ed Brown for two million dollars. Before showing his wife, even, he called up Marvin at his office. Pacing around the back patio, he told him about the check. "I want to drop the case. I'm really in no mood to see that guy ever again. And I wouldn't know what to do with more money anyway. This much is going to be hard enough to manage."

"Dad, you'll be a fine millionaire."

"Well, we'll see about that. For your help I want you to have a hundred grand. At least."

"I won't take it."

"But Marv, that would be a great down payment on a new house or something. You deserve most of this, really."

Marvin told him he liked his house just fine, and that the only reason the check had arrived was because Dan feared for his life after nearly being choked to death.

"Eh," Ed said, swelling up with pride. "More likely he knew he'd have no chance in court against a natural born lawyer like you, son."

"Dad, please. I'm just a rookie. And I don't deserve any of your money. You need every penny of it, I'm sure."

"Then you'd better be prepared for an awfully big present this Christmas," he said.

"That's fine, Dad. I can handle a Christmas present."

After Ed hung up the phone, before venturing in the living room to show Susan the check, he stood there in the kitchen trying to see into the mind of Dan Cook. Surely the local judge wouldn't have ordered a verdict of such a large sum. And Dan had admitted looking forward to a trial as an excuse to get away from his trailer. Ed knew right then there was a missing piece to this puzzle, some secret the developer must be certain he could keep hidden behind his money. So after showing his wife the check, and feigning that he shared her jubilation, he climbed the stairs to their bedroom. There he slid the check into the drawer of his beside table, promising himself he wouldn't cash it until he uncovered exactly what it was Dan was attempting to hide. Ed's intuition was telling him that the developer was a very smart man, and had covered his tracks well, so that calling his bluff by refusing the settlement and going to trial was the wrong path to take. The only thing to do was wait and see what bubbled up to the surface.

ELEVEN

WHIL the check from Dan Cook burnt a hole in the drawer of his bed stand table, Ed and Jack fell into a comfortable rhythm, a cadence made possible thanks to Javier. Ed wanted to maintain his role with the morning milking, so Javier began arriving by bicycle around eight in the morning. The Brazilian worked tirelessly all day, visibly frustrated when Jack wanted to stop for lunch. He refused any food offered to him, instead snacking on strips of beef jerky pulled from various pockets. He worked all day, six days a week, without a grimace or any sign of fatigue. Jack knew Javier left the farm on his bike and went to his dish washing job downtown without stopping to shower, finishing that shift close to midnight, then arriving back at the farm by eight the next morning. They worked side by side repairing fence lines, moving the cattle from pasture to pasture, cleaning stalls, baling hay, harvesting corn, and overseeing the digging of the new well. When Jack stopped to wipe the sweat from his eyes or drink a glass of water, he'd shake his head over the machine-like capabilities of their employee, a manpower boost that made August bearable for the first time he could remember. Javier had limited English skills, but possessed a natural optimism that Jack came to rely on during the course of that hard, hot month.

"What are we going to do with Javier once the season ends?" he asked his father one evening after supper.

Ed sighed, something he was doing more often those days. The money was a heavy weight on his shoulders. And he'd been lacking the energy, after his long days on the farm, to investigate the hidden motive behind Dan Cook's too-easy settlement.

"You like that little guy, don't you?" he asked his son.

Jack nodded enthusiastically.

"He gives me the willies for some reason," Susan said from across the table.

"Oh Mom, he's harmless. I mean, back in the day down in Rio I bet he killed a man or two – but with fair reason, I'm sure. He's got a good heart, trust me. And he works harder than a Mexican!"

"That's the truth," Ed chimed in. "This place is humming along better than usual this time of year. Maybe we'll keep him on through the fall."

Susan got up to clear their plates, obviously struggling to hold her tongue.

"And tomorrow Jack and I are heading out towards Ithaca to pick up our new tractor - "

"Yeehaw!" Jack shouted out.

"Which means it'll just be you and Javier around here all day," Ed continued. "So do your best to make him feel comfortable."

He didn't tell either of them he'd be putting the tractor on the American Express card. Both Susan and Jack assumed the check was in the bank.

The next day Susan accidentally slept late. She picked up the bedroom as usual, then cut her time in the bathroom short. Her husband and son had already left on their pilgrimage west to buy the new tractor. She peered out the window above the kitchen sink, scanning the property for any sign of the long-haired Brazilian. He was nowhere to be seen, so she started tidying up the kitchen. Instead of making tea, though, she warmed up the rest of her husband's pot of Folgers. Before long she was twirling around the kitchen, dancing in whirls to the Vivaldi playing on NPR, thoroughly enjoying a rare caffeine buzz. When the dishes were done she moved to the bright living room in the front of the house to spin some of her wool from years past into yarn.

From the chair at her spinning wheel in the living room Susan kept glancing through the kitchen at the door leading into her office. She wondered what projects lurked in the windowless room. Lately she'd been choosing to focus more on the domestic side of life. Over her years at the farm there had been a constant tug of war going on inside her, a nagging voice insisting that no matter how good it felt to be a wife and a mother, to nurture and take care, she had to fulfill a promise she'd made to herself upon leaving school to marry Ed, a pledge that she would accomplish tangible achievements out in the world. But here she was in her late fifties with little to pin up on the refrigerator, where her children's homework once hung, besides a Volunteer Appreciation Award and some newspaper clips. She wondered if her mother, the suburbanite Jewish diva, had been secretly disappointed with the path she'd chosen. Although Susan felt most herself in the kitchen preparing a shepherd's pie, and looked forward to the whirl of the spinning wheel and the soft wool passing through her fingers as a reward for her cooking efforts, the office room always lurked, a portal of desks and books and computers linking her back to college, and the endless pursuit of acceptance into the elite club of career-driven intellectuals, a membership she'd long ago passed up.

Today it was easier than usual to ignore the office in favor of her wool. It was the first time she'd been alone at the farm with Javier. She needed the comfort of the soft, brown and white strands of yarn passing through her fingers. Susan knew Ed and Jack loved the guy, and he seemed like a hard-working, honest man. But there was something about him, something contained in the long, deep scar running down his cheek, or in his black, unblinking eyes, that made her uneasy. Jack's comments that Javier had possibly killed a man in Brazil years ago didn't help, even though her son insisted he was joking. To Susan, the man seemed to have a ferocity to him that he channeled into hard work, a fierceness born out of a tough life in the slums outside Rio. Javier had a past life in Brazil none of them knew a thing about, aside from the fact that he had three daughters, to whom he sent the major-ity of his paychecks. So when she wasn't glancing at her office door, or focusing on the wool threading onto the spool, Susan caught herself peering out the windows, looking for any sign of the Brazilian. She hadn't seen him all day. There was noth-ing unusual about that, she told herself, trying to ignore her persistent uneasiness. His tasks around the farm rarely took him anywhere near the house.

Over an hour later she was still working the wheel. Even though she could feel her aging hands beginning to ache, all the Christmas presents she aspired to knit over the next few months kept her going. The coffee helped too. And the clas-sical music spilling in from the kitchen. Now it was a flute and harp concerto by Mozart, something she used to play for Marvin when he was a baby. A single gunshot then shat-tered the melody, echoing off the ridge line. Susan froze stiff in her chair, waiting for the the next thing to happen. Maybe the radio was the reason she didn't hear the door open in the kitchen, didn't hear Javier's footsteps across the wood floor. He appeared in the doorway between the two rooms like an apparition. His otherworldliness was amplified by the dead wolf he was holding by the neck, lifting it above his head so the tail barely brushed the floor. Susan dropped the ball of raw wool she'd been clenching in her fist. She struggled to breathe. Dizziness overwhelmed her. She wanted to fall on the floor, except her need to get this man and that dead animal out of her house gave her the strength to resist fainting, to stand up and scream.

"What the hell are you doing in my house?! The wolf – you killed the wolf!? Get out of here, right now. Out!!" She shouted the last word at the top of her lungs, jabbing her finger towards the back door.

Javier's eyes widened in horror. "Senora, please, I only, it go across the field, near to barn -"

"Get out."

He backpedaled towards the kitchen door. "I protect the cows," he said in a final plea of innocence before stepping out into the bright midday.

Susan slammed the door behind him. Pacing the floor, frantic with nerves, she peered out the windows and watched with shocked disbelief as the little man climbed on his bike and pedaled off down the driveway, the dead wolf draped behind his back. She thought he'd be lucky to make it to wherever he lived before being thrown in jail. But there was nothing she could do. She was consumed with rage over her memory of the wolf's blank, dead eyes, that majestic creature she'd regularly imagined loping through the property like a primordial vision of wild.

Ed and Jack came home from their expedition buzzing
with joy. The tractor would be delivered the next day. They
couldn't wait to share their excitement over the new addition
to the farm with Susan. Ed wanted to tell her about the special
implements he'd splurged on, including a post-hole digger and
a rototiller. Jack was more eager to discuss the enclosed cabin
with air conditioning and a stereo system, a feature that made
him think he might actually enjoy haying season for once in
his life. But they didn't see Susan anywhere. After wandering
around the first floor calling out her name, Ed climbed the
stairs and found her in bed, her head sandwiched between
two pillows.

He sat down on the edge of the bed and rubbed her back.
"Are you sleeping?"

"No," she said, her voice strained.

Susan rolled out from between the pillows. Her eyes were
puffy, her face streaked with dried tears.

"Suzie, what's wrong?"

She told him what had happened. While she spoke her
tone shifted between relief and fear. Listening, Ed oscillated
between contrasting emotions, relieved the threat of the wolf
had been extinguished but fearful for Javier's safety. Prison
time for killing an endangered species could be five years
or more. For an illegal immigrant it would mean immediate
deportation.

"I'm not going to fire him," Ed said after a long silence.

"I don't expect you to. He was only doing his job, at least
that's how he considered it, I'm sure. There's just something
about him that makes me nervous, Ed. And, besides, I really
liked the idea that a wolf was around. It was the most beautiful animal I've ever seen. Even dead."

Ed hugged her head into his chest as her sobbing
returned.

"I never would have imagined I'd be crying over a wolf!" she lamented.

Ed rubbed her head. He was far from shedding any tears over the dead predator, but let her have the mourning she needed without interrupting.

When the lurching sobs quelled he finally spoke up. "So, assuming we can keep him out of jail, what are we going to do about you and Javier? You can't go on being scared of him. He's a very gentle man, Susan."

She sat up, wiping her eyes dry with her sleeve. "I'm going to teach myself Portuguese," she said firmly. "That will be a good start."

"I agree."

That night, after Susan had calmed down, after a dinner of steak and red wine to celebrate the new tractor, Jack took a ride down to the restaurant where he knew Javier worked as a dishwasher. It was the nicest restaurant in town, a place called Mika. Walking up to the bar he wished he'd dressed a little nicer. He could feel the stares of well-heeled patrons on the back of his neck. But as he settled into one of the leather stools the bartender gave him a welcoming smile, sliding a coaster under his nose.

"Evenin', pardner. What'll it be tonight?"

"Jack on the rocks, please. Oh, and let your dishwasher know someone at the bar wants to talk to him."

The bartender looked nervously towards the kitchen door. "Uh, the staff isn't allowed out here." He leaned closer to Jack in order to whisper. "Especially the illegal ones."

"Ahh," Jack said, nodding.

"You're welcome to go in there and chat with the little guy, though. He's one hell of a worker."

"Oh, I know."

The bartender poured him a tall drink. Jack swirled the whiskey around a few times before taking a healthy swallow.

"Think I'll finish this drink and then go on back there - "

"Good call. You'll fit in better with a nice little buzz on, trust me."

The bartender moved away to attend to other patrons. Jack settled in over his drink, trying to adjust to the atmosphere of polished wood and candlelight, piano notes from a distant corner, abstract works of art, china and crystal. It was like stepping into some fancy New York city establishment. As he was nearing the end of his drink the bartender approached him. A clean cut kid around his age, Jack struggled to place the hint of recognition he felt.

"Hey, man, you go to high school here?"

"I did. Chris Wilson. Class of '06"

"Oh yeah, I remember you. In my brother's class. Prom king, valedictorian, most likely to succeed - "

Chris snatched Jack's glass with a sip of booze still sitting in the bottom. "Another drink?"

"Uh, sure, I'll have one more."

The bartender tossed out the ice and refilled it with a plastic scooper. Jack watched the four counts of whiskey chug over the square cubes of ice.

"Hey, man, I didn't mean anything by what I said – I was just tryin' to figure out who you were, since I thought I recognized you and all."

Chris dropped the drink down with a new napkin. "Eh, don't worry about it. Everyone expected so much from me, but here I am, stuck in this goddamn country town pouring drinks for second homers."

"You went to college, right?"

Chris nodded. He scanned the bar to make sure no one else needed anything.

"Cornell. Ivy league. Actually majored in agriculture, thinkin' I'd come back and help my mom save the farm. But I failed." His voice sunk with the statement.

Jack winced. Obviously Chris didn't know he was a Brown. He wanted to talk about Sunset Valley, but wasn't going to bring it up out of respect, so he waited for Chris to continue.

"My old man shot himself when milk prices dropped for the fifth straight year."

"I remember that," Jack said flatly.

"Mom's okay now that we sold out. She works at the town hall as a secretary to make ends meet. Sister's in California. Never calls."

Jack looked down at his drink.

"Luckily I didn't quit my day job. Or night job. Whatever you wanna call this gig. That developer paid us a lot more than the farm was worth, for sure. But we needed to get a high price just to pay off all our debts." His eyes did a slow scan of the dining room.

Jack stood up. His drink was still full. "Well, I'm gonna head back there for a minute and chat with Javier. But you and I need to talk some more."

"Oh yeah? Why's that?"

"I'm Jack Brown."

Chris' face lit up. "No! Ed Brown's son?"

"That's right."

"Holy shit!" Chris practically fell over the bar as he leaned out to slap Jack a high five.

Everyone in town got their milk from the Brown farm. The only dairy farmer within a hundred mile radius to survive the lowest of the low milk prices, Ed Brown was a legend in town.

His epic status was heightened by the fact that he rarely made an appearance on Main Street, and had reportedly just won a very large settlement from the builder of Sunset Valley. If Ed had been close to being a local hero before, now he was a hero for sure.

"Whiskey's on me, Jack Brown."

"Thanks."

Jack walked back into the kitchen through the swinging wooden doors. He was confronted by fluorescent lights and stainless steel, sizzling pans and the roaring hum of a dish machine. Standing there with one hand on the handle of the machine's sliding door was Javier, beaming an innocent smile as Jack approached him.

"Oi, senor Jack!"

"Hello, Javier."

"Please, senor," the little Brazilian said, reaching up to lay one of his strong hands on Jack's shoulder. "I sorry for today, your momma, so mad, I only - "

Jack placed his own hand on top of Javier's. The machine had stopped its cycle. Jack could see what appeared to be the head chef staring in their direction. He knew he didn't have much time with the prized dishwasher.

"Javier, no problema, okay? Forget it. But you have to tell me . . .where is the wolf?"

"Mi apartmento, senor."

Jack nodded. He could see the chef was making his way over to them.

"Can you bring me there when you've finished here?" he asked Javier.

"Sim, senor. No problema. But late, muito late, senhor."

"It's okay. I'll wait. Me and the other Jack. Mr. Daniels!"

Javier's forehead scrunched in confusion.

"Never mind. I'll be at the bar, okay?"

"Sim."

Jack turned around and bumped into the substantial belly of the head chef, his face swelled red with anger. "Sorry, chef - I was just leaving."

"Good," the big man grumbled.

While Jack sipped his second drink, Chris made time to come over for more conversation. This time, though, he leaned in close, lowering his voice. His face was tense, drawn tight with nerves. To Jack he seemed like an entirely different man than the one he'd been talking to before.

"I have a confession to make, Jack Brown."

"Oh yeah?"

Jack didn't like the sound of the word confession. He took a healthy gulp of whiskey.

"I ain't no priest ya know."

Chris didn't smile at the half-joke. "It's not a priest's ears I need. Only a Brown can hear what I have to say. What I need to say, so that I don't end up sharing my father's fate."

Jack might have dashed out of the bar right then if it weren't for his responsibilities to Javier and the wolf carcass. So he slammed back the rest of his drink. "All right, then. Unload on me, man. I'm ready."

By the time Jack left the bar the place had been closed for an hour. Javier's apartment was just a few blocks up the road, so Jack walked alongside him while the little Brazilian pedaled slowly down the sidewalk. Two whiskeys and a beer deep, Jack was struggling to ingest what Chris Wilson had just poured into his ears. So far the only effect was the incessant pounding of his heart, and the strange feeling that his skin might not be able to contain his raging blood. After a walk to the outskirts of the sleeping town they climbed a set of wooden stairs to the one bedroom apartment Javier shared with the two Colombians Jack played basketball with. Line cooks at the restaurant, the two had finished work an hour before Javier, and were in the bedroom they shared. Jack could hear the sounds of a soccer game on TV spilling out through the cracked door. The couch was obviously Javier's bed. He showed Jack a couple bent photos of his daughters back in Rio.

"They're beautiful," Jack said, welcoming the distraction.

The place could have been messier. It could have been cleaner too. It smelled like chilis and lime juice.

Javier motioned for Jack to sit in the lawn chair next to the couch. "A drink, senhor Jack?"

"Water please, Javier. Obrigado."

While Javier retrieved a glass of water for his guest and a Corona for himself Jack scanned the place for any sign of the wolf carcass. Javier brought over the drinks and sat down on the couch.

"Muito bem," he said. "T.V.?"

Javier reached for the remote on the beat up coffee table covered with religious statues, newspapers in Spanish and Portuguese, and a Playboy.

"Javier," Jack said, his stern voice halting the Brazilian's arm.

"Senhor?"

"Where is the wolf?"

After a momentary pause, glancing towards the bedroom, Javier turned and pointed at the one closet in the room. Jack got up and opened the flimsy door to the closet. He gasped at the sight of the carcass hanging there on a hook, it's yellow eyes gleaming straight at him. There was a gaping hole behind one ear, the fur stained red around it. He staggered back a couple steps before recovering himself.

"Javier, you can't keep this here. We have to bury it. Tonight."

Javier nodded in solemn acceptance of his boss' edict. Even after Mrs. Brown's passionate disapproval of his action he was still proud of what he'd done, still believed he'd been doing his duty to protect the farm.

"Soon as you finish that beer we'll go get my car, come back and pick . . . him up . . . and bring him to a place I know. Okay?"

"Okay, senhor."

They walked back to the restaurant parking lot to retrieve his truck. Jack had already abandoned his plan to head to a defunct gravel pit he used to play in as a kid, located between town and the farm. He'd figured they would bury the wolf easily in loose gravel using the emergency snow shovel tucked behind his driver's seat. The relative obscurity of that location promised the carcass would not have been found anytime soon. But his thinking was narrowed by the whiskey, and an alternative vision for disposing of the carcass had been brewing ever since leaving the restaurant. This new idea was the only thing that somewhat calmed his furious heart. After helping Javier load the carcass into the back seats Jack drove right past the dirt access road to the gravel pit. He didn't stop as they passed his driveway either. He saw Javier begin to stir beside him.

"Senhor . . .where we go?"

"You'll see," Jack said, icy and cool in his determination.

Once past his farm there was no turning back, an almost literal truth since the narrow country road cut through dense forest, offering no good place to turn around. Beyond this swath of state land the road dead-ended at the former Wilson Dairy Farm. Emerging from the forest into the open expanse of space, Javier beside him, the dead wolf behind him, Jack was now entirely blinded by rage. The wolf's death saddened him on a much deeper level than the loss of the cows had, and the need to lash out at something, or someone, had taken over. Driven by his gut, Jack made the effort to suppress the nagging thought that instead of acting out this way he should take the incident as a sign it was time to leave, that life on the farm was a tame version of reality, a place where a creature of the wild wasn't welcome, where he was suddenly feeling like a prisoner enslaved by milk and the expectations of his father. If only it was that simple. Thanks to Chris Wilson's testimony, the developer up the road had become more than an enemy. In Jack's mind Dan Cook was now a force of evil that had descended upon the family from another world, a foreign reality where greed was the only rule worth following.

He parked the truck beside the giant welcome sign to Sunset Valley, eerily lit by a pair of flood lights amidst the scalped landscape that was void of any other light source aside from the clear stars and a half moon hanging low in the sky. He climbed out, reached in the back of the cab and grabbed the carcass by its neck. Javier circled the truck, persistently loyal, ready to follow Jack wherever they needed to go, to do whatever had to be done. After reaching back into the truck to grab his flashlight, Jack led them ahead as if he knew where he was going. They stumbled along the dirt precursors of winding paved streets, each awestruck by the barren, apocalyptic setting punctuated by right angle walls of concrete foundations. After wandering around for half an hour trying to find the right spot to leave this curse he was putting on the development, Jack decided the best place was back where they'd started. He circled them around to the truck, where he crouched beneath the huge painted sign. Javier took the wolf and obediently climbed up on his back, draping the carcass over the top of the sign with a perfect toss. After Javier got down off his back Jack stood there, hands on his hips, taking in the sight of the magnificent animal hanging down over a picture perfect sunset, rolling green hills, and little white houses.

"Dear God," he said out loud, still not sure exactly what he meant by that loaded three letter word. "Please accept the soul of this beautiful animal into heaven." Jack paused. He wasn't sure about heaven either, but decided that paradise for a wolf would probably be another chance at life in a wilderness without being shot. "Forgive Javier for his innocent mistake. He was just being a loyal employee. And also, God, understand that I'm doing this to kill this horrible place, because I know that losing our water is only the beginning of what will befall our family because of this development. This wolf was innocent. Dan Cook is not. So, God, since I can't murder him, please help me extinguish this hideous creation of his."

Jack closed his eyes, took in a deep breath, then released it slowly into the night. "Amen," he whispered, using the only word he could think of to signify that his prayer was finished.

Neither man said a word all the way into town. As they neared his apartment Javier finally spoke up. "You no like that place, eh senor?"

"Sunset Valley? No, I hate it. They stole our water, Javier. And killed our cows."

"I see. So it is war?"

Jack stopped beside the curb in front of Javier's apartment building. He turned to face the little Brazilian. "Yes. It's a war."

Javier nodded. His dark face was very serious. "I fight war with you. No problema."

Jack smiled. "Obrigado, amigo. Oh, there's one more thing."

"Que?"

"I need you to give me your pistol."

TWELVE

A T sending the settlement check to Ed, Dan Cook was confident the money would bring down a permanent veil surrounding the technicalities of his ownership and development of the Wilson tract. Now he was trying to come to terms with the fact that winning Susan for himself was no longer a reality. When it came to pursuing a woman, his wealth was his source of confidence, what he believed a real man should always be able to provide for the object of his desire. In Dan's mind, his offer of ultimate stability had been his only shot at her. During the days in his on-site trailer, and well into the nights at the motel room he was living out of in town, he ignored the duties of business, spending most of his mental energy trying to decide whether or not to finally give up this hopeless crusade for the love of a married woman. Dan wasn't used to failing, but a week after mailing Ed the check he decided to give up. Having reached his position of success by making one of his few golden rules be to never mix women and business, the direct result of this rare failure was that he poured himself into Sunset Valley.

He began showing up at his trailer by five in the morning, two hours before his crew managers arrived. So naturally he was the first to find the dead wolf. He squealed his Prius to a stop in front of the sign, not believing what was hanging over the top of it. He'd watched enough Discovery Channel to know exactly what kind of animal it was, even in the half-light of dawn. Overcoming his initial shock, he maneuvered his car directly under the sign. He got out and scampered up onto the roof. Eye level with the wolf's shoulder, he could see the bullet hole wound in its neck. Dan was struck by an instinctual kind of certainty, something much more than a hunch that told him the Brown family was responsible for this. He left the dead wolf hanging there and got back in his car. Heading towards town and the police station, Dan was no longer surrendering anything more to Ed Brown. His brief fight for Susan, and the water issue, had only been battles, small skirmishes between two men. Now it was war.

Even though the check from Dan Cook weighed as little as any rectangular piece of paper that size would, the monetary significance of it was lead heavy in Ed's mind. On the morning after his journey with Jack to buy the tractor, cleaning his plate of bacon and eggs with the last of his toast, even the darkness before dawn outside the kitchen windows lacked its usual promise of light. To him it could just as well have been midnight. As he got up to put his dishes in the sink and pour a second cup of coffee, he tried to tell himself it was only a matter of perception. But from his depths he knew it was more than that. Two million dollars threatened to change his life drastically. He would have to surrender to the sudden reality of being a millionaire first, and a farmer second. What worried him was that his first purchase, the thirty thousand dollar tractor, was only making him feel worse. And he hadn't even paid for it yet. He'd loved sliding on his back under the old Massey Ferguson he'd known so intimately, to tinker around until he'd fixed the latest mechanical problem. He always fixed the problem. Even if the job took him late into the night, it was time well spent. But this new John Deere wouldn't break down for years. And when it did, even if he was physically capable, Ed would have no clue how to repair the computerized, hydraulic-ridden machine anyway. He decided that morning he disliked having a surplus of money as much as he hated the inevitable forward march of time. Maybe that was the real reason he'd yet to deposit the check.

When Jack plodded into the kitchen hints of daylight were already creeping across the polished tree-trunk chopping block. Ed had finished his coffee, and was waiting at the table.

"Late night?" he asked his son.

Ed already knew the answer to his question. His sharp ears always let him know what time his son had made it back home.

Jack poured a cup of coffee. "I guess. I was hangin' out with Javier. Went to his restaurant in town. Saw his place."

"Ya' see the wolf?"

Jack nodded. Ed knew his son had done something with the dead animal, but he didn't prod him any further. Jack sat down at the table, huddling over the coffee mug.

"What's wrong?" he asked his father.

"Why do you think something's wrong?"

"Look out the window, Dad. We never milk this late. You either wake me up or go out there yourself and then give me shit for the rest of the day."

Ed cracked a quick smile.

"Gettin' soft on me now that you're rich?" Jack asked playfully.

"Don't ever call me rich!" Ed snapped.

"Sorry."

Ed got up and walked over to the sink. "I just, I have to deal with a lot of things now. Complicated things."

Jack stood up. "I know, pops."

Ed stared out the window above the sink at the long barn. With Javier back to being a part time employee, Ed was able to take part in the milking once again.

"We should get out there and start milkin'. We can talk," Jack said. "I've got something to discuss too."

Ed slapped the soapstone sink. "All right then!"

"I'll take my joe with me," Jack said, moving to pour a second cup.

In the barn, while Ed cleaned teats with the spray hose and Jack tossed down some bales of hay from the loft, the two men decided they would offer Javier a big enough raise to lure him away from the restaurant. Then he could arrive in time for the morning milk all year long. While they spread flakes of hay into the stalls and filled up the troughs with water from the new well, Ed shared his reluctance to entirely give up participating in the morning milk, his second favorite part of the day.

"I understand that, Dad," Jack said while they moved along from cow to cow, attaching the mechanized milker four teats at a time. "But it's time you focused on other things - coordinating the new wells, and making Marvin's bedroom into an office like you talked about."

Ed nodded, trying hard to accept the necessity of this upcoming transition. He had a farm to manage, and he couldn't let hanging onto routine distract him from making sure they were successful.

"So, Dad, now that we have a new tractor, what's next?" Jack asked.

"Replacing the girls we lost, and maybe more."

"Can we get more Angus too?"

Jack had been urging his father to speed up their transition into the beef business even before the settlement money had come in.

"Maybe. We'll see. I'll have to look into prices."

"Okay. Just stay away from the porn when you're online in that office of yours."

Ed smacked his son on the back of the head just hard enough. "Then, after all of that is done, I might take your mother on a real vacation."

"Seriously?" Jack said, jiggling one of the plastic tubes to clear out a pocket of air bubbles that was slowing the flow of milk.

"This November is our thirtieth anniversary."

"No shit!"

"It's true. So, after the check came I got this crazy idea that I'd take her on a vacation."

"I didn't even think the word vacation was in your vocabulary," Jack said.

"It wasn't, son. But it is now."

As they neared the end of the line of cows, Ed felt the weight of the check possibly lifting just a little. Up until that moment he hadn't thought past November.

"Then what?" Jack asked.

"Then . . . I don't know. Christmas, that's what. Then everything starts all over again."

"Except you'll still be a millionaire."

"You know I don't like that word."

"I know. That's why I said it."

They made their way into the bright room that held the shiny steel refrigerated holding tank for the milk, where they checked on the gage that told them how many gallons had been pumped in. Ed stopped abruptly in front of the tank.

"Didn't you have something to talk about?" he asked his son.

Jack shrugged his shoulders. "Oh, it's nothing really, pops. Just girl stuff."

"Girl stuff, huh," Ed said.

Jack was a bad liar, and they both knew it. But instead of pressing him for the truth, Ed just tried to lighten the mood.

"Pregnant girl stuff?"

Jack chuckled. "No Dad. I'm a firm believer in condoms."

Ed nodded once, sharp and approving. He bent down to check the gauge. "Ninety eight gallons. Just right."

THIRTEEN

WH Jack entered the kitchen the following morning he was surprised to see his father still reading the paper. Ed never lingered over the morning news. He usually just glanced at the headlines and saved an in-depth reading for his hour of digestion after supper. But this morning something had his full attention. He didn't even notice Jack right away. At the sound of the coffee being poured into a cup he spun around and stood up.

"What the hell were you thinking?!" Ed shouted at his son's back. He was holding up the front page of the paper. The headline read "NEW DEVELOPMENT VANDALIZED BY TIMBER WOLF CARCASS." Underneath the giant headline was a black and white photo of two construction men holding up the wolf carcass between them, a shot taken during a police investigation of the site.

Jack lingered by the coffee maker, staring at the floor.

"Answer me, Jack. What were you thinking?"

Jack was frozen in the corner. "I wasn't thinking."

"Obviously."

"It'll blow over, Dad."

"It better blow fast. Dan Cook had nothing to do with this wolf's death. You didn't accomplish anything by doing this. You know that, right?"

Jack nodded. He slurped down most of his coffee, then refilled his cup before approaching the table gingerly. "Dad, I have to tell you something. You should be sitting down for this."

Ed sat down.

"I wanted to tell you yesterday, but for some reason I kept it inside. When I went to Mika the other night to find Javier, I ended up chatting with the bartender for a while. Chris Wilson is the bartender. When he found out who I was, for some reason I'll probably never know, he decided to spill his guts while I drank my second whiskey. Turns out, you're not gonna believe this, Dad." Jack paused for dramatic effect. "Turns out the deed on their land gave us a right of first refusal on any offer to buy."

Ed grabbed onto the table and started to rise. "What?"

"Dad, please. Sit back down and let me finish."

Ed sat back down, shaking his head. "It's been my dream to get a shot at that land, ever since I was your age, son."

"I know, pops. You've told me that many times."

Ed motioned for Jack to continue.

"Chris said that his father had the clause added on years ago because he respected you more than anyone, and wanted you to have the first shot at his farm if he was ever to lose it. When Dan offered double the assessed value of the property in exchange for overlooking this detail, Mrs. Wilson accepted."

"That bitch," Ed snarled.

Jack raised his eyebrows at his father's unprecedented profanity.

"It was their only chance to get out of debt. Chris said he protested, but his mom wouldn't budge. Since she worked at the town hall she was able to locate the public copy of the deed, which she burned in her wood stove along with the original. So that's why Dan was so quick to send us a check. And that's why, after hearing all of this straight from the source, I kinda lost control. I must have thought that somehow what I did would frame him for the death of the wolf, and then we'd have some kind of payback. Of course that was a stupid idea, inspired by the whiskey. And now I'm just scared."

Jack breathed heavily from the exertion involved with relating this disturbing revelation to his father.

Ed was staring at the kitchen wall. His mouth hung open. Eventually he turned to face his son. "Did you ask this Chris Wilson if he would testify in court?"

"I did. He won't. Because of his mom. But he said if there's anything else he could do he would."

"Eh," Ed muttered. "You know I haven't deposited that check yet?"

"What!? Why not?"

"Because, son, I knew there was something lurking underneath that two million, some catch that might have given me the land instead of the money. That land is what I want."

"But Dad, it's not even a farm anymore. You've seen it. There are foundations, and roads, and -"

Ed held up his palm to stop Jack's words. "Oh Jack, never underestimate the ability of nature to reclaim what is hers. I'd take five hundred acres over two million dollars any day. And I hope you would do the same."

Jack hesitated, unable to say whether or not he would indeed do the same.

"Well, it ain't an option now, so no point dwelling on it. Plenty o' work on the three hundred acres we've already got, I guess. Speaking of work, are ya' ready to milk?"

"I am."

"Let's go."

Jack swallowed the rest of his coffee, and left the cup behind.

Susan wasn't sure why fall always made her nervous. She thought maybe it had something to do with having been an overly serious student. Perhaps the cool air made her nervous the same way the first day of school always used to. For her, fall was more about change than any other season. Changing was something that had never come easy to Susan. For some reason this fall took its time more than other years, a lingering shift she actually caught herself enjoying. Like it did every year the season brought a crisp clarity to the dance between man, beast and nature. Each day was content with itself, each another increment in the change from summer to winter. The Brazilian had given two weeks' notice to his restaurant, so Ed was able to maintain his role with the morning milk a little longer. When Javier arrived around eight, instead of working on projects around the farm all day her husband would head back into the house. She was surprised by this disruption of her regular routine. Ed responded to the palpable tension by sequestering himself in the upstairs room designing his office. Occasionally he tracked her down in some part of the house to ask her opinion of something. She never wanted to talk about it, so her answers would be short and gruff, sending him retreating back to the room.

Susan had no grudge about Ed setting up an office. She'd always had one of her own in a room off the kitchen, a domain all to herself where she maintained various intellectual projects, things like editing a local arts newspaper and writing letters to politicians on farming and environmental issues. What bothered her wasn't really Ed's presence in the house during the midday hours, but rather the inevitable result of his endeavor. Following a common yet unspoken American tradition when a child goes off to college, Marvin's bedroom had remained untouched, preserved like a museum installation exactly the way he'd left it. There were posters of

New York City sports stars like Alex Rodriguez and Michael Strahan. Gold trophies stood on the dresser from his achievements in basketball and tennis. An award from the National Honor Society hung above his bed. There were pictures of his high school girlfriend Sam pinned in various locations. Susan couldn't help envisioning Ed dismantling all of this. For days she left him alone with his task, feeling like she was losing her son all over again. Lying in bed one night, in between reading their books and falling asleep, she listened as Ed broached the subject for the first time. He recounted parts of his experience converting their first son's old bedroom into an office. He told her about the frequent breaks he took to sit on Marvin's twin bed, where he'd stroke the afghan she'd knitted out of wool from a few sheep she used to keep in one corner of the barn.

"It's the softest thing I've ever felt in my life," he said.

"Softer than my skin when you were courting me?" she asked playfully, hoping to change the subject.

"Well, not quite that soft, I guess."

Ed told her how he liked to look up at the ceiling where the glow-in-the-dark stars he'd helped Marvin attach almost twenty years ago still remained. How he would peer out across the desk beneath the large window that looked out at the barn and pastures beyond. He told her how he thought it was ironic that Marvin's room had a view of the barn while Jack's only window faced the front yard and the driveway. The opposite would have been more in line with how things had actually turned out. As the posters came off the walls, the trophies got loaded into boxes, and the clothes that still smelled like Marvin were folded into plastic crates, Ed told his wife he'd felt a deep sense of happiness for his first son. Winning a settlement so large from a corporate developer had put him on the map of land rights attorneys. Taking apart the room seemed to finalize Marvin's departure from the nest in a healthy way. Susan's distance, even though she was lying right next to him, told him she felt otherwise.

"You should come take a look one of these days, Suzie. I think you'd feel better about it if you did."

"Okay," she whispered.

The next afternoon Susan stopped in the doorway of the new office. Everything was out of the room except the desk, a chair, and a small table with a lamp. Ed was standing in the middle trying to formulate a plan.

"I used to come in here sometimes," she said.

Her voice startled him. He turned to face her, lifting his eyebrows.

"Some days, when I really missed him that first year, I would lie on his bed, thinking I was going to take a nap, but I usually just ended up crying."

Ed walked over to her.

"It took me a year to realize I was crying more for myself than for him," Susan continued. "So I stopped coming in here. There must have been so much dust after all these years."

Ed hugged her tight for a minute or more, then stepped back. He reached down to grab the check from its new resting place on his office desk, a small step closer to the bank. He held it out in front of her as evidence of his internal conflicts. His hand was shaking in the air.

"You haven't deposited it yet?" Susan asked, her blue eyes opening wide with distress.

Ed hadn't told her about his hunch, even after Jack had confirmed it to be true, and defined its specifics. After hearing about Chris Wilson's secret Ed knew it was time to put the check in the bank and move on. The Wilson tract would never be his. But that brought up a new problem. Finally he looked directly at his wife, shaking his head. His face was strained.

"What is it, dear?" she asked.

"It's just . . .I don't want to walk into the credit union with this check – Meghan and Sue there at the counter, the ones that have taken my small deposits, our milk money, every week for all these years . . .what will they say?"

Susan reached out a hand and cupped his cheek. "Ed, they already know about the money. Everyone does. The word is out, so to speak. They'll say the same things they always do. They love you. The whole town loves you. And two million dollars in your bank account isn't going to change that."

"No?"

"No."

Ed sat down at his desk. He opened the top drawer to retrieve a deposit slip from his check book. He started filling it out. His hand was no longer shaking. "Welcome to my office, Suzie."

"It's a wonderful office," Susan said. She stepped back until she was standing in the doorway. "Ed?"

"Yes?"

"Do you want me to go to the bank with you?"

Ed signed the deposit slip. He looked out the window at the view of his red and white barn, the blue silos rising up behind it. He was shaking his head. "No thanks. This is something I have to do on my own."

Susan slipped out soundlessly, leaving him alone with the check, and his view.

FOURTEEN

O Javier started showing up every day by five-thirty in the morning to milk with Jack, Ed became officially lost, stranded in a kind of no man's land. His body was still programmed to rise at quarter till five in the morning. He still left his wife in bed and headed downstairs to cook breakfast. The only difference was now he kept his pajamas on, a self-imposed practice designed to keep him from going out to milk, since a third man was unnecessary and could only get in the way. The first few weeks were the worst. Ed would fight waves of jealousy as he watched Jack pour a second cup of joe, say goodbye, and head out the back door towards the barn, leaving him alone with coffee he didn't want to drink and a paper he didn't want to read. During these moments alone at the kitchen table, stuck in farmer purgatory, Ed often wished he'd never gotten the money. Then the luxury of hiring Javier full time wouldn't have been an option. Now he understood why his own father had dreaded retirement, always telling the family he wanted to work right up until the moment he dropped dead. As soon as his office was completed he'd have to get more Jerseys, making his own presence for the milking a necessity.

On one of these mornings, dawn inching steadily into the kitchen, his wife asleep upstairs and Jack out in the barn awaiting Javier, Ed decided it was time to do what any man in his position would. He needed to take a vacation. Although he'd told Jack about the idea, in truth he never intended to follow through. Vacations just weren't in his nature to contemplate. He'd denied himself this luxury, among all others except coffee, for his entire adult life. But with their thirtieth anniversary coming up the following spring, there couldn't be a better excuse for a trip. He knew right away the destination would be Hawaii, the only far away place Susan ever mentioned wanting to experience. He felt better all of a sudden, aware that when the day came to leave the farm for a week or two on an island he'd have to force himself onto the plane, even if they went in March, his least favorite month of the year. The thought of leaving the farm for a string of days felt like death. And the memory of what happened the only time he and Susan had gone away loomed ominous in his mind.

Satisfied with the condition of his office, proud that his diligent spending had brought the project to completion without surpassing his self-imposed five thousand dollar budget, Ed wanted to splurge on this anniversary trip. He felt more than justified in doing so. He revealed his plans to his wife during one of their bedtime talks, in between reading books and falling asleep. Having realized years ago that talking to Susan was his version of praying to a god, his voice always took on a calm, almost sacral tone during these moments. He spoke into the darkness above the bed. "I want to take you away. For our anniversary. It can be like the honeymoon we never had. What do you say?"

Susan's exhaled a long breath of air. "Oh my," she said. "I guess we do have a little money to spare." She sat up, turning to face him in the darkness.

"Where do you want to go?" he asked bluntly, having already guessed her destination of choice back when the idea had first struck him.

"Hawaii," she said with certainty.

The next day Jack was walking towards the house from behind the barn. He was feeling confined by the browns and grays of an early winter. The drab sea of monotonous color had a grip on the farm, and were weighing down Jack's spirits more than in years past. Nearing the house he glanced up at Marvin's old bedroom window, where the glow of his father's flat screen monitor, displaying a scene of some tropical landscape, was visible through the glass. Jack fantasized about one day taking a vacation of his own, maybe with Katie, a tropical escape like the one his father was fine-tuning up there in his office. Or maybe something long-term, a wandering adventure that could last for years, flying solo, relying only on himself. He'd been telling himself that when a window for such an escape appeared, one that wouldn't give the false impression that he was running away from responsibility, he'd seize on the opportunity. That had been the message imparted upon him by the wolf, and he vowed to remain loyal to it. After some time away, however much he needed, he'd come back to stay. The only hitch to this idea was Katie.

Jack was taking his usual mid-morning break. He looked forward to the hard-earned respite, when he'd have himself a snack and then curl up on his bed with a book. He allowed himself half an hour, knowing Javier was content to be working away on a project, maybe pausing briefly to gnaw on some jerky and slug back some water. This morning, after a snack of a banana and yogurt, Jack stretched out on his bed with The Old Man And The Sea. He was nearing the end of the story, and the old fisherman was dominating his thoughts these days. It would be hard to stop in twenty minutes and venture back out to work. But he put the book down soon after picking it up when the sound of a car pulling into the driveway caught his attention. He leaned up on his elbows and pulled open the blinds on the window above his bed. A dark blue police cruiser was winding its way towards the house. Jack scrambled to his feet. He bent down and reached under the mattress. His hand found the cool steel of Javier's pistol. He thought about searching for a new hiding place for the weapon, but then decided against the idea.

Jack left the handgun where it was and headed for the kitchen. There he bumped into Ed, who had seen the trooper car as it pulled to a stop beside the house. Susan was peering out from her office room. Her eyes were wide with fear.

"What's going on?" she asked the men.

Jack shrugged his shoulders unconvincingly. Ed glanced out the window above the sink. Two state police officers were bending down to inspect the tire treads of both trucks in the driveway.

"We'll find out soon enough, won't we son."

"Yup."

"C'mon, let's cut 'em off at the pass! Don't want their donut breath stinkin' up our kitchen."

Ed opened the back door and waved for Jack to follow. They stepped out onto the back patio. Susan closed the door behind them. Beneath their wide-brimmed hats, under the same polished uniforms, the two officers were hard to tell apart, except one spoke and the other didn't.

"This the Brown residence?" one of them asked as they approached the house.

"Yes it is, sir," Ed replied.

"I'm Officer Sarcowski, and this is my partner, Officer Jordan."

"I'm Ed Brown, and this is my son Jack. What can I do for you gentlemen?"

Sarcowski pivoted and scanned the property. Ed and Jack followed his gaze, both wondering if Javier was the object of this visit.

"We have a warrant to search the premises," he said, beckoning his partner to hold out the official looking document.

"Well, okay," Ed said, giving Jack a confused look. "If you don't mind me asking, what exactly are you searching for?"

"A gun."

"What? I own a shotgun and a twenty two, weapons I'm fully certified and trained to - "

Sarcowski held up a gloved hand. "We're looking for a pistol, Mr. Brown. The one that fired the bullet that killed a timber wolf found at the new development up the road. In case you don't know, it's a felony to kill an endangered species. Then there are the trespassing charges associated with its disposal. Anyway, we have reason to suspect a resident of this farm. A logical reason, given the threat a wolf obviously poses to your livelihood. Now, if you'll step aside, my partner and I are going to search the house. Is there anyone else inside?"

"My wife," Ed said.

The police officers stepped up to the door. Jack, looking out towards the barn, saw Javier walking closer. As the troopers entered the house he directed the Brazilian back to the barn with various hand signals.

"I don't like this one bit," Ed whispered to Jack.

In the kitchen Susan did her best to act calmly while the two officers pawed through cabinets and pantry shelves. Jack slipped down the hallway to his bedroom. Susan offered the men food, which they politely turned down. They declined Ed's offer of coffee as well, but he set himself to brewing a huge pot of it even though he didn't want any either. The gurgling sound of the machine failed to have its normal calming effect on him. Ed had never liked cops. Having two of them in his kitchen was

very unsettling. Then came the sound of breaking glass in the
direction of Jack's bedroom. Susan gasped, drawing a palm into
her chest. Ed closed his eyes. The troopers drew their guns and
stalked down the hallway towards Jack's bedroom. Ed ignored
his wife's pleas not to follow. Reaching the bedroom door he saw
the window above Jack's bed was shattered to pieces. A pistol lay
on the pillow. And there was no sign of his son.

"Should I go after him?" Jordan asked, speaking for the
first time.

Sarcowski held up his hand. "No. We've got what we came
for. The kid'll turn up."

After holstering his own gun he reached down a gloved
hand and grabbed the pistol. His partner dug out a thick plastic bag and held it open as Sarcowski dropped the evidence
inside. Ed stepped firmly into the room.

"That's my pistol," he said, holding out his wrists. "I'm
your man. Cuff me."

Sarcowski chuckled under his breath, pushing Ed's hands
down. "That's sweet, Farmer Brown. Trying to save your son
and all. But you already told us about your guns, and this one
didn't make the list. Soon as we get the prints off this sucker,
then match it to the bullet they found lodged in the carcass, we'll
know who our man is. Based on what I've been hearing around
town, it seems you have yourself a fine lawyer. So after we leave
you might want to call him up to ask about the penalties for har-
boring a fugitive. Even if the fugitive is your own son."

The men walked out of the room, heading back towards
the kitchen. Ed slumped down onto Jack's bed. He picked up
a shard of glass. Cool outside air spilled into the room. He listened to his wife offering the policemen coffee in the kitchen,
heard the reluctance in their voices as they turned her offer
down. Then the cruiser's engine started, and a siren pierced
the crisp fall day. Ed propped his elbows on his knees, dropped
his face into his hands. He fought the hints of shame and fear

that were trying to penetrate his skin. Jack had simply been protecting Javier. There was nothing shameful in that. And those policemen were no match for Jack's sensibilities. There was nothing to fear, yet the emotion managed to crawl its way partway into him as he sat there, staring into the warm pink darkness of his palms. As the siren finally faded into the distance Ed realized it wasn't his son being caught that he was scared of, but the opposite. Jack's escape from the law would no doubt result in his long-term absence from the farm. Ed lurched up from the bed. He had to call Marvin, so they could be prepared should Jack be fortunate enough to get himself caught, because losing him indefinitely was a prospect Ed didn't know how to face.

After smashing through his bedroom window Jack ran, stopping only twice within town limits. The first stop was deep in the woods, when he paused long enough to bandage the slice in his arm that was gushing blood, using a compaction of striped maple leaves lashed tight with his belt. He laughed out loud at himself, amused by the absurdity of leaping through his window when he could have simply opened it. He decided the primal rush of his escape had been worth it. The trail of blood eliminated, he circled back around to Katie's backyard. He knew she was at work. But Smitty was home, evidenced by his company truck parked in the driveway. With a degree of stealth he wouldn't have previously thought himself capable of Jack scaled an ivy-cloaked lattice, then shimmied up a gutter pipe to the flat rooftop outside Katie's window where he'd spent so many long and glorious nights. He opened the window and slipped inside. The apricot smell of her sheets struck him as he moved to her desk. Jack was ready to leave everything behind except her. The farm and his family would still be there when the air had cleared and it was time to come back. But Katie's love, the genuine affection she washed over him in constant waves, was something he couldn't imagine would just wait for his return. Torn between the need for his own escape into the unknown and the warm soft promise of a lifetime spent with Katie, Jack forced himself to sit down at her desk and scratch out a note on a page of her butterfly-fringed pad.

Dear Katie,

I don't know where I'm going, only that I have to go, and that you can't come. There is some growing up I need to do that won't happen here. If you wait for me, I'll be the luckiest man alive. If you can't wait -

Before Jack could finish the note Smitty threw open the door.

"What the hell are you doing here?" His voice boomed with the question.

Jack chose not to waste time answering. Luckily he'd left her window open, and didn't have to break another pane of glass as he dove out. He scampered across the roof and dropped to the ground.

Smitty shouted down at him. "You've got one hell of a nerve sneaking in here like that!"

Back in the woods Jack heard Smitty's truck rumble to a start in a futile attempt to track him down on the roads. He didn't plan on being on any roads longer than it took to dash across them. Jack ran for hours, heading southwest, his trail no longer marked by spots of blood. Instead he left tiny drops of moisture on the ground, tears that dried quickly, leaving no trace of the pain that would be his constant companion for years to come.

II

THE ROAD

FIFTEEN

TH only contact Ed and Susan had with their son were the random postcards sent once a month from various corners of the west, all of them secured to the old GE fridge with magnets in the shape of cows. The couple hung on each postcard's arrival, the bent gloss photo with ragged corners, usually a pristine scene of some natural landscape. They might have been pictures of another planet for all Ed was concerned. While reading about Jack's obsession with the desert on the back of one card, a shot of red rocks and cacti that seemed it might glow in the dark, he was momentarily furious. What value could there be in that moonscape land? No corn would grow there. No hay could be seeded in that sand. Cows would die there in a matter of days. Jack insisted the New Mexico wilderness was the most beautiful place he could ever imagine, confirming for Ed that his son was indeed going crazy. As most fathers would, he contemplated tracking his boy from state to state by following the monthly trail of postmarks, as Jack never alluded to his exact locations, but quickly let the idea go. His son would stop running at some point. He had to believe this in order to keep going everyday, to convince himself Jack was going to be okay.

Susan focused less on the content of Jack's words and more on the look and feel of them. She'd trace the individual letters with the tip of a finger, following the indentation made by a ball point pen. She would close her eyes and feel the shape of his letters, trying to elicit a clue to the state of mind he might have been in when writing. Some postcards were scrawled with jagged letters pressed firmly into the thick paper, evidence Susan took to mean her son had likely been having a stressful day. But then next month's card would arrive with round, graceful words visibly penned with care, giving her as much motherly relief as she could squeeze out of the few sentences likely written a week or more before she was reading them. These monthly postcards were the couple's life support, little shots of hope to keep them going.

Close to a year after Jack's departure the couple decided to go ahead and take their vacation to Hawaii. The only thing they knew about Dan Cook was that he'd put Sunset Valley up for sale, although construction hadn't been halted, and his Prius was sometimes seen speeding up the road around the morning milk time. Otherwise Dan hadn't re-entered their lives since the check had arrived in the mail. Already bent out of shape over Jack's vanishing act, Ed's body had a physical reaction to leaving the farm, one that began a short way into their drive to the airport. He kept turning up the heat as goosebumps covered his skin and shivers passed through him in waves. He had trouble taking in a full breath. When they stopped at a rest area he could barely feel his feet on the ground. Susan kept asking if he was okay. Ed would grunt that he was fine, hoping the sun and the sea would help ease his panic over this separation from the farm. He'd accepted Marvin's offer to cut his hours in the office, to stay at the farmhouse and watch over Javier and the Colombians. Ed would never have asked his first son to do this, but when Marvin proposed the idea himself, Ed figured he was up to the task. Besides, even though he'd deny it, milk ran through Marvin's veins just like it did for every Brown.

Although she tried not to show it, Susan was having an opposite reaction to leaving their home. Her blood bubbled like popped champagne. Her excitement about being able to finally detach herself from the daily domestic toils of life was overwhelming, occasionally leaking into her voice while conversing with her nervous husband. Susan understood that her elation, which was catching her by surprise, was dependent on the knowledge that they were only to be gone for ten days, during a time when the muddy transition from winter to spring always felt like it would never end. Life had taught her that she needed the routine of what the farm demanded of her, that she'd long ago chosen her fate even though, at the time, she'd simply been choosing love. And Susan could also understand why her husband felt the way he did. The burden of their survival had always fallen much more heavily on his shoulders. Even with their recent financial windfall, their future still depended on the land and the cows, the grasses and chickens. Maybe the settlement money guaranteed their physical survival, but the farm gave them the rest of their sustenance, things that when added up together equaled something close to happiness, even in the wake of Jack's vanishing act.

After a day and a half of travel they finally made it to the thatch-roofed bungalow Ed had reserved for them in the jungle behind a remote beach on the island of Kauai. The vacation became the honeymoon they'd never had, just like Ed had promised, a gift to themselves so much more precious now than it would have been thirty years ago. They fell into little routines during their eight days in that tropical paradise, surrounded by more shades of green than either thought existed, lulled to sleep at night by the rhythmic murmur of waves lapping up the beach. Ed most cherished the midday hours, when it was too hot to be on the beach or walk in the jungle. He'd climb into the hammock on the shaded front porch of their bungalow, sip an iced tea, and swing gently while reading one of Jack's novels he'd taken on the trip. During these hours, his senses lulled by breezes infused with flower-blossom nectar and sea salt, he was able to forget about the farm entirely.

Susan's favorite time was the transition from late afternoon into early evening, when she'd stroll the dirt path into the little town about a mile from their bungalow. It was on one of these walks, with Ed accompanying her, that she noticed Rising Moon Yoga Center. Drawn by the carved, pastel-blue butterfly sign and the long driveway under a canopy of palms and bromeliads, she wanted to investigate. But these walks were Ed's least favorite time of day, when his moving body resumed its ache to be working on the farm, a longing he was mostly able to quell during his beach and hammock time. So she stored the name in her memory, vowing to look it up when they got back home.

On their last night, lying naked atop the sheets of their bed inside a billowing white mosquito net, sweating and breathing hard after an hour-long lovemaking session, their conversation was slow to take shape. With voices softened by the moist air and memories polished smooth by the constant sea, they reminisced about the early days of their relationship. Between junior and senior year of college Susan, emboldened by her experiences with the Wellesley Outing Club, had taken a job on a trail crew in the Adirondack Mountains, what was supposed to have been an adventurous hiatus before burrowing into the thick books of a medical school career track. Ed had discovered the Adirondacks the year before, and was seizing any chance he could to escape his workaholic father for an overnight in the vast wilderness early that summer.

"You sure were sexy in that forest service outfit," Ed recalled.

"I thought you smelled funny," Susan said, giggling.

"I smelled like manure."

"I know that now, honey. I remember your arms too. How strong they looked."

"I remember you were the only one of the girls on the crew wearing lipstick."

"There were only two other girls!" Susan said in her defense.

"Yeah, and they looked like boys."

She slapped him playfully on the thigh. "You sure were persistent. I'll give you that much."

"Was I?"

"Like a bull."

Ed had abandoned his father every weekend that summer, hiking in to camp near the interior cabin Susan shared with the other girls. They hiked out for ice cream cone dates in Lake Placid, sometimes getting a motel room but always sleeping in separate beds. Without saying it out loud, they'd both agreed their courtship would have an old fashioned quality.

But on the last weekend in August Susan decided to share his tent, what was an unprecedented move at that point.

"That was a nifty trick you had, zipping our sleeping bags together before I even knew what was happening," Susan recalled.

"I didn't see you unzipping them," Ed countered.

"It was cold!"

They shared a long laugh. These memories, filtered by time and the surroundings, acquired a luminescent quality. Ed's passionate monologues on the benefits of the farming way of life, how its rewards surpassed any she could expect by graduating college, had culminated in a speech he made in the afterglow contained by the tent that night. These words, emboldened by the confident passion of youth, were a source of anxiety between them that was never fully addressed. The fact that his natural love for farming had altered her direction in life so dramatically lurked persistently on the outskirts of their otherwise rock solid relationship. Susan had trouble separating the early stages of her love for Ed from an intellectual curiosity about everything he represented, a rural life so different than anything she knew at the time. For some reason it took going to Hawaii for them both to see that this element of the past had long ago become irrelevant. And so too had Dan Cook.

The tropical island's intoxicating effect not only cast a golden hue on their collective memory as a couple, it also allowed them to pass through entire days without a single thought about Jack, which was a rather stunning occurrence. During the initial year following his disappearance it had been rare than an hour went by where one or the other didn't entertain a concerned thought about his whereabouts and safety. Allowing themselves to indulge in this temporary amnesia was a relief to their bodies and their minds, as the stress surrounding his absence had begun to settle in their bones and lurk in the shadows of their every thought. Frolicking together in the warm green-blue sea like born-again teenagers, the couple erupted into true laughter for the first time since that fateful day of the shattered window. Sharing the deserted portion of paradise together, the only witnesses of their giggling fits were a pelican, a few crabs, and the sun.

SIXTEEN

THAT first year Jack wandered by any means he could. After maintaining a steady jog during his initial days on the run his exhausted body had succumbed. So he used a portion of his minuscule budget to purchase a Greyhound ticket to Cleveland. The muddy skies above the gray city mirrored Jack's mood so perfectly that he stayed for a few months, quickly finding employment as a carpenter's helper. He moved up the ranks fast, and after three months Jack was leading a crew on a renovation job. His nickname among his fellow workers was Skills, due to his remarkable adroitness with a skill saw combined with the fact that he didn't tell anyone his last name. At night he'd burn off whatever steam he had left in the city's many pool halls, honing his natural talent for the game. Before long he was considered a shark. But as soon as the job he was leading had finished Jack took his money and ran. He did the honorable thing and told his boss the truth, that he was a fugitive from the law. His boss was hardly surprised, and urged Jack to stay, citing the many convicts he'd employed over the years. But Jack knew it was time to move on. Hoping to avoid another period of hard labor for as long as possible, Jack sought out free forms of transportation as he ventured further west. At first he stuck to hitchhiking, enjoying the random conversations and the simple hope contained in an outstretched thumb. But after riding two hundred miles with a trucker who gave him the willies, Jack was wooed by the subtle art of hopping freight trains while laying over for a night in St. Louis.

James 'Mic' McFarlan was a redheaded, red-bearded Scotsman, a first generation immigrant who'd traded a truck-driving career for the wanderlust lifestyle of train-hopping. Jack met him in a St. Louis pool hall, a dark and dingy place Mic frequented as a place to hustle cash from Budweiser-buzzed pool sharks, none of whom ever suspected a Scotsman capable of possessing that kind of ability with a cue. Jack caught his attention by taking all the money Mic had won that night. He felt bad hustling the Scottish hustler, and used a portion of his winnings to buy Mic a Guinness. They sat together at the bar. Letterman was on mute above them, distracting their attention from one another from time to time.

"So," Mic said, his accent thick and scratchy. "I can't help meeself from asking, wood ya mind showing me a thing oor too about this game sometime?"

Jack grinned, proud of this talent he'd never imagined himself possessing, a surprise equal to his natural prowess with a skill saw. "Hey, sure thing, Mic," he said. "Ya got anything to teach me in return?"

The sturdy Scotsman spun around atop the bar stool. His gaze extended beyond the grimy walls of the bar, towards some special place that made his face brighten. "Yee ever hopped a freight train, young Jack?"

"Can't say I have."

Mic tipped the pint glass up and downed the second half of his beer, the black stout contrasting sharply with his thick red beard. He brought the glass down onto the bar with a loud thud. "Meet me at the freight yard on the West Side, corner of Lafayette and Newell. Tomorrow night. Sunset." Like a true guru, Mic didn't wait for Jack to accept the invitation. He got up and marched out of the bar. "Danks for the brew," he shouted without turning around.

"My pleasure," Jack said to himself.

The bartender grabbed Mic's empty glass, lingering in front of Jack, shaking his head.

"Mic's a legend, kid. Rumor has it he hopped an Amtrak back in his prime. You're one lucky son of a bitch. A man who can hop a train has the most freedom of anyone. If I were you, I'd definitely show up tomorrow night. 'Nother beer?"

"Give me a whiskey on the rocks," Jack said, figuring he'd need a good buzz to find sleep on the park bench he'd set his sights on earlier that day.

Jack fell easily under Mic's tutelage. The two of them formed a classic mentor and disciple relationship, a bond built out of Jack's respect and Mic's dedication to the obscure art of train-hopping. They spent a month on purely physical training, wind sprints and pull ups, squats and push ups, before Mic finally deemed Jack ready to jump a train. The day of his first hop Mic took him shopping for what he called a Rookie Outfit, a span-dex body suit designed for running track events. Jack protested briefly, until Mic shared a story about another first timer he knew of, a kid who'd caught his pant leg on the wheels of a box car and suffered a shattered femur and three broken ribs.

"Once yee get the knack of it, yee can wear whatever ya want. Okay?"

"You're the boss," Jack said, eliciting a rare smile out of the Scotsman.

Jack would remember the night of his virgin train hop for all his life. His pumping adrenaline and surging endorphins while he sprinted just behind his mentor gave him a kind of high he was never able to recreate. The shriek of steel-on-steel would echo in his ears forever, always tugging him back to that moment even years later, while hopping his one-hundredth freight train. Jack, one car behind his teacher, was able to perfectly mirror Mic, emulating the Scotsman's form in front of him. When they reached target speed, sprinting as fast as the train was moving, Mic lifted a bent left arm to signal it was time. They each grabbed the metal ladder running down the side of their respective cars. Gripping tight, Jack sidestepped a couple steps, leaped up and swung his torso around, hooking his feet on the bottom rung of the ladder. He climbed up a few steps. Mic turned to acknowledge his pupil's success with a thumbs up and another grin. Jack arched his head back and released a deep, bellowing howl of joy.

Jack and Mic celebrated their success the next night by hustling a new pool hall together, making off with five hundred bucks apiece while narrowly escaping the brawl they'd instigated. After finding a safe haven on Jack's park bench, Mic asked him what he was going to do with his winnings.

"I'm gonna ride the rails east before I head west again, Mic. There's a fellow I heard about in the Blue Ridge mountains, makes banjos by hand. I'm gonna wait there while he builds me one. It's time I learned how to play an instrument."

"Sounds like a darn goood plan, mee friend Jack. I'll miss ya, though."

Jack draped an arm around the Scotsman's shoulders. "Did you really think I'd stick around this city, breathing beer brewery fumes and crashing on this bench, after you taught me how to jump a train?"

Mic nodded slowly. "Noo, Jack. I deed not. But there is one more thing yee should know, an unspoken rule upheld by our community of hoppers."

"What's that?" Jack asked.

"Once you have perfected the art of hopping yourself, yee must share dee knowledge with anoother. Is that clear?"

"Yes, Mic. Very clear."

The Scotsman stood up, backing slowly away. "And one other thing," he said, unable to completely shed his role of master teacher. "If yee ever find yerself in need of a community of hoppers, ride the rails to Sacramento. There yer'll find immediate friends. Jest stay away from dee poker tables."

SEVENTEEN

IN Asheville Jack expanded upon his carpentry resume by working on a crew building timber frame houses. In reality he was just passing time until his handmade banjo was finished. Instead of indulging in pool table exploits after work he chose to pursue the company of women. Feeling like he'd never officially broken up with Katie, he justified these adulterous inclinations as a necessity for survival. His memories of Katie were a constant force calling him back to Springtown, a siren beckoning his spirit to give up its flight, urging him to return even if only for one more soft kiss, one more chance to stare into her brown doe eyes. The dangerous thing for Jack was that his mind was almost able to convince his soul that experiencing these lost treasures just once more would be worth years of jail time. So, to help him silence the tempting prospect of a return home in the name of love, he decided to try his hand at the art of wooing the opposite sex.

Unlike his train-hopping apprenticeship, this new endeavor he would have to teach himself, using the only method he could think of – trial and error. His first dozen attempts resulted in failure, which Jack expected given the fact that the only girl he'd ever dated had been his friend before he'd kissed her on a whim. After being timid at first he gradually grew bolder, enduring not only the pain of rejection but the sting of a slap across the cheek from one potential date and a wad of spit launched into his eye from another. Gaining a deep respect for these Blue Mountain girls, Jack dug his heels in and stepped up his game with each potential new conquest. Transcending the stereotype of luck, number thirteen proved to be the charm. She was a biker chic named Lou who liked whiskey and pool as much as he did. She kicked his ass at pool, and drank him under the table. But she also complimented his lovemaking skills to such an extent, in between hearty, full-throated moans, that the floodgates of Jack's romantic confidence flew wide open.

After her departure for the Sturgis rally in South Dakota, after nursing the leather burns on his inner things resulting from her insistence on keeping her chaps on while riding him, Jack unleashed a new, masculine swagger upon the twenty-something female denizens of Asheville. He quickly discovered that when the confidence inspired by his recent erotic success was added to his striking dark looks and sky blue eyes, failing to get a date with a woman he'd targeted just wasn't an option. But as soon as his banjo was finished, a beautiful instrument of supreme quality, he quit the timber framing job, left three girls anticipating a second date, and jumped the first freight train heading west. Following the number one rule he'd set for himself in order to survive this period of his life he didn't look back for a second.

During this first year away, in moments when the rush of new experiences receded enough for him to contemplate things, Jack's grief at leaving oscillated with a kind of relief. Maybe it wouldn't be so bad not to smell another cow pie squished beneath the sole of his work boot. Sleeping past five in the morning was pretty nice too. He was learning new skills, things he never thought himself capable of mastering. The heartache from leaving Katie receded slowly, a glacial retreat that allowed his freedom to blossom gradually. As time went on he relished the hardening of his self, like molten metal solidifying into steel. He welcomed pain, knowing from his days in the high school weight room that growth hurts, whether physical or spiritual. No pain meant no gain.

At first the exhilaration of a constant new horizon, the expansion of his self into the wide open west, was a daily exercise in forgetting where he'd come from. He became the blacksmith of his own spirit, forging new identities based on his whim of the month. But at the same time he couldn't deny that his core remained, a bedrock sturdy as stone. His past life, growing up into something close to a man on the farm, was the foundation supporting his soul-searching endeavors. These ties to home supplied him with a constant source of built-up strength, gave him the confidence to dangle from the cliffs of the unknown, to dabble with various professions, hobbies, and women. But slowly, steadily, this inherent connection to the place he came from began to descend further down into his core, becoming harder to tap into the longer he was away. He understood that eventually this pursuit of freedom in exchange for true happiness would no longer be an option, and a choice would have to be made. Until that time came he made himself a promise to fully indulge in the absolute liberty of his spirit.

EIGHTEEN

DAN Cook felt like a captain going down with his ship. He'd recently converted his trailer office into a living space, allowing him to remain on site for days at a time. He dreaded his bi-weekly trips into town for groceries. When he drove past the Brown farm he'd lift a palm up to the side of his face, preventing the possibility of catching a random glimpse of Susan. He devoted all his waking energy to Sunset Valley. A year after the wolf incident, half the houses were up and the rest were framed. But thanks to a housing crisis that appeared to only get worse with every passing month, new home sales were in a continual free fall. He only had twelve deposits out of a hundred houses for sale. To ease the panic constricting his throat, refusing to accept a business failure on top of the romantic defeat he'd also experienced, Dan strapped on a tool belt and joined his shocked crew, banging nails and hauling sheet rock and whatever else they directed him to do. This made sleep come to him easily on the air mattress inside the trailer. But still there was always Sunday, when the crew stayed home, and Dan struggled to kill time while trying to ignore the fact that his houses just weren't selling.

It was an extreme phase for the developer, working alongside his crew in hopes of burning up the frustrated excess of energy percolating every hour he spent in his office. His laptop became a demon, hellbent on bombarding him with bad news. Sales of new homes down to the lowest level in eighteen years. Home prices sliding further every quarter. Credit markets seizing up. Mortgages becoming increasingly difficult to obtain in the wake of the sub prime meltdown. He stopped opening his computer altogether, abandoning the hundreds of email connections that helped him feel less lonely. He no longer turned on the nightly news, even though Brian Williams had been the most dependable human presence in his life for years.

But still Dan couldn't escape the calamity. His crew brought it up at every break, stressed as they were about their 401K's and job stability. It was Dan's duty to reassure them, which he tried to do convincingly, hiding the doubt underlying his words. After selling twelve homes before breaking ground he hadn't had another serious buyer come forward since, leaving eighty-eight percent of Sunset Vally unspoken for. Not one to seek solace in drugs or alcohol, Dan struggled for ways to cope. He tried to develop new habits that could help him survive this crisis. He pushed his body to the brink, jogging for miles even after a hard day of pounding nails. He quit coffee and sugar, and rented instructional DVD's on Yoga and Tai Chi, which he followed religiously during his long nights alone in the trailer. He even tried Buddhist meditation, training himself to let go of unhealthy thoughts as soon as they arose. In this way he was able to move forward, the only direction he knew how to go.

On one Sunday he went into town, planning on strolling the peaceful streets for a couple hours, browsing in the little shops before settling in for a fine meal at Mika, the only restaurant chic enough to make him feel like he was back in the city. Tired of the loneliness haunting him while he strolled through town, trying to ignore the happy couples and content families lurking on every street, Dan sought refuge inside Mika right after it opened at five o'clock. Instead of taking a table in the empty dining room he settled in at the polished wood bar, anticipating a superficial chat with the young bartender in a tuxedo. Chris Wilson made him a Grey Goose martini, straight up with olives in a large frozen glass. Dan sipped the vodka happily, eager for a little buzz to get him though the rest of the long day. Chris was polishing wine glasses in one corner of the bar.

"You make a damn good Martini, young man."

"Thank you, sir. Glad to hear I'm good at one thing."

Dan took a long sip. A few patrons were being seated in the dining room.

"I'm sure you're good at something else, eh?" the developer asked.

Chris shrugged his shoulders. "Thought I'd be good at farming. But I wasn't. So here I am."

"Did you have a farm?"

"My folks did. Second to last dairy farm in the county. Thought I could save it, for my mom. But we had to sell out. I took off while the deal went down. Couldn't watch. Now our farm is being turned into just another ugly subdivision. It's called Sunset Valley. Fitting name."

Dan tried to quell the dread collecting in his stomach. Mrs. Wilson had mentioned having a son who'd returned from college intent on saving the family farm. But he'd never met Chris Wilson, and it seemed the kid had no idea who he was. Sunset Valley was becoming his prison, trapping him in an identity he no longer wanted, the final verdict on his fate.

"I'm sorry," Dan said, and thought of adding something about the risky nature of farming, but decided to hold his tongue. Even building houses was risky these days, with the economy in its seemingly endless free fall. Now more than ever it was every man for himself.

"I'm over it," Chris said, although his thin voice suggested otherwise. Then he waved at some patrons entering the restaurant. "Speaking of farms, there's Ed Brown, and his wife Susan. They own . . ."

Chris kept talking, but Dan Cook didn't hear a word he said. His body had gone numb as he tried to build up the courage to glance in the direction the bartender was looking. He decided to keep his back turned for now, hoping the martini would impart him with the strength to take in the sight of the only woman he'd ever wanted yet had not been able to possess.

An hour later, making his way through a steak and another martini, Dan finally turned in his chair to take in the sight of Ed and Susan at their table. It took less than a minute of witnessing her interact with Ed for him to realize the couple shared a kind of love he would never know. Their connection was visible to anyone with a hint of perception, two spirits attuned to one another, gliding through the evening with a natural harmony. Watching them, feeling like he could see their love hovering about the candlelit table, Dan came to the dark conclusion that Ed would have to die before he'd have any shot at Susan, and it would be an awfully long shot even then. Although he had a few mafia connections thanks to his line of work, he wasn't the kind of man to have a rival knocked off, especially a romantic one. Unable to bear the sight any longer, Dan asked Chris to wrap up the rest of his steak. He downed the last sip of his martini and slapped a black Amex down on the bar. "Charge Farmer Brown's meal on my card too, will you?"

"Sure," Chris said, reading the silver letters on the card, choking on the name as he took in the identity of his patron. "Mr. Cook."

Now the secret was out of the bag, and Dan couldn't wait to be out the door. After tipping Chris a hundred bucks in cash, a gesture that failed to erase the scowl etched on the kid's face, he walked briskly out the restaurant with a palm along the side of his face, blocking his view of the sickeningly happy couple. The next morning he booked a flight to Belize, intent on never coming back. He didn't care what happened to Sunset Valley. It could sit there like the unfinished masterpiece of an artist with a tortured heart, because that was precisely what it was.

Lying in bed later that night, digesting their three course meal, Ed and Susan tried to figure out Dan Cook. He was a person like no other they'd ever met.

"He is persistent, you have to give him that," Susan observed.

"He persists at the wrong things. He paid for our anniversary dinner! Did he think that would get him anywhere?

She reached over and cupped her husband's chin in the palm of a hand. He kept his gaze lowered like a shy school boy.

"Was I persistent?" Ed asked, still avoiding her eyes, once again repeating his favorite question, as if he needed constant reassurance that he indeed possessed this noble trait. She gave him the same answer she always did, the one that reliably produced a glowing smile.

"Like a bull," she whispered. "Now kiss me."

NINETEEN

THE next four years were relatively placid ones, defined by the steady growth of the farm and Javier's full acceptance into the inner folds of the Brown family. He became like a third son to Ed and Susan, and a second brother to Marvin, partially filling the void left by Jack's absence. His shy confidence and easy smile helped keep everyone up-beat. As the years passed Jack's postcard updates dwindled in frequency, and finally stopped arriving altogether. Ed found himself trying to accept the possibility that his second son was never coming back. Even though the Brazilian was hardly ten years younger than Ed, and showed no signs of intending to have children of his own to take over when he grew old, Ed managed to block out his worries about the farm staying in the family. With Marvin close by, and his bank account still flush from the settlement money, he maintained an optimistic attitude that things were going to work out in the end. And there was always the chance that Jack would come home one day, more enthusiastic than ever about running the farm.

After winning the settlement for his father, Marvin began shifting his focus towards specializing in land rights cases. Still taking mortgage contracts and bankruptcy filings in order to pay his bills, he worked overtime for low rates, practically donating his time to conservation groups, state agencies, and, his favorite clients of all, farmers. He had to sacrifice more than his time and hourly rate to take on these cases, as many of them involved long-range drives and nights away from his comfortable house in Springtown. But the weekend excursions to investigate cases he otherwise never would have had access to proved to be worthwhile on a career level. His practice was in a continual state of expansion, forcing him to hire another attorney as well as a secretary. The first person to show up for an interview was a woman named Katie Dobson.

When he first let her in the door of his lobby he didn't even recognize her, hadn't thought twice about his past familiarity with that first name. But it didn't take him long to see the same girl he'd known before, underneath the woman she'd since blossomed into. In his office room he sat in a leather chair behind a clutter-free glass desk. She was seated on the sofa across from him, hands clasped over her crossed legs. She wore a black velvet skirt and a white blouse. Her hair was mostly up, with a few stray, golden brown curls falling across her shoulders. The only blemish Marvin could detect in her appearance were the hint of dark blue circles under her eyes that she'd made no attempt to cover with make up.

"So," Marvin began, feeling like he was trying to cut through the awkwardness in the room with his words. "You must have known it was me when you applied for this job."

"I did," Katie said, nodding assertively. "Since I have no experience with secretarial work, I figured the . . .family connection, so to speak, might improve my chances at getting the job."

Marvin glanced down at her resume, more to avert her soft brown eyes than to check-up on her qualifications. But he did take note that she was already working four nights a week as a nurse. "Will you be able to handle a day job on top of what you're already doing at the nursing home?"

"Yes," she stated abruptly. "I need another job, Marvin. I'm a single mother."

"Oh," Marvin said, trying hard to hide his shock, remembering her new last name on top of the resume. Up until that moment he'd still been seeing her as Jack's girlfriend. "Well, Katie, I don't see why we can't give it a shot."

Katie jumped up to her feet, smiling, her hand extended over his desk. He shook it, noticing the lack of any ring.

"When do I start?" she asked eagerly.

"How's tomorrow?"

"Perfect."

Marvin skirted his desk, ushering her towards the door. He hadn't planned on having a secretary by the next day. His answer had been a spontaneous one, inspired by his desire to see her again as soon as possible. Simply her presence in his office during the interview had given the space a breezy lightness. The prospect of this feminine kind of warmth becoming a part of his daily life, a quality that had been lacking for far too long, was too good to let pass by, even for a single day. He opened the thick door. They stood there for a moment, face to face. There was only one word in Marvin's mind, one name echoing back and forth. The name was demanding release before the moment could come to a close, and what he'd just set in motion could continue forward. But he couldn't bring himself to utter it.

"Have you heard from him?" she prompted.

"Jack?" Saying his brother's name for the first time in years made him freeze up inside. He paused, wanting her to say it too.

"Yes. Jack."

Marvin shook his head.

"Me neither," Katie said, glancing down to the ground. "Not that he would even know how to get a hold of me if he wanted to." She shuffled her feet on the polished bamboo floor, glancing over her shoulder towards the front door.

"Well, congratulations Katie, you're my first employee," Marvin said, eager to move the subject away from his long-lost brother.

Katie smiled graciously. Marvin felt his neck flush with a shameful kind of heat. This was his brother's ex-girlfriend. In the old days Katie had been Jack's girl. Nothing more and nothing less. He'd never taken much note of her physical appearance one way or the other, except the basic reality that she was quite pleasant to look at. Noticing anything more than that would have gone against some kind of ancient code. Now he was taking in every aspect of her. He let his focus follow the lines of her hips tucked snugly in the skirt. He appreciated how her dirty golden curls contrasted with the bright white top. The small brown freckles that splashed across her cheeks seemed so perfectly placed. He was distracted by the whiteness of her teeth, entranced by her easy wide smile. The way she'd asked about Jack, how her voice had become thin and hesitant all of a sudden, was proof she still had feelings for him.

"Thank you, Marvin," she said, reaching out to shake his hand.

She walked out into the day. Marvin felt his gaze lingering on her butt as it swayed from side to side within the skirt's tight confines. He closed the door and walked back to the desk, knowing he was far too distracted to get anything done. He only hoped that pushing some papers around or checking his email might allow him to ignore the corner he'd just so recklessly boxed himself into.

TWENTY

MARVIN didn't tell his parents about this new development, deciding to keep it as a secret until he'd established a solid working relationship with his new secretary. Katie quickly became the highlight of his days. He usually showed up at seven, and spent two hours in furious anticipation of her arrival. She would make them coffee, and water the plants, bringing the office to life with her movements. If Marvin wasn't busy with a client they'd have lunch together, him with his takeout sushi, she with her hummus wrap from home, sitting on the back porch of the building, surrounded by trees and the soft babble of the creek. Sometimes they'd just sit quietly, sharing the moment. Other times their conversation would meander through a variety of topics. He talked about his time at law school and the big city career he'd cast aside to come back to Springtown. She told him about nursing school, and the marriage she'd finally given up on. No matter the subject their words would always circle around to wind up on the farm and, inherently, the subject of Jack. Katie seemed eternally fascinated with the concept of his mysterious disappearance. It was a topic Marvin much preferred to be left unspoken, a dual strategy to ease the pain of his brother's absence as well as allowing him to perpetuate the burgeoning fantasy that he and Katie might one day be together. He fought hard to keep his romantic feelings under tight wraps, concealing his hand like an experienced poker player, day-dreaming about the possibility of someday going all in.

He let her work part time, on her three days off from the nursing home. He told her it was no problem to take off after lunch to pick up her boy from preschool, and suggested that she bring him back to the office rather than paying for a babysitter. Marvin felt his dormant fatherly urges emerge when her son, a sweet and shy boy named Greg, was around. He started stocking the little mini-fridge in the lobby with snacks for the kid, juice boxes and pudding cups and fruit roll ups. On one Saturday, hoping to quell the unrelenting desire just to lay his eyes on Katie that so frequently disrupted his weekends, he built Greg a tire swing off the back deck of the office. Marvin let him hang the bird feeder he'd built at school out back, and soon found his loneliness in the days Katie didn't come in quelled somewhat by the song birds feeding outside his window. After almost a year of this, having finally told his parents about the situation, he one day found himself enduring her lunch-break recount of a string of unsuccessful dates. Marvin then took a plunge into mysterious, unnavigable waters. He would later justify this leap into the unknown by telling himself she pushed him to do it by following up her talks of romantic failure with a question about his own love life.

"So, are you seeing anyone?" Katie asked, her tone innocent, void of the motives he would later attribute to her question in order to justify where it led him.

"No, I'm not. I was dating a girl in the city, but she couldn't commit to moving up here, so we split up. Since then I just haven't met anyone all that . . .inspiring around here."

She nodded, flashing a shy smile. "Yeah, I know what you mean. The Springtown dating pool is awfully shallow."

For the first time Marvin held her eyes longer than a few seconds. He was looking for a sign in them, something beyond her words that told him the risk of what he was about to propose was entirely worth taking. He took the fact that he wanted to dive into her eyes, to float in their light brown pools, as all the sign he needed.

"Maybe we should go on a date one of these weekends, just for the hell, heck, of it."

The surprise flashed across her face. Marvin watched it settle in her clenched fists resting on the table.

"Marvin, I . . .gosh, I have no idea what to say. You're my boss, and Jack's brother."

The truth of this first identity was undeniable. The second one was more complex. He was Jack's brother. But who was Jack to her? Jack had let her go so long ago. There had been another man, and a baby, in between. And, above all else, he'd been gone for over four years by that point.

Marvin reached out to cup one of her trembling hands. "I think we're both old enough to know that life doesn't come with a pause button. And loneliness can be fatal. At least it feels that way to me."

She started to speak, stopped, then started again. Marvin saw only her lips, nothing else, pink and slightly moist, her little tongue flicking between them as she formed the words he'd never forget. "Should we, maybe, go to a movie, you think?"

"I think we should."

TWENTY-ONE

JACK didn't have a home, hadn't found one since running away from the farm. He'd been running for five years now, never staying in one place longer than a few months. It was a hard life. His body had a permanent ache. He was bony, wiry, stretched thin by the daily toil of survival. In cities he always felt out of place. But when he fled to the countryside the sight of all the farms only pained him. And the suburbs scared him more than any inner city slum he'd ever passed through. He was lost, no matter how many times he told himself otherwise, cast adrift in a world with rules he hadn't learned to follow, defined by ladders he'd never climbed, crisscrossed by paths to the top of a mountain he'd never known to exist. Every day Jack had to force himself to accept being a castaway all over again. No one was lucky enough to survive as a farmer these days. All the kids had to leave their farms. Why should he be any different? God was not about to make an exception for him, especially after what he'd done back home, murdering those seven cows. Struggling through another month at another odd job in another random city, Jack continually told himself this was his punishment from God. All he could do was make the best of it, and pray that one day he'd again know peace of mind. In this way he got through the days, one by one, month by month, year by year by year.

Jack gradually began to feel vulnerable. He no longer trusted every stranger he bumped into. The next town and the next female conquest no longer swelled with the promise of adventure. As the months stretched into years he felt his well-spring of energy being gradually depleted, to the point where no sunrise or range of mountains or stunning canyon could replenish it. The only thing that restored him, aside from playing his banjo, was to think, and to dream, about the farm. But still he stayed away, always reminding himself of the police car, and the pistol. He remained constantly aware that, in the end, freedom was the most precious aspect of being alive. Spending five years in prison just wasn't an option. So he kept running, living like a nomad, butting his head against the Pacific, eternally frustrated by the physical limitations of his destiny.

One art form Jack mastered during his years away, in addition to carpentry and the banjo, was seduction. After Asheville, and his chap-wearing love-tutor Lou, he challenged himself at finding a lover in every new place he landed, testing his wooing abilities in a wide variety of arenas. He found dates in biker bars and brothels, Sunday church and the art museum. He dated a painter in Santa Fe, a bronzed wildcat who liked to use his torso as a test canvas. In San Francisco he successfully courted a welder named Jane, with biceps as big as his own and a blowtorch libido. There was the marine biology grad student he stumbled upon on the Mexican coast who taught him how to befriend sea turtles while skinny dipping in the warm Pacific. He wooed a nineteen year-old in Baton Rouge studying to be a Baptist minister, who belted out multiple hymns during her orgasms. And there was the bartender from Tuscon addicted to sky diving, who initiated Jack into her own version of the Mile High Club.

There were all of these and many others in between. Jack was able to hone his skills as a lover, becoming confident in his ability to satisfy the physical needs of any woman. But he remained afraid to test his aptitude at pleasing the other, more intangible desires of these women, things like companionship and commitment. Jack never stuck around in one place long enough to test these kinds of waters. He always left right before love came into play, telling himself that if he didn't fall in love with anyone he would somehow be remaining faithful to Katie. Even though he'd given up on everything they'd had together by leaving, keeping his heart attached to his memories of her was another thing that kept him going, kept him surviving long enough to see the next horizon. Throughout his journeys he maintained a distant hope that the last horizon would be the farm. Then he would stop.

By his fifth year away Jack had become a prisoner, trapped deep in the maze of his running, a new pistol lodged in a holster on his hip. He was working like a slave picking grapes in Napa Valley for minimum wage and a roof over his head. The only two bright spots in his life were drinking Coronas with his Mexican bunkmates and his few dates a month with Jane, the welder in San Francisco. When picking season finally ended, sun burnt and aching and lonely, he remembered the advice of Mic McFarlan, his Scottish train-hopping guru, and headed towards Sacramento in need of community. There he found a hardscrabble village of train hoppers eking out an existence on the outskirts of a freight yard.

The hobo camp provided him with the only lasting feeling of community he'd found during his years of running. He made friends there. There was always music, and plenty of good food cooked over wood fires. And the nights were never too cold, even in the dead of winter. But within this comfort zone Jack made the mistake of letting down his guard, breaking one of the rules he'd set out for himself to ensure his survival as a fugitive. The rule was to never fall prey to addiction. All the whiskey and the sex he'd indulged in never blinded him. He always knew when to stop these behaviors before they got out of his control. This was something that his cohorts, at least when it came to whiskey, had trouble doing. Believing himself immune to this mortal weakness, after experiencing some early success in the all-night, lantern-lit poker games at the freight yard, he began gambling with wild abandon. Jack refused to listen to the warnings offered by his friends at the yard, men who'd seen too many others vanish in the night after racking up huge debts. Worst of all he forgot Mic's last words to him in St. Louis, when the Scotsman had warned him to avoid the infamous Sacramento yard poker matches at all costs.

"These guys you're playing with now, Jack, they're not like the rest of us," advised his buddy who went by the name of Jones, a black man with bushy white hair and a penchant for accompanying Jack's banjo with his mournful harmonica melodies. "They just high rollers minglin' with hoppers, man. They come in here and take guys like you for all you're worth. Ya' gotta stop, brother, before it's too late."

Jack appreciated his friend's concern, but his advice didn't register. Completely unaware that he'd lost all sense of reason Jack plowed forward night after night, going all in even as his beginner's luck started running out. The hardest of the hardcore gamblers Jones had been referring to, tough men

who swooped in for a few weeks to hustle the newer, unsuspecting hobos out of everything they had, were the Russians.
Blanketed with tattoos, shrouded in cigarette smoke and
vodka fumes, they made quick work of many. But Jack managed to hold his own as the weeks went on, not afraid to keep
up with them shot for shot and smoke for smoke, brandishing
his pistol when he felt it was necessary, backed up by a crew
of wary yet loyal bums fronted by Jones, one of the toughest
men in the camp. Unfortunately for Jack, their appreciation
for his reckless bravado led to them loaning him thousands of
dollars to keep playing night after night.

Close to a month of nightly matches culminated in one
final, twelve-hour binge of poker. Jones made an appearance
at the table in hopes of balancing the sides, keeping one hand
on the long blade strapped to his thigh throughout the match.
The two Russians, Vlad and Niri, had loaned Jack five grand
before the match started, giving him a chance to double the
money and break even before they left town. By the time daylight arrived, doing little to cut through the haze surrounding
the table, Jack went all in on what he thought were two pair,
but was really only one. Blurred by too much vodka his vision
saw double, and his brain was too muddled to realize the
impossibility of two pair with the same suits.

Vlad, the larger of the two Russians, smacked the table
and laughed out loud as he dragged the last of their five grand
back. "Now you owe us ten, mister Brown. How do you plan
on paying us back?"

Jones, who'd stayed sober all night, gave Jack a look that
said it was time to draw their weapons.

"Yeeah," muttered Niri, a tightly-wound wolverine of a
man. "Least I kneew, riding treeains deedn't pay much."

Both Russians had a good laugh at that, laughing so loud they didn't hear the sound of Jack's pistol cocking or Jones' knife sliding out of its sheath.

"Maybe we have a job for you, Brown. To earn the money back working for us. You think so, Niri?"

"Peerhaps we do."

"That won't be necessary," Jack said, giving Jones a quick nod. The black man lunged at Niri with his knife. Jack stood up, drawing his gun. As the knife plunged into Niri's bicep Vlad's fist slammed down on Jones' arm, splintering bone and knocking the knife down on the table. Jack lifted the table and launched it at the two men, grabbed Jones by his good arm and ran. He turned back once to fire a shot at the table the men were using as a shield. There was a loud scream of pain, and a shower of bullets followed, kicking up dirt and dust around their feet. Jack and Jones headed towards the shouts of some friends. They dove behind a warehouse and saw a train leaving the far end of the yard. Jack lifted Jones onto his back and sprinted to the open door of one car. Running alongside it he rolled his wailing friend in and jumped up a second later. The train slowly gathered speed as it chugged north towards Oregon.

TWENTY-TWO

Aғтеr a midnight arrival in Portland Jack escorted Jones
to the ER, promising to come check up on him first thing in
the morning. While stumbling through the back streets of the
city, in search of a place to catch a few hours of sleep, Jack met
a long-legged woman in a red leather mini-skirt, fishnet stock-
ings, and a rain coat. She was stone sober, heading home from
work, eager for some quiet time to decompress from the night.
After a brief encounter in a back alley, an interaction just long
enough for him to realize her line of work and for her to deduce
he was lost, she took him home. The next morning it took him
a moment to get his bearings. He was lying on a water bed in
a penthouse apartment with cathedral ceilings and two story
windows looking out on the Portland skyline. Lying beside
him, wide awake and smiling, this nameless woman was by far
the most sensual creature he'd yet to encounter.

She was lying on her side. He let his eyes take in her naked
body. Her dark brown skin contrasted sharply with the white
sheets. Her breasts, adorned by long, erect nipples, had a

gravity of their own, loyal to her torso instead of the ground. Her belly button was a round pool of shadow in the middle of a smooth, toned stomach. Jack's attention froze on her hips. They rose up off the bed in a dramatic, arching curve. Her entire body was a buildup to this curving landscape of skin that culminated in an ass like none Jack had ever laid eyes on, round as a basketball. Her pussy was perfectly shaved, glistening in the morning light. Jack felt himself harden. His focus traveled back up to her face, lingering for a moment on her wide, full lips before finding her eyes. They were cat-like, with dark hungry pupils fringed in yellow.

Jack sat up, riding the little waves his movement created in the bed, and scanned the surroundings. "I don't even know your name," he whispered.

"It's Mariela," she said, smiling.

"Nice to . . .meet you. Great place you've got here."

"Well, if I'm going to take my clothes off in front of bald men drooling over cheap steaks while swinging upside down on a pole, the least I can do is pamper myself by living in a place like this," she said as she got up and slipped into a silk robe.

"Makes sense."

"Speaking of pampering, I want to make you breakfast in bed."

Jack grinned like a goofy schoolboy as she glided off towards the kitchen. He scanned the room. In one corner was a universal gym set. Beside it a shiny silver pole rose from the hardwood floor to the ceiling.

"I use it to practice," Mariela explained from the open kitchen on the other side of the vast room.

"I see."

Jack didn't tell her it was his birthday. He was twenty-eight years old. He quickly decided that this woman making him breakfast in bed would be the best present he could have ever imagined. He didn't remember Jones until much later in the day. By the time he made it to the hospital they told him his friend had been released late that morning. Jack wondered if he would ever see the old hopper again.

Over the next few months Mariela would guide him into uncharted realms of sexual satisfaction, outdoing all the other women Jack had experienced during his years away. She made him aware of body parts he'd never thought could possibly be pleasured, like the space between his littlest toes, and the cleft of skin along the top of his ear. Her endurance and enthusiasm astounded him, and he let her lead him to new heights of ecstasy. He never wanted to see her perform at the strip club, and told her so. But even though he requested it many times, Mariela wouldn't do any of her routines for him on the practice pole in her penthouse. So he was left to imagine what all the men saw when she was on stage, reminding himself how lucky he was to be the one waiting on her water bed when she got out of work.

As his twenty-ninth year unfolded, Jack was nagged by the undeniable reality of his youth receding into the past. Having treated his time on the road as the youth he'd never had, indulging in the freedom of being permanently twenty-something, he was shocked by some slow and steady changes going on in his body. The rush of new experiences, even these unexplored realms of pleasure he was discovering on a nightly basis, weren't enough to keep him going all of a sudden. Instead of pursuing situations that made the top of his scalp tingle with excitement he began to crave something firm beneath his feet. He wanted to stop moving. Settling right then and there, marrying Mariela and finding some career to pursue in Portland, tempted him daily. If he felt this way at twenty-eight, what would thirty feel like? Time was having a different effect on him now, and Jack wasn't sure he liked it at all. One of the early signs that he was in danger of developing feelings for this stripper who defied his stereotype of the profession was a burgeoning habit of telling her things he would have normally kept to himself. These confessions usually happened during late-morning, post-coital cuddle sessions under sheets dampened by their sexual escapades. They made love in the mornings, because after work Mariela liked to just watch a movie and fall asleep, trying to move past all the glazed-over eyeballs of lonely men staring at her body parts. During one of these morning moments, his long wiry body entwined around her tiny soft frame, Jack disclosed a heavy burden that had been weighing him down every day, making his freedom an illusion.

"Ya know those train-hoppers I was telling you about down in Sacramento?" he said, inhaling the sweet scent of her moist neck.

"I do. Your only friends in the world. Besides me."

Jack chuckled. "Yeah, well, I'd only call a few of them my friends. Others became enemies."

He felt her body tense up slightly. For a stripper she was extremely sensitive.

"Why do you have enemies there?" she asked bluntly.

"Because, baby. I lost one too many games of Texas Hold 'em."

She released a long breath.

"How much do you owe?"

"About ten grand."

She wriggled out of his arms and sat up, tossing the silk sheets towards the foot of the bed. "What!? You haven't even been working since I met you. How do you expect . . .oh no, don't even think I'm gonna give you a loan for ten grand, no sir." She was shaking her head from side-to-side, her long black curls flying out.

"Baby, don't worry. I've got a gig at a bakery on the coast. I'll be able to spend my days off here with you, while I work up enough cash to head back down there and win what I need to."

"No. I don't want you gambling again. Once you save up five grand I'll match it, so you can just go pay them off once and for all."

Jack reached up and pulled her back down onto the bed. He rolled on top of her. He could see the worry and concern etched into her face, and knew right then she was already in love with him. He couldn't decide what was the bigger trap, owing thousands to some shady men with connections to thugs up and down the West Coast, or having this ferociously loyal, hot-blooded Latin stripper falling in love with him.

"Well, I've been living like that Sherman guy who marched through Georgia in the Civil War, burning bridges for five years. I've got you, and my boys down there at the train yard village. Nothing else."

"You've got a job lined up at that bakery on the coast, right?" She covered her breasts with her hands.

Jack nodded. "I prefer my duties in your bed, though," he said, removing her hands with his.

She giggled, reaching towards his crotch. "Well, it looks like now it will only be a part-time gig for you." She clasped one hand around his penis. The other hand cupped his balls.

Jack arched his back and closed his eyes. "I can live with that," he mumbled, moving a hand down to gauge her readiness for his entry. She was soaking wet, and writhing now beneath him.

"Take me, Jack," she whispered. "I'm yours."

TWENTY-THREE

MARVIN and Katie's wedding, scheduled for an October weekend, grew to become an unspoken symbol among the family representing the now very real possibility that Jack was never coming back. And, given the union that was poised to take place, maybe he'd be better off not returning. None of them wanted to see what his reaction would be, so they pushed this possibility out of their minds in order to fully celebrate the momentous occasion. A high pressure system passed through on Friday, clearing the air and leaving crisp blue skies garnished by wisps of clouds. Susan's sister Margarat, whom she never saw except on Christmas day, was the first to show up to help, taking a few days off from her work as a fashion designer to drive up from Manhattan. Aside from the embarrassment of having a new Lexus SUV parked in her driveway, Susan was happy to spend some quality time with her only sister. She arrived Friday afternoon in high heels and a close-fitting dress, bearing bottles of fine wine and fancy champagne, brushing off Ed's insistence on reimbursing her with a casual flip of her jewel-studded hand.

"Just because you can afford to give me money now doesn't mean you should," she said.

"Fair enough," Ed said, knowing he'd never taken a dime from his sister-in-law even during the hardest of times on the farm.

Susan had never admitted to the yearly check Margarat always slipped her at Christmas, money she'd stashed in a reserve fund for her boys' future needs. She'd often been forced to tap into the money for other things, though, like hiring a plumber behind Ed's back when he'd be too proud to admit his inability to fix a leaking pipe.

"Hope you brought some other kinds of clothes," Susan said, taking in her sister's outfit.

"Of course! I just feel like I have to dress up when I drive the Taconic. It's important to look hot on the road."

"I guess," Susan said, ushering Margarat towards her office room off the kitchen which she'd rearranged into a guest bedroom. She was thinking about a famous Robert Frost poem. Two paths had diverged in the woods of their childhood. Susan had taken the dirt path less traveled, her sister the paved highway, and neither had looked back since.

Katie arrived a short time later, eager to pitch in and help Susan with food preparation. She'd been over for a few Sunday dinners during the past six months of dating Marvin, and had quickly grown accustomed all over again to both Susan and her kitchen. The three women spent two days, working well into the nighttime hours, preparing the feast for a guest list nearing one hundred people. The labor was divided naturally according to the comfort zones of each woman. Susan worked the stove, preparing sauces and stocks, rues and gravies, soups and stews and casseroles. Katie assumed the roll of prep cook. She chopped and diced and minced, peeled and mixed and marinated. Margarat set up a station at the kitchen table, where she worked on elements of presentation, lining bread baskets with cloth, arranging dried flower petals on plates, tying silverware up in ribbons. And whenever they needed new materials or ingredients she readily volunteered to make the drive into town, each time changing back into her original city-slick outfit. The first time she made this dramatic costume switch Katie looked over at Susan with a puzzled expression.

"Hard to believe she's my sister, right?" Susan asked.

Katie nodded.

"Someone got switched at birth," Margarat said, a line she used often.

While the women worked tirelessly in the kitchen, Ed, Javier, and Marvin were busy with the physical logistics. First they drove an hour in Ed's truck to rent three refrigerators, which they set up outside the back door of the house for the women to fill up with food. In the large space between the barn and the house they set up a giant tent, fifty yards long and twenty wide.

"I feel like I'm in the circus," Marvin said at one point as they all worked to erect the center pole.

"Let's hope we don't feel that way on Sunday," Ed added.

"What is circus?" Javier asked.

All three burst into laughter. Ed always took pleasure in responding to Javier's childlike questions with long-winded, detailed answers usually embellished by a personal story or two. But the pace of the wedding preparations was much different than the regular work around the farm, so the concept of a circus was left for the Brazilian to imagine until some other time, as the men focused all their attention on the tasks at hand. After the tent was up they scrounged enough spare lumber out of the barn loft to construct a stage just in front of the tent. It was small, square, and slightly elevated, a simple design that took them the second half of Friday to build.

On Sunday the focus was on parking logistics, posting signs and arrows to guide traffic where they wanted it to go. Then came time for slaughtering. When all was said and done they had twelve chickens gutted, plucked, and drained of blood being quartered in the kitchen for various dishes. Then it was time to butcher Nina the goat, an honored descendant of a long line of the quirky hoofed animals living on the farm, employed through the years in various brush-clearing endeavors. Both Ed and Javier had grown quite fond of Nina. Javier and Martin held the squirming goat down on top of a rock in the lower pasture. Ed straddled its torso and brought the blade of his machete to its neck. Javier winced.

"Is necessary?" he asked gently.

"Yes Javier. It's symbolic, to honor Marvin and his bride. Like a sacrifice, kind of. For good luck."

"Ah, yes, we do same in Brazil. Now pray?"

Ed shrugged his shoulders. "If you want, Senhor."

"Sim. We pray," Javier chimed in. "To Dios!"

As prayers were being uttered in Portuguese the blade sliced quick and clean. An hour later the three blood-soaked men hauled the skinned animal to the fire pit behind the barn, where it would roast all the following day on a bed of coals, visible only to those curious enough about the smoke and the smells to venture back there.

That night Ed and Susan lay wide awake in bed for hours. They waited for sleep to come. With the busy preparations leading up to the wedding day, neither of them had been able to allow the intensity of the upcoming event to truly strike them. Now it permeated their bedroom, the invisible presence of an unspoken dream shared by two parents that was about to become flesh-and-blood reality. Both were made sleepless by the jubilant expectation of tomorrow. Susan felt the tingle of her skin as goosebumps spread in waves from scalp to toe. The lullabies she used to sing Marvin to sleep with echoed in her ear. Ed's primary symptom was hearing the pound of his heartbeat. Having never been to the hospital, visiting a doctor no more than once a decade, he usually made it a point to ignore the involuntary systems of the body, especially the beat of his heart. So he listened to the sound of its steady rhythmic pounding with a kind of rapture, as if he'd forgotten that he possessed the organ in the first place.

Each knew the other one was awake, but neither spoke. Susan was consumed with the mother's joy of having a happy son and, although she hesitated to admit it, the slightly selfish relief of a daughter-in-law. A lifetime spent raising two boys had led to an intense yearning for at least one of them to bring a nice, respectful girl into the folds of the family. She'd always thought Katie would be a perfect fit. The only thing that had changed was which one of her sons had invited her into the family. Katie was down to earth, intelligent, and possessed a great sense of humor. Ed was filled more with a father's kind of pride, a deep wellspring of satisfaction that had finally been fully tapped now that his first born son had built a complete life of his own. And he couldn't help that little corner of his farmer's brain telling him how important another generation was to the future of his farm, a significance much greater than his newfound fortune. Of course he was aware of the chance that any sons of Marvin's would grow up to be professionals of some kind. But if he got enough time with them on the tractor, he believed there was a shot he could turn at least one grandchild into a farmer after all. And there was always Jack's offspring to consider, something he'd maybe already started working on for all Ed knew. But there was a certain quality to the way his heart pounded in his chest that made him wonder about the inherent expectation of the first born son. He wondered if his father had felt the same way about him all those years ago. Trying to remember if he'd been aware of any such pressure growing up, Ed finally fell into a gentle sleep. An hour later he woke up to the first light of morning and Susan puttering around the room.

"What are you doing?" he asked her.

"Waiting for you to get up so I can make the bed."

"Did you sleep?"

"No."

Ed rolled out and onto his feet. "I think I got an hour, no more."

Susan set herself to making the bed.

"Need help with that?" he asked.

She looked up at him curiously. "Help? No, I don't."

Ed wandered over to the bedroom window. Looking down, the tent was a surreal sea of white.

"This is a big day," Susan said, trying to find things to do. She was waiting for him to change out of his bed clothes so she could fold them away before heading to the bathroom.

"I miss the morning milk," Ed lamented. "Having Javier and the Colombians is great and all, but doing the milking always kept my chin up no matter what else was happening."

"I know. You just need even more cows, honey. Enough milking to keep all four of you guys busy."

"Maybe."

Susan was standing beside him. She reached down for his hand. "But it's no time to think about all that. Our son's getting married today. So take off your pajamas, get dressed, and go wake up my sister. It's good for her to get a taste of farm life."

"Pff," Ed said, turning to kiss her. After the kiss he held her face in his hands and looked into her eyes. "I love you, Suzie."

"I love you, Ed. Thank you, for this life you've given us."

Ed blinked a few times, hoping he wasn't about to cry. He'd made her a farmer's wife long ago, but part of him still sometimes wondered whether she yearned for some other, more cultured existence. The way she said thank you told him that if she'd ever had that sort of longing, those days were in the far distant past.

The wedding day was a success. The guests parked where they were supposed to, guided by Javier's hand signals. The ceremony itself was conducted by a local Quaker pastor, and took place in the pasture beside the creek that the Colombians had cleared and mowed in preparation. The buffet spread under the giant tent delighted the taste buds of amateur chefs and satisfied the appetites of teenagers. The roast goat that emerged in sections from behind the barn drew many compliments, as did Susan's homemade bread. The bluegrass band played for hours, from sunset well into the night, and almost everyone danced. Smitty, Katie's father, was the most enthusiastic dancer of all, leading waves of people in spontaneous square dance sessions under the tent. Speeches were given and toasts were made. The keg was drained and all Margarat's bottles of wine were drunk. Ed gave tours of the farm to little kids on his new tractor. Javier taught Portuguese lessons to curious cousins. Susan brought waves of guests into her house to show off her knitting projects and spinning wheel. Margarat got drunk and flirted with most every male over the age of twenty, eventually winding up in the hay loft with Mark Ridley, Ed's lonely veterinarian. Delighted by the opportunity for an authentic roll in the hay with a certified doctor, her inebriated giggles startled the cows into fits of snorting that could be heard all over the farm.

When the night finally ended, when the last car pulled out of the driveway, Ed and Susan curled up to sleep with Greg at the foot of their bed, Marvin and Katie returned to the spot in the pasture below the pond where their vows had been made. The stars exploded in the sky above them. They lay down in the cool, dew-laden grass mowed short as a golf fairway.

"Wow," Marvin said. "I've never seen the stars quite like this here."

Katie didn't share her immediate thought, that she'd regularly seen star-filled skies that rivaled this one during her nights with Jack on the rooftop outside her bedroom. She guessed Marvin's perceptions were being heightened by his first experience of love. Her own emotions were more muted, less intense, having already given her heart away twice. Katie was relying on the third time being a charm. After going out on love's limb one more time, she knew there would be nothing leftover to try again.

Her hair fell down around his shoulders. He curled up beside her. She enveloped him in her arms. The earth spun, but the stars stayed still. And so did they. They were still for a very long time, becoming one, more joined than in any moment of lovemaking they'd shared so far. And the little creek gurgled past them, indifferent, as if they were a boulder in the field. They relished in the moment, drinking deeply from it, both of them knowing there would be many instances down the road where they would need to reach back to this place of shared memory and harvest its strength.

TWENTY-FOUR

ALTHOUGH he'd found the best lover of his life there in Oregon, Jack had managed to lose the only constant aspect of his transient existence since leaving the farm. He'd lost his freedom. No matter how bad things had gotten, how much he hated a job or a city, there was always another train to hop, another town to head for, where a new series of adventures awaited. It was his own fault, getting caught up in a web of debt. Jack realized he was trapped in a kind of triangle. One of its three points was Mariela, with her warm and radiating love, the kind of love that jogged his spirit back to Katie, to memories he'd thought were forgotten. The second point of his triangular prison cell was his new job at the bakery. It was a cozy place on a quiet bay along the luminous North Oregon coast. There he slogged through a grueling six day week mixing doughs and sweating in front of a bank of ovens, wielding a wooden paddle. There were moments of bliss, when perfectly crusted loaves of sourdough cooled on a rack, licked by the dawn sunlight filtered through sea mist and a flour-coated window. But overall the work bordered on slavery. Jack woke before three in the morning, and fell asleep before nightfall. His boss was a German cyclist named Gregor, whom Jack respected even while putting in more hours at the bakery than he did. Somehow every Monday he'd haul himself to the bus station and ride into Portland for a day and a night with his woman. The third point of this vast triangle of containment, a location not fixed in space, was the gang of Russian gamblers no doubt scouring the West Coast for the banjo-playing train hopper who owed them ten thousand dollars.

So after all these years of running, hanging onto freedom when he'd had nothing else, Jack was trapped, imprisoned by the trio of love, work, and debt. While it struck him that most adults his age were likely in the same basic scenario, ensnared by these side-effects of responsibility, Jack had always prided himself on being different from the majority of his fellow humans. If he was going to commit himself like this, to one woman and one job while grinding away at a debt, it needed to be in the name of farming. This fact hadn't changed with time, and was now rising up again as soon as he started to feel caught in this three way entanglement. But going back home was still not an option. Naturally his mind drifted towards possible escapes.

These mental fantasies circled back persistently to a book he'd read in high school, written by a man who'd gone to Northern Minnesota to live with wolves. Jack sensed that he might find some closure up there with the wolves, the completion of this circle he'd been navigating for so many years. Of course this meant skipping out on another boss, and ditching another girlfriend. But Jack cared about both Gregor and Mariela too much to repeat this pattern with them. So he figured he'd ask each of them for a break, vowing to return after his three-month sabbatical in the wilderness. Before he could announce this intention, however, life stepped in the way.

Jack was working a giant piece of croissant dough across the wooden table in the bakery. Gregor had just arrived, and the two men were chatting about the weather, one of the German's favorite subjects.

"Haven't seen a cloud in tree days, Jack. Vwat is going on, I vonder?"

"Calm before a storm, maybe," Jack said, pounding the buttery slab of dough with a giant rolling pin.

"Yees, perhaps zee storm is coming."

Jack turned to look out one of the square pained windows. His gaze stopped short of the ocean. Hunkered down among the boulders where land met sea, just across the two lane road from the bakery, were two men he recognized immediately.

"Fuck!"

"Vat is it?"

Gregor moved to the window. Jack dropped the rolling pin. He spun in circles, trying to decide on where to exit the bakery.

"Those men in the rocks are Russian gangsters. They're here for me."

Gregor clenched his fists. "I hate zee Russians." He turned to face Jack. "But vwat have you done to them?"

"It's a long story, Gregor. How do I get out of here?" Jack asked, reaching for his faithful banjo hanging on a coat hook by the back door.

The baker put his coffee cup down on a metal cooling rack. Approaching the wooden table he bent down to the floor, waving for Jack to do the same. Underneath the table was a hatch door.

"I learnt zis from my parents, who survived zee holocaust. Always have a tunnel, for escape. Even in America. You never know."

They crawled under the table. Gregor lifted the hatch door and climbed down a wooden ladder leading into the ground. Jack followed close behind.

Jack didn't want to leave, not in this way, forced to run from the closest thing he'd found to home since leaving the farm. He didn't want to abandon another boss, let go of another relationship. But he had no choice. There wasn't even the chance for a goodbye kiss with Mariela, for a we'll-be-together-again kind of pledge. He couldn't risk luring the Russians to her doorstep. Jack circled his way to the train yard on the edge of the small coastal town he'd come to know so well, stopping only to buy a bottle of champagne. It was an ironic purchase, as he was hardly in a celebratory mood. But Jack decided he had to force himself to recognize the significance of his upcoming ride. By his calculations he'd successfully hopped ninety-nine trains up to that point, making this ride a monumental one to say the least. He decided that he had no choice but to recognize the occasion, one he'd been saving for a special day in order to relish it more, but events beyond his control had forced him to undertake it sooner than he'd planned.

This yard was well known to be hot, hopper lingo for a risky scene, where a hard nose bull named Rocko roamed about. Although just a security guard employed by the train company, a bull had no problem exerting a hand-cuff level of authority upon any hopper caught red-handed in a hot yard. Jack had always used extra caution during his weekly commuter rides back and forth to Portland. But on this day he skulked about in broad daylight, his banjo hanging off his shoulder, the bottle of champagne clasped in his hand. In a way he wanted to be caught. It would force him to stay in this life he was having so much trouble leaving behind.

So when the outgoing junk train, loaded with lumber cars, started chugging its way out of the yard, Jack had to use all his dwindling willpower to hop it. His legs were concrete. His hands almost slipped off the metal side ladder. But he hung on, because he had no other choice. Life was pushing him back east. Leaning against a towering pile of sawed off tree trunks he closed his eyes and thought about wolves.

Jack wondered if his one hundredth train hop would also be his last. The end of his train-hopping career would more likely be one final ride home when it was time. For now he was simply looking forward to satiating the intense longing for wilderness that had been consuming him lately. He was completely certain that his wandering days were done. Feeling sexually satiated from his months with Mariela, Jack hoped it would be enough to sustain him through what turned out to be a long, solitary journey in search of the kind of spiritual sustenance that had the chance to last the rest of his life. All the full-time hoppers stuck to the more southern routes, never riding the line Jack had chosen, one that originated in Seattle before passing through the Eastern Oregon yard where he'd jumped it, taking him through Montana and South Dakota on its way to Minnesota. On his second night, rumbling east across the northern prairie with two hobos for company, a couple of scruffy drunks that might have had him up all night regardless of his restless mind, Jack reached back through time to the last night he'd spent with Mariela. After twelve sumptuous hours together they'd watched dawn arrive from the porch of her downtown condo. It had been the first sunrise Jack had seen for many months, and the sight had made his urge to be with the wolves stronger than ever.

There on the train Jack thought about the contrast in extremes between that week-old memory and his current situation. The hard wood floor of the box car vibrating into his bruised ass, and his sore back grating against a steel wall, was the opposite of Mariela's flower-scented, billowy bed, and swinging naked under her fleece blanket in the back porch hanging chair. Everything about the two settings couldn't have been more different. The sound of the bums snorting and farting in the dark corner versus the soft sleeping breath of his brown-skinned lover. Dawn's light breaking across empty wheat fields with an endless curving horizon versus the pine forested slopes above the Portland skyline. A stale biscuit to look forward to versus fresh coffee, orange juice, and eggs. If Jack had had any regular friends instead of his random, fleeting alliances with fellow hoppers, they might have told him he was crazy to give up the soft for the hard. But if they really knew Jack as a friend, which no one truly did, they would have understood that the key to his existence lay in maintaining a constant balance between hard and soft, steel and skin, exhaustion and rest.

TWENTY-FIVE

As a boy Jack Brown had always fantasized about hopping freight trains in the same way he'd dreamed of becoming a cowboy, a distant kind of hope he never believed would actually come true. So when he was celebrating his one hundredth ride, uncorking a bottle of Veuve Cliquot with the two drunks he shared the rattling box car with, Jack took a moment alone with his champagne. He gazed out the open sliding door at a vast prairie bathed in moonlight, and finally let himself feel a glimmer of pride. During the five years that had passed since leaving the farm he'd learned many things. How to survive on a dollar a day, a mastery of the banjo, and every kind of construction skill possible to acquire. He could jump a train traveling twenty miles an hour, make a home for the night in any kind of freight car, and had survived ninety-nine rides.

The bums he was sharing the box car with were pestering him to play some tunes on his banjo. Eventually they succeeded in distracting Jack from his melancholic pondering. Fully aware of his banjo-strumming reputation among the train-hopping lifers, as he called them, Jack knew they expected to hear a sample of his near legendary banjo skills among the community. He couldn't disappoint them, especially on this anniversary ride. The Montana prairie lands stretched out into the distance, halted only by the jagged, shadow-cloaked Rocky Mountains jutting up into the clear night sky. All Jack wanted to do was watch. He'd chosen the date for his landmark ride intentionally on the full moon, precisely so he'd be treated to the scene stretching out in front of him at that moment, a scene that topped any a movie theater could possibly provide.

"C'mon over here, then," he called out to the two drunks, waving them to emerge from the dark corner of blankets, inviting them to join him at the open side of the car. "And bring my banjo!" he added, noticing they were carrying only the half-full bottle of champagne. He had to shout above the steel-on-steel rattle that surrounded them, a constant soundtrack Jack only heard when trying to hold a conversation of some kind. The jostling metallic grating sounds used to keep him awake all night. It had taken less than fifty rides to cure him of that problem, along with the help of a medicinal shot or two of whiskey before climbing into his old, duct tape-patched sleeping bag and curling up atop whatever cargo he happened to be sharing quarters with. Sacks of flour were the best he knew of, followed closely by rice and beans, in that order. Sometimes he and his fellow hoppers would fantasize about the utter luck it would be to land in a car with sacks of all three. Everyone would get a good night sleep and, assuming they had water and a camp stove, things Jack always carried, each could look forward to the luxury of burrito dinners.

Jack took the banjo from the toothless hobo and sat down cross-legged on the floor of the car, facing out. He started picking a slow, remorseful tune he'd written a few weeks before. The drunks stood behind him, draping their arms around each other less to stabilize themselves against the rocking train than to ensure that the bottle of bubbly never drifted far out of one's reach while the other one drank. Jack focused on the huge round disk of a moon hanging above the knife-edged peaks while his fingers worked the strings, teasing out a mournful melody, his instrumental version of a wolf howling at the moon. The image of a wolf came to him while composing it. But the anticipation of his next destination couldn't hide the underlying source of this sad ballad, his endless yearning for the farm, a deep longing for the place made stronger by his efforts to suppress it. He'd thought that turning this sadness into a song might bring him a kind of relief more long-lasting than a whiskey buzz or a western sunrise, and gear him up for what awaited him in Minnesota.

But when he finished the tune, one of the hobos sniffling back tears above him, Jack felt worse than before he'd started playing. He accepted a turn with the dwindling bottle of champagne, eager to pick out a new song to help change the mood in the car. Inside, though, he couldn't deny that something had been shifting lately. The gravity of his soul was pulling him back home with a renewed strength. This time the tug was more substantial than he'd felt it ever since getting past the first year of his excommunication, a period he didn't consider to be in the same category as the four more years that had since followed. During these long stretches of time the reality that he'd been cast out of his Garden, the place he belonged to in the world, became more evident every day. Now some force was speaking up, telling him the time to return was near. As the two homeless train-hoppers danced a jig arm-in-arm beside him while he strummed his favorite

Nanci Griffith tune above the moonlit Montana prairie, Jack recognized this mission to spend time with the wolves would be his last adventure, one final chance to discover another piece of himself.

Before heading off into the wilderness, after outfitting himself in Minneapolis, Jack stopped at a pay phone downtown to call Mariela. He timed his call during an hour he knew she'd be working, knowing that if he told her his plan instead of leaving it in a voice mail she would have become frantic, would have begged him not to go through with it. The sound of her voice on the recording inspired shivers of doubt to course through him. He almost hung up before leaving a message. Instead he tried to speak like a man of action, belying a solid confidence in the direction he was heading. He wouldn't use the Russians as an excuse.

"Hi, it's me. Jack. I'm in Minnesota, about to head into the woods up north, to be with the wolves. Not sure how long I'll stay up there. As long as I need to, I guess. I'm not calling to say goodbye, that I want it to be over. Just want you to know where I am. I'll call again when I come out."

Jack almost said I love you, but stopped himself short.

He spent the rest of his day in Minneapolis using his bakery savings to stock up on enough gear and provisions to last for three months in the wilderness. By evening he was rolling north out of the city on a Greyhound. The next morning, after switching buses twice, sore and sleep-deprived, the northern landscape was intoxicating him even through the thick panes of the bus windows. The pine trees enveloping the road were deep green and towering, the sky an intense shade of blue. There was a kind of clarity to the light of morning that he hadn't seen since a stint in the Rocky Mountains the year before. On the farm he'd always felt poised between two worlds, the wild and the civilized, tasting both but fully immersed in neither, burdened by his duties to domesticated creatures. During his travels Jack had spent most of his time in towns or cities, craving intimacy with the many variations of human culture, from pool halls to art museums to strip clubs. Now he was headed in an opposite direction, seeking a bond with a wild place, and hopefully more than a glimpse of the creature that had so profoundly altered the course of his life.

TWENTY-SIX

JACK got off the bus at the last stop, an outpost of a town consisting of a general store, a post office, and a canoe outfitter. Shouldering his one hundred pound backpack, his banjo strapped to the outside, Jack took a moment to breathe in the fresh, crisp air before making his way down the lonely road toward the outfitter. He left his pack leaning against the front steps and walked into the rustic building. Kayaks and canoes hung from the ceiling and walls. Life jackets and paddles and camping gear filled the shelves. A young, bearded man with glasses was filling out some paperwork behind a wooden counter. Jack stepped up and extended his hand.

"Jack Brown. I'm here to rent a canoe from you. Sir."

"Okay, Mr. Brown. Steve Dwyer. Owner and head guide." The young man was slightly taken aback by Jack's boldness, the kind that bordered on recklessness at first impression. "For how long do you need the canoe?"

"Three months."

Steve coughed into a fist. "Um, we don't rent canoes for that long. You'd be better off just buying one."

"Fine." Jack pulled out his wallet. "How much?"

"Well, it depends on which model. Can I ask you, Mr. Brown, what your plan is?"

"You can. I'm heading into the Boundary Waters to hang out with wolves."

The guide shook his head. "No you're not."

"Of course I am. What are you talking about?"

"I can't let you go in there alone, for three months. You won't come back out. That I know. You'll have to find a canoe someplace else. Period."

Jack spun in a circle, restless, and slightly frantic. "Congratulations, Steve. You just lost a customer."

"I know. Better than you losing your life, though."

"But I'm going in there anyway," Jack protested.

"Not if you can't find another canoe."

Jack winked. "I'll find another canoe, Steve-oh. Even if I have to kill a man, I'll get myself a canoe before this day is over."

He spun around and marched out of the store, struggling to resist his urge to turn back and witness the guide's reaction to his Clint Eastwood-style statement. But Dirty Harry wouldn't have looked back, so neither did Jack.

That afternoon Jack was paddling himself up a feeder stream that would lead him into the vast network of rivers within Boundary Waters National Park. The canoe belonged to the owner of the general store in town. Jack had noticed it leaning against the side of the building on his way to the outfitter's, and the owner had gladly parted with it for a three month rental fee of two hundred dollars, no questions asked. Entranced by the setting, getting high on the fresh air and the mysterious possibilities of the next three months, Jack's face set itself into a constant grin, a smile that lasted for hours, not fully leaving his face until that night, tucked inside his tent, cocooned in his sleeping bag and the one hundred square miles of wilderness surrounding him. What caused his grin to finally dissipate was the distant howling of a pack of wolves, so faint that at first he wasn't sure if his mind was making the sound up. But the back and forth howls went on for some time, long enough for Jack to know they weren't a figment of his imagination. Hearing the calls of the animals he came there to get close to, even though they sounded days of paddling away, stole the elation that had defined his day. His ecstasy was by no means replaced with fear, but rather a sense that the mission was a serious one, with a deep purpose demanding he honor it at all times. Jack knew if he did not allow a sense of reverence in, the wolves would keep their distance, and he might not see a single one. So he said a prayer, out loud in the safe womb of his tent.

"Please, God, allow me the opportunity to be close to those wolves, so that I may have the chance to see you in them, to feel your presence once more, like I did in the pasture all those years ago, face to face with that wolf, with You. I promise to kill my ego during these next few days on the river, so that when I reach those wolves I just heard I will not be Jack Brown, but just a man, heart and mind wide open, ready to witness whatever You choose to show me. Amen."

Jack paddled all day long during the next four days, plunging himself deep into the heart of the wilderness. Each night he heard the howls of the same wolf pack. Each night they sounded a little closer. On the fourth night they were all around him, so close he imagined their bellowing calls might shake the walls of his tent. He set up camp on a knoll jutting out above what had become a wide, fast-flowing river. He spent a couple days making his perch feel like home, complete with a laundry line, an outdoor cooking fire, and a bathing pool in an eddy of the stream below. His hammock strung up between two long hemlock trees completed the scene.

But Jack didn't allow himself to be lulled into the pastoral sense of relaxation contained in his idyllic campsite setting. Dismayed about the fact that although the wolves were all around him, a fact they made clear every night, he had yet to witness any sign of their presence, not even a track in the sand of the river's shore. It was becoming clear to Jack that if he wanted any kind of contact with the animals he was there to see, it was going to take more effort than he'd already expended. He came to the conclusion that what he needed to do was undertake a seven day fast, hoping such a sacrifice would show his god that he was willing to do whatever it took to open himself up to a connection with the wolves.

So on the morning of his fourth day at the base camp he stopped eating. The first two days were the hardest. He strung all his food high up in a tree, then spent the majority of his time trying not to think about what was up there. By the second day the pains in his stomach distracted him from every task he attempted. His legs grew so weak that even the short climb up from his swimming hole left him exhausted and short of breath. He barely slept the second night, kept awake by a combination of hunger and adrenaline, as the wolves sounded closer than ever, seemingly just beyond the edge of his camp. But every time he stuck his head out of the tent to shine his flashlight into the woods the howling would stop, and all he would see were the trunks of the nearest trees.

At some point during the third day of his fast Jack felt a shift take place inside. It first came upon him as a feeling of complete and utter lightness. He barely took note of the ground while walking around his camp. He no longer felt hungry, had no more daydreams of food. His legs were neither strong nor weak. He focused on small endeavors, minuscule tasks that he allowed himself hours to complete, fully present in the center of every moment, content with carving a statue out of cedar, sewing up a pair of ripped shorts, collecting rocks on the beach. After a solid night's sleep, unconcerned that it was the first night he didn't hear the wolves, Jack woke up on the fourth day of his fast feeling like he was high. He passed the whole day in a state of absolute bliss, convinced he never had to eat again if he didn't want to. His world sparkled. Everything was sharper, clearer than normal. Crystalline sunbeams magnified the texture of bark. Clouds moved in slow motion, morphing into the shapes of all kinds of creatures. Sounds were amplified. The river roared, thunderous in his ears. Birds sang in perfectly clear, flute-song melodies. Breezes tingled his skin as if tempting him to lift off the ground, to join them as tributaries of wind gusts and circle the world.

Towards the end of this hallucinatory day Jack was spread out on his back beside the river, eyes closed, imagining the water rushing in one ear and out the other, cleansing his mind of all its random, unnecessary thoughts. Then he felt something on his neck, a hot breath that brought up memories of his dad's dog Jill during the rare times she gave him any attention. Jack snapped his eyes open. He was staring face-to-face with a wolf, six inches above his nose. He wanted to scream, then run, but he did neither, choosing instead to remain frozen still, to drink in the moment, the flaming yellow stare that was piercing his soul. The wolf snorted, pawed at the sand beside Jack's neck. Its huge head and broad shoulders loomed, bushy and gray, casting a large shadow across Jack's upper body. Now he wanted to reach up and touch the great animal, but resisted that urge as well. Finally, unable to hold the wolf's stare any longer, feeling unworthy of whatever challenge the animal was engaging him in, he closed his eyes again, surrendering fully to the moment. Jack felt one hot snorting breath where his neck met his shoulder, followed by the brush of a wet nose, then a splatter of sand against his cheek. He snapped his eyes open to a view of the early evening sky. He sat up, scanned every direction, but the wolf was gone, leaving behind a set of tracks heading into the water. Jack spent the remaining hours of daylight studying them on his hands and knees, tracing the contours of claw marks, following the outline of the great paws with his fingertips.

Over the final three days of his fast Jack saw that same wolf every day. He watched it cross the same place in the river, towards the end of each day. The alpha wolf would always pause to glance up at him perched on the embankment above, the meditation circle Jack had settled into for the majority of his final days of fasting. He took note of how scrawny the animal was, with protruding ribs and sharp hip bones, how it moved with the urgent gait of animal that hadn't eaten in a long time. On these first two encounters the wolf won their staring contests, as Jack would eventually glance away, unable to hold the bright yellow eyes with his own any longer. But on the seventh and final day of his fast he locked eyes with the wolf below, refusing to let go, until finally the animal snorted and dashed across the river as if surprised by the defeat at its own game. Jack couldn't help but chuckle to himself. It was a perfect ending to his fast. He built a fire on the beach that night to celebrate. The pack came closer than ever, engaging him in a back-and-forth round of howling. At one point during the course of the night, peering into the woods on the other side of the creek, Jack saw the flames of his fire reflected in three pairs of golden eyes. His heart pounded against the

walls of his chest. The stars swirled above him. For a stretch
of moments he was fully immersed in the heart of a cosmic
dance, at one with all creation. Then the eyes vanished, the
howls abated, and his fire burnt itself down. So Jack waited
for dawn, and with it his first taste of food in eight days.

Before sunrise he scrambled up to his camp and made his
way immediately to the large bag of food he'd strung up high
in a giant hemlock. The rope was exactly where he'd secured
it, but when Jack looked up into the branches he saw that
his bag had vanished, as if a monkey had snatched it away
and escaped across the coniferous canopy. He spun in frantic circles, cursing himself for not having kept an eye on the
stash. He'd ignored it as a strategy to keep his mind off of
food during the fast. Dropping to his knees, tugging at his
hair with desperate frustration, he noticed a set of claw marks
leading up the bark, evidence that a young bear had scaled
the hemlock and expertly spirited away his bag of food without leaving behind a single scrap. As the mental control he'd
so diligently maintained over the week slipped away, his belly
contorted with sharp pangs of hunger. He rolled on the ground
clutching at his stomach, moaning. After some minutes of
indulging in his agony he got up to assess the situation. He
was confronted with the reality that his body was incredibly
weak. He'd barely moved during the last three days of the fast.
Climbing the embankment that morning had taken the last
burst of his remaining energy supply. Paddling his way out
was simply not an option. The only weapon he had to hunt
with was a pistol. He quickly decided that the best use of his
time and energy would be to construct himself some kind of
a fishing pole, as he'd seen schools of trout in the river below.

A few hours later Jack had a crude fishing pole made of a pine sapling, his sewing thread, and a hook fashioned out of an aluminum can. He dangled the line, using grubs as bait, in the creek's pools all afternoon and into the night without luck. In desperation he fired a couple rounds at a few of the larger fish with his pistol, missing terribly. Somehow he managed to crawl up the embankment and drag himself into his tent. He heard the wolves that night, but their calls came from a great distance, sounding miles away, concerning him greatly. Jack liked to know they were close, taking a strange sense of security from their proximity. But the next morning he was growing very worried about his likelihood of survival. On impulse he gobbled down some of the same grubs he'd been fishing with, followed by a couple mushrooms growing near his camp. Less than ten minutes later he was vomiting in violent spasms, spewing out not only the food but also most of the water in his stomach, making matters even worse. Jack dropped to his knees. He was waging a battle with his own mind, which was urging him to give up, to build a giant fire in a last minute effort to draw attention, then curl up in the tent to wait for help, or death, whichever came first. He was tempted by the idea.

Towards the end of the day, staggering around the camp collecting armfuls of wood, his vision blurry, his breathing rapid and constricted, he felt himself losing his tenuous grip on reality. Unable to make it down to the fire pit by the river he constructed the bonfire in his meditation spot, a pile of sticks and logs taller than he was. Not caring if he ended up starting a forest fire he set it ablaze, watched the flames roar up into the canopy. Plumes of smoke surged high into the air. He staggered backwards from the heat, dropped to his knees, and crawled into the tent. Sprawled on his sleeping bag, the gray nylon walls spinning around him, Jack felt ready to surrender to death. But not inside a tent, contained within the false security of man-made fabric. So he dragged himself out to lie on the ground far enough from the bonfire so as not to feel its raging heat. If he was going to die, he didn't want his body to go to waste. Although he knew they weren't scavengers, he wanted the wolves to eat him, and figured they would. At that moment Jack couldn't think of a better destination for his body than the empty digestive tracts of a few starving wolves. According to his personal philosophy, a private religion that had finally solidified during the past week, what happened to one's body after death mattered little compared to where the soul was headed. And he knew without a doubt his spirit would be heading straight back to the farm, taking a direct trajectory towards his favorite upper pasture.

Lying on the dirt, listening to the roar of the great fire, Jack kept his eyes wide open. If death was coming for him, he wanted to see it before it took him away. But at some point he closed his eyes to let sleep, death's cousin, claim him. He fell into what he thought was a dream until days later, looking back through hindsight, realizing he must have entered the space between dreaming and waking, a place normally inhabited by shamans and medicine men. He became a wolf. He was running through the woods with the pack. It was night but he could see, as if wearing night vision goggles. His low, canine body was filled with power and strength. He was running just behind the alpha male who'd been visiting his beach. Two other wolves ran along beside him. Jack knew they were chasing an animal of some kind, although he couldn't see the prey in front of him. The trees shot by in streaks. The pine needle forest floor was soft under the pads of his four feet. And then he saw it, a large deer bounding just in front of the lead wolf, darting in a zig-zag path in an attempt to avoid being caught. Jack saw the alpha leap into the air, front paws outstretched, jaw open. It landed atop the deer's hindquarters, dragging the animal down. At that moment he snapped out of his vision, returning to the ground outside his tent.

The bonfire had burnt itself down to a mound of red glowing coals. His skin was damp from the dew that preceded the dawn. A few of the brightest stars lingered in the sky. After getting over his surprise at still being alive, Jack lurched up. Clutching his stomach he hollered with pain. He was then confronted by a strong smell, what could only be the rich, earthy scent of blood. He scanned the ground around him, his eyes quickly settling on the sprawled out carcass of a large deer. Jack pounced on the animal, fearing it might get away. He realized then it was quite dead, and missing one of its hind legs. He stood up, scanning the forest. And then he saw them, through the trees, about fifty yards away. The alpha wolf, two other adults just behind him, and four cubs beyond them, wrestling with the hind leg of the deer. Jack shook his head in disbelief. The lead wolf seemed scrawnier than ever, the other two adults not much better off. On impulse he flipped open his pocket knife and sliced off a chunk of meat from the deer's remaining hind quarter. Holding the bloody meat in his hand Jack walked towards the wolves. But the closer he got the more the alpha retreated, snapping at the other two adults to do the same. Jack stopped, engaging the leader in one more staring contest, blood dripping off the meat in his outstretched hand. The wolf turned for a moment to watch the pups devouring the leg, then looked back at Jack as if to confirm his awareness that the pups were taken care of, that he was fulfilling his duty as leader of this pack. The wolf stared straight into Jack's eyes, ignoring the meat, ignoring the other two restless adults waiting for permission to accept what was being offered. Jack then heard a voice in his head, a voice much different from the normal sound his mind gave to his own thoughts. It was the voice he would have imagined answering one of his prayers over the years, if one of them had ever been answered.

> That meat is for you.
>
> Without it you will die.
>
> I can catch another deer.
>
> When you are strong, go home.
>
> Something has happened there.
>
> Your family needs you.

Jack dropped to his knees. He wanted to laugh and cry at the same time. But instead he brought the raw, warm meat to his lips, and the alpha turned away to lead his pack off into the forest.

"Thank you," Jack shouted.

He sunk his teeth into the bloody muscle. He devoured the entire piece right there, then staggered back to camp, where he set about resurrecting his fire atop the substantial bed of glowing red coals. For the next three days he did nothing but eat and sleep. He drank the bone marrow and slurped out the brains, ate the heart and liver raw, and smoked the best cuts using layers of damp moss. While portioning the meat he came across the large tooth of a wolf. After cleaning it off he stored it in the bottom of his pack, a perfect souvenir to bring home. Jack never heard or saw the pack of wolves again. On the fourth day he packed up and headed downstream in his canoe, setting a direct course for his return to civilization.

TWENTY-SEVEN

As if fate was trying to restore the tenuous balance of joy and grief at the farm, less than a year after Marvin's wedding the height of summer brought a new darkness to the family. It wasn't yet August, but for some reason Ed declared it was time to cut the hay. Javier hid his objection and went out into the fields with his boss to cut grasses that were way too short. The purple clovers and long green blades of pasture grass weren't much more than a foot tall. But Javier didn't say a thing, trusting completely in every decision his boss made. A few days later, when the cut grass had dried out sufficiently, Javier scrambled behind the tractor attempting to gather the scraps from bales that wouldn't form. Finally Ed stopped the tractor and stepped out to assess the situation. He wiped the beads of sweat off his brow. The heat was pounding down on them with a gravity of its own.

"Javier, how about some water?"

"Sim, senhor."

Eager to get a break away from this strange situation, the Brazilian hurried off to the house. But instead of getting water he found Susan in the living room, where she was reading.

"Senhora?" he said tentatively.

"Hi Javier," Susan said, lowering her book onto her lap, acknowledging the deja-vu permeating the room. But there was no dead wolf this time. "Is everything okay?" she asked him calmly.

Javier shook his head. "Grass only this high," he said, bringing his hand down to the middle of his shin. "Not ready for hay. Bales broken."

Susan took in a quick breath. She stood up, letting her book fall to the floor. Javier backed out of the doorway as she stormed past him and up the stairs. "Excuse me, Javier."

She dashed up the stairs to Ed's office room. She stepped up to the window that looked out on the barn and pastures. She saw her husband pacing in circles around the tractor and baler, fists clutching at his hair, broken bales scattered about. Susan grabbed the binoculars sitting on the desk that Ed used to observe wildlife. She focused in on him. Like Javier reported, the grass was barely a foot tall. Even she knew, without ever being a part of baling operations, that this wasn't high enough. And, in addition, the forecast was for rain that evening. Susan found his face in the binoculars. It was scrunched up tight with anguish. His eyes were watery and bloodshot. His mouth opened and closed. But when she reached to lift the window pane she could hear he wasn't making any sound.

"Honey," she shouted out to him. "Is everything okay?"

Ed shook his head. Susan closed her eyes for a moment. All his life her husband had never admitted to anything not being okay. He had his silent rages over things, but possessed an undying optimism that never failed to impress her.

"I'll be right down," she shouted, backing away from the window. Something was horribly wrong. Her first thought, one that would be proven that evening after she forced him to go to the hospital, was that he'd caught his death.

Ed could never have imagined his life would end like it was, wasting away in fast forward speed, his brain being rapidly consumed by cancer. Now imagining anything beyond the present day was impossible. Susan tried her best to help him see into the future.

"There's still a chance you can beat this," she'd say almost every day while bathing him in bed. Her words, heartfelt as they were, began to sound more hollow each time she uttered them. Her husband was dying. This fact had been confirmed by three second opinions. As long as the five years had felt to Jack, the opposite had been true for Ed and Susan. These years had passed in blinks of time. Like a river approaching a waterfall, it seemed to both of them that life was rushing towards a conclusion with gathering speed. Even as each grew more certain of this fact they never discussed it together. The topic was better left unspoken.

Six months after the diagnosis Ed was largely confined to bed. The cancer had spread to other organs. His entire body throbbed with pain all day and into the night, when he allowed himself the indulgence of a single morphine patch. Getting up and moving around only made the pain worse. He felt so lucky to have his wife there by his side, the woman he'd shared his life with ushering him out of it instead of a hospice nurse with a face he didn't recognize, hands sheathed in plastic gloves that didn't know his body. Susan had dropped all her projects, devoting every ounce of her energy towards caretaking her husband. Javier and his two Colombian friends, employees of the farm following Jack's desertion, were maintaining things beyond the walls of the old farmhouse. Susan was taking care of the inside world, hardly noticing the steady green progression of spring occurring beyond her windows. Marvin did all the grocery shopping, and showed up every day to sit with his father.

Susan treated her husband's illness the way she'd always treated winter, as a beast that could not be avoided, facing it head on, remaining entirely present in every moment. She didn't allow herself to retreat into the relative safety of her comfort zones, the office room or the kitchen. She viewed his cancer as a dark, cold night, a never ending freeze that demanded she endure it, to experience it as fully as possible, while maintaining the wood stove warmth of her love for the man that had carved out the overall form her life had taken. The cancer spread slowly through his brain, taking a little part of him every day. Susan didn't bother tricking herself into thinking her love could be the chemotherapy he'd so stubbornly resisted, that bathing him with her care had a shot at halting the ferocious disease hellbent on destroying him. But she doused him with love anyway, providing a kind of comfort the morphine could never give him. The soothing caress of her presence beside his bed wasn't able to mask the pain, but rather allowed Ed to accept it as part of his makeup, like a new limb, a deadly appendage that could be embraced even as it was ushering him out of the life he'd so loved.

During the rare moments when his wife was absent beside him, leaving him alone with only his disease for company, Ed would become a fighter. He'd squirm in the hot bed consumed with a kind of rage he'd never thought possible, a fury lacking an outlet for release. Without some physical task to attack out on the farm, what had been his lifelong method for channeling his sometimes overwhelmingly dark moods, bursts of frustrated energy inspired by life's inherent limitations, there was nowhere to turn but inward. Ed couldn't help wondering that if he'd taken some time to discover religion, dying might have been easier, his suffering more tolerable. Having always replaced prayer with work, and the need for God with his wife's loyalty, when left alone with his lurking death Ed struggled to keep doubt from inflicting him with its own unique symptom of regret. Thrashing in the sweat-soaked sheets, replaying all the choices he'd made over the years in fast-forward, his hindsight refused to make room for regret to establish any kind of hold. Everyone was alone in the end. He told himself this over and over while riding out the darkest hours, surviving until his wife returned and restored order to his soul. Her gentle peace reminded him all over again, every day, that being alone was much different than being lonely. He'd always been alone, like every man. But thanks to Susan, loneliness was something he'd never had to suffer through, and never would.

One day within the hazy pain of sickness Ed woke up feeling giddy for a reason he couldn't place. The feeling was undeniable, and surprised him into questioning its source. It had been so long since he'd known an emotion resembling happiness. His smile caught Susan by surprise as she came in from the bathroom after emptying out his bedpan. His pale white face and bald head and wide goofy grin turned him into a clown. She giggled for a moment before catching herself, ensnared by the guilt that kept laughter always just out of reach. She sat down on the edge of his bed. Their bedroom, renovated a year after Jack's disappearance, had a wall of windows looking out on the property. Mid-morning light was streaming into the room, striking the pressed bamboo floor, illuminating the stitches of the brown and white quilt she'd knitted for his sick bed.

"You're smiling," she said.

"I have no idea why."

Susan glanced out the windows. Seeing him smile made her want to cry. But looking out at their farm wasn't any easier of a view to take in. The scene only reminded her of Ed.

"Maybe you're happy about spring," she said weakly.

"No. Trust me, spring is the last thing a dying man wants to see."

He closed his eyes. His smile shifted into a subtle expression of contentment. Susan moved to look at his upper arm, searching for evidence that he'd put on a pain-killing patch in the morning for some reason. There was nothing there. Ed snapped his eyes open. He sat up. Susan reached out a hand.

"Honey, careful, not so fast."

"I know what it is, why I feel so good today. I had a dream about Jack."

"Oh, Ed. Our boy."

Susan brought her hand in to her chest. She used to dream about her missing son all the time. But it had now been almost two years since she'd last seen Jack in her sleep.

"In my dream he came home, to see me, before I . . .he came home, Suzie."

Ed rolled over and curled himself into her lap. She stroked his bald head with both hands.

"That must have been such a nice dream, honey."

He smiled up at her, watching the tears fill her eyes.

"I'm sorry," Ed said.

"Sorry for what?"

"For making you a farmer's wife, the kind of wife that doesn't get a honeymoon until she's put in over thirty years on the job. Most of all I'm sorry for dying before you."

"Stop." She leaned over and placed her lips on his forehead, holding them there, trying to keep from trembling. "I chose this life," she whispered with urgency, as if he might die right then, before she had a chance to say these words. "I chose you. Those Wellesley girls can have their big city careers. I've had so much more, Ed. Never forget that. Okay?"

He nodded. She sat back up.

"Jack is coming home," he said in a matter-of-fact voice.

"How do you know? Because of the dream?"

Ed shook his head. "That only confirmed it. There are some things a father just knows. I know he's coming. He is on his way."

TWENTY-EIGHT

JACK stood at a pay phone in downtown Minneapolis. It was the same phone on which he'd called Mariela before heading off into the woods three months before. This time he wanted to hear her voice. He tried to ignore the rush of the city all around him. His senses had been heightened by such a long stretch of time away from civilization, and every sound penetrated into his core, rattling him into a state of stress. She picked up after two rings, and eagerly accepted the collect call.

"Jack . . ."

"Mariela."

"You're alive."

"You thought I wasn't?"

She answered with silence.

"I want to see you," Jack continued.

"Come to me. I'm waiting. I've been waiting the whole time."

Jack shook his head, even though she couldn't see the gesture. "I can't."

He didn't know how to tell her he couldn't go back there. He missed the life he'd created in Oregon, his relationship with Gregor, the satisfying romance with Mariela, the relative proximity of his friends in Sacramento. The delicious comfort of her penthouse apartment. It was all so enticing. But the wolves had told him what he needed to do.

"But Jack, those Russians are long gone, I took care of them when they came by here."

"You did?"

"Of course. I couldn't survive in my business without some pretty shady connections. My boys took care of it."

Jack smiled. He could have loved this girl forever. In another lifetime. "Thanks baby. It's not the Russians, though. I have to go home. If I go west again, I might not ever make it back to the farm."

"Why do you have to go home now, Jack?"

"Something has happened to one of my parents."

He heard her draw in a quick breath.

"How do you know?" she asked urgently.

"The wolves told me."

Jack figured she likely thought he was going crazy. But if Mariela did think such a thing, she hid it very well.

"I see." Her tone had shifted, as if she sensed the inevitable fact it was over, and was already trying to move on.

"Can you get a flight to Minneapolis? We could have one more night - "

"I don't think so, Jack," she said firmly. "I'm not a one more night kind of girl."

There could have been much irony behind that comment, but Jack didn't hear it. She was a stripper, but she wasn't a one night kind of girl, even if there had been so many nights before. He should have known better than to propose the selfish idea.

"I just didn't want to say goodbye to you over the phone."

"Me neither, Jack."

She hung up, eliminating the possibility. The dial tone pounding in Jack's ear was a clear line, an east-west border dividing his spirit the way the Mississippi divided the country. The west had nothing more to offer him. He would never see Gregor, or his fellow hoppers in Sacramento, or Mariela, ever again. The line had been drawn. Home was calling him back. It was time to jump his last train.

Riding east through the mid-western heartland, surrounded by vast, fertile farms, Jack's mind wandered back and forth through time. Five years earlier, before breaking out his bedroom window, his only expectation for life had been that he would become a dairy farmer married to his high school sweetheart. Now here he was, fifty lovers and a hundred box car rides later. It had been half a decade spent living a transient life of extremes, fasting and whiskey-bingeing, praying to god in the empty churches of every religion, feasting on the carnal delights of every kind of woman. Jack squinted into the sun rising in a red half-circle above the gentle arch of the Ohio horizon. A farmer was driving a large tractor through a distant cornfield. Jack had one hand on his worn Bible, the other on his heart. He shouted out loud to the sun and the tractor and the corn.

"I have become a man!"

His audience was nothing and everything at the same time. The next words he didn't shout out, choosing instead to whisper them softly, a quiet promise to himself.

"I will become the Farmer."

Over the next two days the train skirted just south of the Great Lakes, through Erie and Cleveland, past Buffalo and, finally, rolled into Springtown. Jostling along behind Main Street on tracks Jack used to play on as a kid, weary and worn from three months in the woods and two nights in a box car, he almost rolled right out of the wide open door when the tracks branched sharply and the train made an abrupt turn to the south. Beyond the outskirts of town Jack could see the narrowing valley to the north, rolling ridge lines on either side making shadows across the forested valley floor. Somewhere in those shadows was the farm. Jack couldn't see much of anything through the stand of trees he was staring into. All that mattered was that the train was rumbling away from his home. This line no longer stopped at Springtown, since there was nothing there to stop for, which meant he would have to attempt something he'd only tried a few times.

In the practice of train hopping it was called a dismount. He'd been halfway decent at it, usually drawing applause from any veteran hoppers unable to perform dismounts at their age, men who'd become proud and astute observers of the art. Except it had been years, the embankment beyond the track was steep, and the stones that formed it jagged and sharp. But by far the worst part was that it would be the first time he dismounted from an empty car, meaning he'd have to launch his backpack, including his well-padded yet delicate banjo, out of the car just before he jumped. He picked up the large green hiking pack, held it by one end, and tossed it out. A second later he bent his legs, pushed off, and jumped. He fell to a crash of limbs and tumbling rocks. Thrashing to a halt, bloody and bruised but with no bones broken, Jack lay on his back, chest heaving, and howled at the cloudy, late afternoon sky. He got up and stumbled down the tracks until he reached his backpack. He lifted it up and onto his back, tightening the shoulder strap. Then he set off into the scruffy woods, heading towards the farm in a steady, loping run.

III

HOME

TWENTY-NINE

Marvin wondered if Katie would believe in the concept of a mid-life crisis, because he was becoming more and more certain that was precisely what was happening to him. His large, solid house on one of Springtown's old, tree-lined streets had been striking Marvin as more lonely by the day. He'd been in the house for seven years now, and still had trouble making it feel like home, even with his wife now sharing it with him. And during the past week, since making the life-changing decision he'd so far only shared with her, the emptiness and sterility of the place was hitting him even harder. When Katie moved in they'd redecorated it together, and the transformation from old New England colonial to sparse, nature-chic wasn't doing it for him. The rooms felt cold and hollow in comparison to his childhood farmhouse. Maybe his slightly spontaneous decision to alter the course of his life as he neared the age of forty had been motivated less by a genuine, heartfelt purpose but more as an avenue to escape a life that wasn't bringing him much in the way of satisfaction. Marvin dared to

wonder if he was making this mid-life change as simply a subconscious attempt to avoid the direction he'd been heading,
into the realm of a settled, middle-age family man. He tried to
shake that idea out of his head, to focus on the need to share
this newfound purpose, one that had so abruptly seized him,
with his father. Before it was too late.

Marvin was making one of his regular daily visits to the farm,
visits that were becoming longer each time. He was finding
it harder and harder to leave his father's side, although leaving his pregnant bride and stepson home was just as hard. It
seemed, not only to him but to Susan and all their friends as
well, that Ed was nearing the end. And the most honest of all
about this inevitable fact was Ed himself. Even so, he always
urged Marvin to make it back to his house in time to have
dinner with his new family. Dinner hour was approaching.
Ed could tell by the angle of light outside the great windows
of his bedroom. Susan was in her customary chair beside
the window, knitting quietly, the only activity besides cooking she was able to engage in. Like her cooking of late she
made frequent mistakes, and was constantly forced to back
up her stitch in order to correct a botched pattern. Marvin
was closer to the bed, sitting in the desk chair he'd borrowed
from his father's office room.

"You should get on home," Ed said, his voice a scratchy
whisper. "Dinner time is the foundation of a family, and you've
already missed more than enough of them on account of me."

"Dad, c'mon. I've got plenty of family dinners to look forward to. What's mom whipping up for you tonight?"

"Nothing."

Marvin glanced at his mother. She nodded in confirmation.

"Haven't eaten a thing in three days now," Ed stated.

Marvin lowered his head. It was getting too hard to look at his father for any long stretch of time. Dark circles swallowed his eyes. The skin hung from his bones. His sudden baldness was surreal. Learning now that the strongest man Marvin had ever known was voluntarily starving himself, inviting death to take him, was impossible to accept.

"Won't you let us take you to the hospital?" he pleaded.

"No!" Ed snapped, his voice suddenly energized. "How many times are you guys gonna ask me that same question? I will not die in a hospital. This land gave me my life." Ed rolled his head over to the side. He looked out the back of windows. "Now this land will take me back. Simple as that."

No one spoke for some time, as if an utterance of any kind might detract from the noble omniscience of Ed's statement.

Eventually Susan broke the silence. "I'll make you something, Marv, if you're staying," she said, pulling Marvin's attention away from his father. "Someone has to eat all those groceries you brought, right?" Susan continued.

"Right, Mom," Marvin said to the floor. Then he lifted his head, brightened by some new line of thought. "Dad?"

"Yes?"

"I have something to tell you, something I decided a while ago but didn't want to bring up until . . .things started getting, you know, serious with your cancer. I decided that I will close my practice and manage this place, in your honor. I already told the landlord of my office."

Susan looked over at her husband, trying to gauge his reaction.

Ed struggled to lean up on one elbow, beaming at his son. "That's so great to hear, Marvin. Can't trust an operation like this to three guys that can hardly speak English, you know? And who else is here to run the show?"

The answer hung heavy in the room

"I couldn't live with myself if this place died with you, Dad."

Marvin blinked his tears back. Ed lowered himself back down onto the pillow, closing his eyes.

"What does Katie think about it?" Susan asked, shuffling in her chair. Her attention had drifted from the needles and thread in her hands to the view outside the window.

"She's okay with it," Marvin said under his breath.

"As long as you keep showing up for dinner," Ed murmured.

Susan dropped her knitting and spun in her chair towards the window.

"Mom! What is it?"

Marvin stood up and leaned over her shoulder to look. They both stared in shock at Javier sidestepping across the back lawn, a pistol drawn up to his eye, the two Colombians marching loyally behind him. Following the aim of his gun their eyes found a man staggering down the driveway beneath a huge pack. With long scruffy hair and a spotty beard, neither Susan nor Marvin recognized Jack. His ripped, blood-stained clothes, bony frame and erratic gait bore no resemblance to anyone they knew. They expected Javier to pull the trigger, and were not about to do anything to stop him. Jack dropped the backpack and lifted his hands above his head. Javier inched closer, keeping the pistol focused on its target. Jack dropped to his knees. Then he turned to look up at the house, focusing on the bank of bedroom windows. When Susan saw his clear blue eyes she lunged for the window and lifted the glass pane.

"Javier!! Don't shoot, Javier! It's Jack."

Javier lowered the gun. He strained to have a closer look at his suspect.

"Senhor Jack?" he murmured.

Jack nodded, then fell to his knees.

"My son," Ed said. He was lying on his back, eyes closed. "My son is home."

Susan went to the bed, where she draped her arms around her husband. Marvin stepped over to the window where he stood statue-like, transfixed by the Shakespearean quality surrounding his brother's dramatic return. Later on he'd look back on the moment as an out-of-body kind of experience. It was only when Jack disappeared below, entering the back door with Javier trailing close behind, did Marvin's senses return. He heard the dink-dink sound of metal striking glass. Looking down he discovered the source of the noise, his wedding ring on a shaking hand was tapping the window pane in rhythm with his heartbeat. He turned to face his parents. They were staring at his hand. Marvin slid the ring off and tucked it into a pocket. Then he left the room, heading downstairs to greet his brother.

After all the commotion surrounding Jack's arrival had quelled somewhat, Marvin corralled his teary-eyed mother in the kitchen, urging Jack to head upstairs and spend a little time with their father.

"It might be your only chance, Jack. Every morning he wakes up is a bonus at this point. He won't let us take him to the hospital."

Jack climbed the dark stairs slowly. His legs were cement. Even though his premonition that one of his parents was in trouble had been confirmed, the reality of his father lying in bed on the brink of death was almost more than he could handle. It took all the force of his embattled willpower to climb the stairs and enter his parents' bedroom. Night had fallen in a wall of black outside the bank of windows. A small lamp glowed beside the bed, casting long shadows across the wood floor. Jack was struck by a peculiar odor, a smell he couldn't place within his memory bank of experience. He walked up to the bed and looked down at his dying father. Ed reached out a bony, shaking hand. Jack held it in both of his.

"Son."

"Dad."

"You look worse than me," Ed said, his thin, pale lips spreading into a slow grin. Jack coughed out a quick laugh, moving to pull up the desk chair close to his father.

"Kind of ironic, huh," Jack said flatly.

Ed nodded. He closed his eyes, wincing against the pain coursing through his body. Jack was having trouble looking at his father. He kept trying to find other things in the room to focus on.

"Right about now is when I put on a morphine patch to get through the night. But I'll wait a bit, so we can talk."

"Whatever you need, Dad, just let me know. I'm not going anywhere."

"Wish I could say the same."

Jack grimaced.

"But enough about me. Where the hell have you been all these years?"

Jack gave his father a brief summary of his wanderings, omitting some of the periods of debauchery while expanding upon those times he thought Ed would be proud of, like his carpentry accomplishments and mastery of the banjo. Jack left out the train-hopping and promiscuity, the whiskey shots and poker playing. He didn't mention the wolves. They both soon realized that it was impossible to play five years of catch up in that one moment. So they gave up, choosing instead to simply share time, hoping the minutes would slow themselves enough to satisfy them. One was much easier to appease than the other. As a dying man, Ed had few expectations from this long-awaited reunion with his lost son. For him, words were unnecessary. Jack's close proximity, scrawny and scruffy but with the same bright, confident eyes, was enough.

"Sounds like you've been doing some real livin' out there son."

"I have, Dad. Now I'm tired."

"You could have come back sooner. I got those cops off your tail in no time. With a little help from Marvin's law skills, of course."

"I needed to go away," Jack said, his voice loaded with the pain of acceptance.

Ed rolled his head to one side, staring out the window at the stars emerging one by one in the night sky, the big dipper rising up above the barn. "I love this view."

"It's beautiful," Jack said, following his father's eyes. "Feels like I'm seeing it for the first time."

Ed had just one request to get out before sleep, and morphine, claimed him. "Son?"

"Yes Dad?"

"When I leave this world, and honestly, between you and me, I'm ready to go – I don't want to be locked up in a coffin. What I want is to be burned out behind the barn, in that pit we used at Marvin's wedding. Then I want my ashes spread across the upper pasture, so I'll be able to rest in true peace, under the snow in winter, under the hooves of our girls in summer."

Ed turned to face his son. Jack forced down a dry swallow of air.

"You're the only one in the family with the balls to carry through on this, which is why you're the only one I'm telling it to. I know I can trust you, Jack. Okay?"

"Yes, Dad. Whatever you want. No problem."

Jack had cried himself to sleep many nights during that first year of his running. Eventually the tears had stopped. He was convinced he'd simply run out of them, and was happy with that notion. Instead the springs of his sorrow had built up into a deep reservoir over those years. There in his parents' room, permeated with the smell he decided must be death, the levee burst. His torso rocked with heaving sobs. Ed offered a corner of his quilt to absorb the tears. Jack apologized over and over for missing the last five years of his father's life.

"It's nothing to be sorry for, Jack. Life takes us in unexpected directions. You're here now. That's all that matters. Although I would be lying to say I didn't miss you terribly, I forgave you the day you left. And my forgiveness has never wavered. Any other guilt you might still have is between you and that god you probably still believe in."

Jack struggled to reign in his lurching sobs. Ed carefully secured the small white patch onto his upper bicep with a shaking hand.

"You still don't believe in any god?" Jack asked. "Even after these months sick in bed, dying?"

Ed shook his head slowly. "Why would death make a man suddenly become religious? If anything, this experience is proving me right. All I have to hold onto is my family and my land. Nothing else matters. That's why, if you follow through with what I asked of you, I'll have as good a shot as any at remaining close to these things."

"I understand, Dad."

They both looked back out the windows. Ed let out a long sigh as the morphine started kicking in. Jack had one more thing to say.

"Well, I won't be going anywhere this time, for sure. I'm here to stay, to keep our farm alive."

Ed closed his eyes, ready to surrender to sleep, and maybe more. "That's good to hear, son. Marvin gave me the same pledge today. Said he's quitting his practice to run the farm."

"What!?"

"Oh Jack, you guys work it out, please. No fighting. Just keep that crazy Brazilian away from a gun. That's all I ask, okay?"

Ed fell off into sleep before Jack could answer. He got up and stalked out of the room, heading for the stairs, eager to confront his brother. Jack fired off his attack at Marvin before reaching the kitchen.

"So now you want to go from lawyer to farmer, just like that, like snapping your fucking fingers!?"

He stormed into the kitchen. Susan backed into a corner. Marvin held his ground at the table.

"What are you doing?" Marvin asked his brother.

"I'm the one who should be running this place. I'm the farmer in the family! You're a goddamn lawyer."

"Jack, please," Susan muttered.

"Stay out of this, Mom," Jack snapped.

Marvin lifted his palm toward her to signal the same. "You show up after five years and have the nerve to act like this? Dad hasn't even passed yet. Who do you think you are?"

"I'm the Farmer. Who are you?"

"I'm your brother, Jack. Your fucking brother."

Jack's body loosened. He stumbled forward and slumped into a chair at the kitchen table. "We shouldn't be swearing with mom around," he muttered at the floor.

"You're right," Marvin agreed.

Susan accepted Marvin's offer of a hug. Soon all three were seated at the table. Susan shook her head, while the brothers warily scoped each other out. Neither was sure if their fight had simply been put on hold because their mother was in the room, or if it was truly over. Of course both Marvin and Susan were deeply aware that the tension surrounding this issue would pale in comparison to Jack's impending reaction over Marvin's marriage to his high school sweetheart.

"This family," Susan said, releasing a quick laugh. "There have been more fights in this kitchen. Now isn't the time to fight, boys. What if your father heard all of that?"

"Aww, he's out cold," Jack said, finally lifting his head. "That morphine kicks in fast. And hard."

"Oh, I know, trust me. The poor guy, so disciplined, even about his death. He'll only put one of those patches on at the end of the day, when he's made it all the way through to bedtime on his own will power."

"Disciplined about his death and specific, too," Jack said.

"Whatta you mean?" Marvin asked, shooting his brother a hooded glance.

Jack took a moment to think about his next words. That their father had entrusted him to carry out the burial procedures gave Jack a leg up on Marvin, at least in his own head. He wanted to keep most of Ed's dying wish a secret, a weapon to use against his brother's position as farm manager.

"Dad just told me how he wants to be buried," Jack stated.

"And how is that?" Marvin asked.

When Jack connected eyes with his mother he saw she didn't know either. They would both find out soon enough, so he decided to withhold the information for the time being, a secret he could share with his father a little longer. Susan just closed her eyes and hummed quietly to herself.

Jack leaned back in his chair. "So, Marv," he said, clasping his hands behind his mop of greasy hair. "You're quitting being a lawyer?"

"Yup. In two weeks I'll be done."

"I'll be damned. So, aside from dad dying and you wanting to be a farmer all of a sudden, what else is new around here?"

Marvin gave his mother a nervous glance, one that implored her to speak up, a look that said he needed a little more time before revealing the secret that couldn't last a whole lot longer. And, given the fact that Jack had to digest their father's imminent death, heaping this other news on top of him right away would likely spell disaster. His hand traveled down the outside of a front pocket until his fingers found the protrusion of the wedding ring.

"Well, our herd has about doubled in size," Susan began. "Dan Cook went away, leaving his half-built development behind. Otherwise you know how it is around here, Jack. Not a whole lot changes. Now I'm sure you have plenty of stories to share."

Jack nodded. "I sure do. They'll come out with time. Of course I'll have to censor some of them for your ears, Mom."

"Okay, sweetheart."

Marvin kicked at the floor, trying to judge whether his brother's anger was fading. "I didn't know you were coming home, Jack. You understand that, right?"

"Yup. Got it."

"I was just thinking about the farm, how someone has to keep it going. Mom can't do it by herself."

"No shit." Jack held up an apologetic hand towards Susan. "Sorry Mom. But Marvin, I'm here to stay. What else can I do besides work this farm? It's what I was born to do. Just turned out I needed some time away."

Marvin slapped his palms down on the table and stood up. "Then we'll both run the place. Expand operations. Right?"

Jack looked at his mother. She lifted her eyebrows.

"Could we pull that off without killing each other?" Jack asked.

"I think so, Jack. I really do."

Jack stood up to face Marvin. They shook hands, strong and firm.

"Welcome back," Marvin said.

"I should be saying that to you," Jack said. "But thanks anyway."

THIRTY

DRIVING home a short time later Marvin was still struggling to make sense of Jack's last comment. Then, nearing his house, it hit him like a sack of rocks in the gut. He barely knew anything about farming. Jack was right. Even after being away for five years it was as if his brother had never left. That's why their father had told Jack about his burial requests, why his comment made complete sense in hindsight. Marvin had been away longer, ever since leaving for college at eighteen. Even in Jack's absence, busy with work and marriage, he hadn't spent more than one or two weekends and Christmas Eve at the farm. Driving towards his house in town, he wondered if Katie was truly okay with the idea. Ever since announcing his decision to her a few days ago she'd been acting strange, essentially ignoring him at the office and around the house. But once she found out Jack was home to stay, the issue would quickly become irrelevant, overshadowed by a situation Marvin dreaded down to his core, fearing the worst.

Seated in a polished Shaker chair in front of a pellet stove, the little front window open to its raging flames, Marvin swirled his bourbon around in a few cubes of ice. He was desperately hoping this nightly routine would bring him some sort of calm. He downed the rest of his drink, coughing on the potent liquor. He got up to add more pellets to the stove, then went to his liquor cabinet in the corner of the great room to pour himself another drink. He never had a second bourbon. Making his way back to the chair, he was startled to see Katie standing in the doorway to the room. She was wearing the linen bathrobe he'd gotten her that year for Christmas. Her brown hair, now long, spilled over one shoulder and down across the cream-colored fabric.

"Surprised to see me?" she asked.

"Yes, actually, I am."

Marvin sat down, beckoning for her to take the other chair beside him. She shook her head. He swirled his drink and stared into the flames inside the stove.

"How's your father?" she asked.

"Worse. He's on his last legs."

They rarely discussed Ed's health. Neither wanted to burden the other with thoughts of death when marriage, and the joint effort of parenthood, was just beginning. Katie gathered her hair in one hand and tossed it over her shoulder. Marvin looked up. It was another of many awkward silences they'd been sharing of late, only this one had a much heavier quality.

"Well, I just thought I'd ask, since maybe I'll be asleep by the time you get upstairs. Is that your second drink?"

"How's Greg?"

"He's fine. Been sleeping for hours now."

"Oh, good. I love that little guy like he was my own son. You know that, right?"

"Yes. I do."

"And I love you, more than you probably know."

Katie stepped into the room. "I love you too, Marv. Baby, what's going on? You're acting very strange."

Marvin took a long, slurping sip of the bourbon. "Jack's home."

"What?" Katie reached back to grab hold of the door frame to stop herself from falling over. "Please tell me that's a joke?"

"Why would I joke about that?"

She approached him, bent down to her knees, and clasped the hand that wasn't holding the rocks glass. "What are we going to do?" she begged, her brown eyes wide with fear.

"I don't know," Marvin stammered. "We should have had a plan for this. It was bound to happen at some point."

"I know. We knew. Oh God, Marvin. I'm scared. What will he do when he finds out?"

"I have no idea. We already had a fight about me wanting to manage the farm. We worked it out though. When I left he was happy. I mean, as happy as he could be, given the situation."

"Right."

Marvin bent forward to kiss the top of her head. He whispered softly into her hair. "I think we have to wait until after my dad dies. It's going to be soon. I don't want to overwhelm Jack. It would just be too much."

Katie nodded. "Yes. Too much."

He watched her eyes settle where the wedding ring should have been. There was no need to apologize for its absence.

"Maybe you and Greg want to get away for awhile. Do you want to go visit your parents in Florida?"

"Yeah, maybe. But we might miss your father's funeral?"

"Yes, but you would have to miss it anyway. Because of Jack. I'm sorry, Katie."

"Don't be sorry."

There was the sound of little feet padding down the stairs.

"Mommy? Where are you? I had a bad dream."

Katie stood up. She wiped her eyes with a sleeve of her bathrobe. "I'm coming, sweetie." She bent down to look Marvin in the eyes. "We'll get through this, Marvin. It's what families do. Okay?"

"Okay."

She turned and walked out of the room.

"Okay," Marvin said again, to himself, his voice hollowed by doubt. He swirled his drink. He inched his chair closer to the stove. Even though it was a mild spring night, he couldn't escape the chill that had been consuming him ever since walking in the door. A damp coldness had settled in his bone marrow, a penetrating freeze that even the strongest, best quality bourbon couldn't palliate.

Late that night at the farmhouse Jack found his mother in the living room reading a book on the couch under a single lamp. At the sight of him she laid the book on the side table and lifted her arms out into a great arching half-circle.

"Come give your mother a hug," she beamed.

Jack approached her, bent to his knees, and hugged her. It was a long, tight hug. When it was over he sat down beside her on the couch. Susan's blue eyes glittered.

"I guess I could have handled things better earlier. With Marvin."

"Yes, well, life never stops throwing things at us. Just think of it as practice for the next surprise that comes along."

Susan couldn't keep the hint of foreshadowing out of her voice. Jack took note of it, but didn't press her for details of something she seemed to know that he did not, but would in due time. Instead he filed her comments away in order to be better prepared for some future discovery that might await him, excited by the mystery of what it might be.

"You know," she said softly, "when I saw you today, up close, I mean, I said to myself that my youngest boy has become a man."

"You think?" Jack asked.

"I do. But not just any man. I see you've become a wise man."

Jack crossed his legs, clasped his hands on top of a knee. "I learned a lot out there, Mom."

"I can imagine. Tell me, where did you learn the most?"

"In Minnesota. With the wolves."

"The wolves?"

Jack nodded.

"Tell me about them, Jack. And I want details."

Jack asked for a glass of milk. Susan got herself a goblet of wine. While they each savored their beverages of choice, Jack told her about his time in the Boundary Waters. Fulfilling her request he didn't leave out any details. When he came to the part about running through the woods as one of the pack he didn't want to call it a dream, but wasn't sure what name to give the experience either.

"It still feels like my spirit was actually there, with them," he said. "Does that make sense?"

"It does."

The certainty in his mother's voice gave Jack the freedom to continue the story along the ethereal thread by which he was weaving it, culminating with hearing the alpha wolf's voice in his head.

"That wolf spoke to me, Mom, in the clearest, most direct language I've ever heard."

He told her the words he'd heard. Or more precisely that he'd felt, in his heart.

Susan nodded slowly as she listened. "And that's why you are wise now, Jack, even at such a young age. You've heard the voice of your god. Very few are that lucky. Most of us spend our whole lifetimes praying without ever getting to hear any kind of answer. Myself included."

Jack smiled. "But you're more wise than I'll ever be, Mom."

"Oh, I don't know about that. The older I get, the less I seem to understand, Jack."

"Exactly."

More than two hours had passed since Jack had started talking. The milk and wine were long gone.

"I only have one question for you," Susan said.

"What's that, Mom?"

"I'm wondering if you could tell me what a pack of howling wolves sounds like?"

Jack scratched his chin. A flurry of answers came into his head. If the full moon had a voice, he almost said, and wanted to speak with the earth. Like the first sound heard by the first humans. Like animals confirming how absolutely alone they are. Or, maybe, the howling wolves had sounded like family. But he settled on one final, all-encompassing reply.

"They sound like god, Mom."

Susan closed her eyes. She nodded her head gently. Her face was soft and warm and aglow with love. She placed a hand on Jack's nearest shoulder. "Lots of people might say enlightenment is the daydream of a hippie, or the false utopia of a detached guru. But to be enlightened is possible, Jack. And you seem to be getting there, in you own way, which is the only way. Now let's get some sleep. Who knows what tomorrow will bring."

These last words could have been heavier than lead given the circumstances, but the way Susan said them allowed the words to float up into the air, to drift outside through one of the open windows, where they could hang between the momentary flashes of fireflies and the constant shining stars.

THIRTY-ONE

THE next morning Ed didn't wake up. Even from her separate bed a few feet away Susan knew the moment she woke, without opening her eyes, that her husband was dead. His presence, the anchor-weight of her life, had exited the room. All that was left was his body, the empty shell of her man. Susan opened her eyes and stared at the ceiling. Other things were gone too. His drawn out, raspy breathing, what had become an entity of its own. And gone was the role she'd become, the constant, care-giving nurse, a job she'd upheld to the highest standards. While pausing there in bed before rising to begin these next days of mourning, a fleeting, guilt-ridden anticipation of freedom passed through her, a liberation that promised to be years in the making. It was the gradual release from a lifelong duty. Exactly what awaited her in this new territory was a great unknown, one that didn't scare her at all. She would treat her widow days like she had all the other days of her life, each to be lived to its fullest potential. That was why she smiled right then, staring at a white spackled ceiling, her husband lying dead in the same room. It was a quick smile, when no one was around to take it the wrong way, before the hours of crying that no doubt lay ahead.

For some reason Susan considered it too early to say goodbye to Ed. A firm believer in a combination of Eastern religions, she understood the importance of not rushing death, that although it seemed to happen in an instant, the process of one's soul completely departing the physical body actually took a few days. This basic time frame was a prescription she planned to follow. Otherwise she had no idea how to handle the burial arrangements. She threw off the covers, got up and dressed quickly. After cleaning him as best she could, cutting his fingernails and hand-washing his face and changing him into a fresh pair of pajamas, she made her way downstairs. She headed straight for Jack's bedroom. Without knocking she swung open the door. Just as they'd been doing with Marvin's old bedroom before Ed turned it into an office, Jack's room was the same as the day he left, with the sole addition of a new window in place of the one he'd broken. Susan shook his foot. Jack groaned himself awake. He sat up, rubbing his eyes with the back of his hands the same way he'd always done. He squinted up at her.

"Dad's dead?"

Susan nodded.

His own words echoed back from across the room, struck him in the chest like wet concrete. The man who'd always defined for him what it meant to be a man was gone.

"Welcome home," Jack muttered.

Susan moved closer. She rubbed his scalp in gentle circles. "He waited for you, Jack. He was ready to go weeks ago," she whispered softly.

"That doesn't make it any easier, Mom."

"Not for us. No."

Jack swung his feet down to the floor, let them land with a heavy thud. "I have to tell you something."

"What's that?"

"Dad wants us to cremate him, in the fire pit behind the barn, and then spread his ashes across the upper pasture. That's what he told me."

"Okay."

Jack looked up, shocked by his mother's reaction to the prospect of a funeral pyre in their roasting pit, the same spot where certain doomed goats had been slow-cooked for various family events. "You're fine with that?"

"Sure. Honestly, Jack, I had no idea what to do. It's not like we have a family church. And I always remember him, even when we were young, ranting about how he hated the idea of being put in the ground inside a coffin we couldn't afford. So it makes sense. I just wonder why he didn't tell me."

"He would have. If I hadn't come home."

"But you did come home."

"I did."

Jack got up and moved to his dresser. Susan backed out of the room.

"I'll call your brother while you get dressed."

"Okay, Mom. Meet ya in the kitchen. Hopefully I can figure out how to run his sacred coffee pot."

"I'm sure you'll figure it out," Susan said, gently closing the door.

That afternoon Susan alternated between dicing and stirring in the kitchen and calling friends and relatives on the phone in her office. Her sister Margarat was due to show up later and pitch in with food preparations for the upcoming two-day wake. Jack and Marvin, after sending Javier and the

Colombians home for a three-day vacation, stood in their parents' bedroom looking down at Ed's body.

Jack nodded at the great expanse of open windows along the back wall. "It's warm today. We've got to get a fan up here or something."

"We need more than a fan, Jack. Mom wants the wake to last two days, which means dad has to make it three full days before the cremation."

"It's only getting warmer," Jack said. "Think we need an air conditioner?"

Marvin scratched under his chin. He took off his glasses and polished them with the cuff of his shirt. "We're gonna have to research this."

Jack nodded. "My instincts say we need to salt him. Like curing meat."

"Please tell me that's a joke. A very bad joke."

"I'm serious. But I haven't researched it. It's just a hunch."

"C'mon," Marvin said. "There's Internet in his office room."

Later, downstairs in the kitchen, the brothers announced their plan to Susan. They decided to leave out Jack's initial hypothesis that the body should be salted and cured. Online they'd quickly learned the realities of cremation. Embalming was one option. The other was much more simple, a natural method the brothers favored.

"Mom," Marvin began, trying to lure her attention away from the stove.

"Yes?"

"We have to find a very large refrigerator. Or else a whole lot of ice."

Susan turned around. She was holding a wooden stirring spoon. A yellow broth dripped onto the floor.

"For dad," Jack clarified.

Susan remembered the large refrigerators she'd rented for Marvin's wedding to store all the food in on the back patio. The catering company she'd used had told her they could get a bigger one if necessary.

"A friend of mine rented some for her daughter's wedding," she told her sons. "I already need to call them to get one here by tomorrow anyway, to store all this food I'm making. I think she said they had ones six feet long."

"But dad's six-four," Jack pointed out.

His use of the present tense made everyone pause for an awkward moment.

"I know, but can't we . . .bend his legs?" Susan asked, feeling herself flush.

"No," Jack said bluntly.

"The problem is rigor mortis, Mom." Marvin clarified.

"Right," Susan said. "I forgot about that. So what are we gonna do?"

Susan was glad she had these two men with her. Together the brothers had a shot at adding up to the amount of man her husband had been. She needed them to realize this collective potential, or else she'd be lost.

"I have an idea," Marvin said. "We can use the refrigerated holding tank that stores the milk."

Jack whooped. "Damn, bro, that's one crazy idea. But I like it!"

"It's insane," Susan said. "What if the health inspector found out? And where are you going to put all the milk?"

Marvin pursed his lips. He obviously hadn't taken the idea that far. Thanks to the larger herd, every morning the tank was filled to near its three-hundred gallon capacity.

"We'll bottle it," Jack said. "And then give it away during the wake. Nice fresh, raw milk for free. People around here go crazy for that. Maybe three hundred people will show up, you never know. Bam, three hundred gallons, sold!"

"Excellent idea," Marvin said, cutting off his mother before she could weigh in on the idea. "Better get two of those fridges, Mom. We're gonna have some serious bottles of milk to store."

Susan went into her office room to dig up the caterer's number. "This family is crazy," she muttered to herself.

"C'mon," Jack said, slapping his brother high on the back. "Let's go out to the barn and see what we're dealing with."

Marvin followed him obediently out the back door.

Jack took his time wandering through the barn, marveling at the improvements and additions his father had made while he'd been gone. The herd's size had been tripled from eighty to over two hundred fifty. There was a second milking apparatus along a new line of track, two more holding tanks, and an automatic manure storage system that converted all the cow poop into electricity. Everything seemed to be lined with shiny new steel. Old school country music, their father's favorite, played out of speakers wired high along the rafters.

"Damn," Jack said, standing in the middle of the cavernous space, twirling in circles. "Dad really went all out."

"He sure did." Marvin was heading for the glass-walled room containing the three refrigerated storing tanks. "Let's go bottle some milk, eh?"

"Maybe we should call up Javier and his hombres to help," Jack suggested.

"No. They're on vacation. First one they've ever had since starting here. Can't go back on that, Jack."

Jack nodded as he followed his brother into the glass room. He was still unsure who the boss was going to be. As the elder,

Marvin had a natural path into being the leader. But Jack was a fighter, and he was the Farmer.

"I'm calling Javier," he said defiantly. His brother lifted his head from inspecting the manual withdrawal nozzle on one of the towering steel tanks. "He can decide for himself if he wants to help," Jack continued. "The Colombians are on vacation, no doubt. But Marvin, we've gotta build a coffin too, you know. And get the pit ready. So I'm going to call Javier."

Jack turned and walked out of the room before Marvin could protest. Stepping into the office and turning on the light, Jack was shocked to see not a shred of dust beneath the bright fluorescent lights illuminating a computer. Not only was there a cordless phone, but Ed had wired the barn with a DSL line. Jack shook his head, marveling at these signs of his father's evolution right up to the end. Dialing Javier's number after locating it in a laminated list on the wall, Jack took a moment to recognize the oddity that humor was somehow making the whole experience more bearable. Laughter, and the tightness of family, was helping them get by. Even in the aftermath of his five year vanishing act and his father's death, the bonds between the three of them were stronger than ever.

"Oi?" came the voice on the other end of the line.

"Javier, oi, it's Jack."

"Ahh, senhor Jack," the Brazilian bubbled. "Como te valle?"

"I'm good, my friend. Nice to see your ass yesterday, even though you almost killed me."

"Sim, sorry, senhor. So sorry!"

"No problema, man. Just doin' your job." Jack's voice then dropped into a more serious tone. "Speaking of your job, are you available to work these next few days? I know my brother told you to take a break -"

"Oh, senhor, I am on my way. Muito bem, I come work."

Jack lowered the receiver and stared at it with disbelief. Javier hadn't even given him a chance to offer double time pay. He lifted the phone back up, planning to announce this intention, but all he heard was a dial tone. The Brazilian was likely already heading for the farm.

"He's on his way," Jack said upon re-entering the storage room.

"And we're gonna pay him forty an hour for the next three days?"

"Yup."

Marvin stood up, a clear glass jar full of milk in one hand. "Who made you the boss around here anyway?" he snapped.

"I did."

"Oh, I see. Well, Mr. Boss, did you happen to tell Javier to pick up the hundred gallon jars on his way out of town?"

"I forgot. I'll go pick 'em up, soon as he gets here."

"Leaving us with nothing to do while you're gone."

"There's something to do," Jack said, reasserting his role as head of operations. "You guys can start working on preparing the fire pit – there's a lot to do out there, as I'm sure you know."

Jack didn't wait for Marvin to challenge him. Instead he headed straight out the back door of the barn to assess the status of the fire pit, where he would come up with some instructions for his brother and Javier to begin implementing. Marvin had no choice but to follow. Preparing the pit was their largest task outside of dealing with emptying the storage tank. Jack listed off detailed tasks that Marvin and Javier could start on immediately.

"Yes, boss," Marvin said, taking a gulp of the fresh milk.

Jack was bothered by the title, but promised himself he wouldn't let it show no matter how many times his brother used it. Better to be called something you are, even if in a

mocking tone, than something you aren't. At the first sound
of Javier's truck approaching the barn Jack left his brother to
head for town in his mother's SUV.

"When I get back I'll start working on the casket," he
shouted as he stepped out of the barn. By assuming this most
important role Jack strengthened his position as master of
ceremonies for their father's funeral.

Marvin could only nod in acceptance of his secondary
position.

Jack took the coffin construction very seriously, approaching it
as a crucial element of the unique ritual his father's funeral had
become. He worked at it for eighteen hours straight, through
that night and all the next day. Drawing on his experience of
stumbling into a Lakota Sundance ceremony in South Dakota
during one of his looser periods of rambling, he began by fell-
ing a giant sycamore bordering the upper pasture. Growing up
the tree had always been special to him. It still held the rotting
remnants of the first tree house his father had built him. Jack
said a prayer thanking the tree for its sacrifice, and made an
offering of tobacco before he dropped the great, silver-barked
tree to the ground with a thundering crash. The earth shook
under his feet like a miniature earthquake.

After sawing off the limbs Jack set about carving rough
boards out of the trunk with his chainsaw. It was dangerous,
challenging work, the kind of task he'd learned to thrive on
during his years away, when conquering difficult situations
had become crucial to his survival. He was glad no one had
climbed up the hill to watch him work, because anyone who
had would have stopped him immediately. By nightfall he had
the boards he needed to make the sides of the coffin. Jack still
hadn't decided how he was going to make the two ends, but

was certain something would come to him. He used the tractor to haul the sycamore boards down into the barn, where Javier was waiting, eager to be of assistance even after working all afternoon with Marvin building the pyre behind the barn. Jack marveled at the towering pile of sticks and logs and dried brush rising two stories into the air, a temporary, combustible monument to Ed Brown. Javier was standing beside it, hands on his hips, a serious expression on his face. Jack rumbled to a stop in front of the barn's back door. He climbed down off the tractor.

"Javier, you're still here."

"Sim. I help, senhor. Whatever you need."

Jack shook his head. He cracked a sad smile, placing a heavy hand on the short man's shoulder.

"I appreciate the offer, my friend. But this is something I have to do alone. Understand?"

The Brazilian shuffled his feet. Jack could tell he didn't want to leave. There was still work to be done.

"I come back in morning," Javier said, walking reluctantly off towards his truck parked down by the house.

"See you then, senhor," Jack called after him.

Inside the barn Jack turned on all the lights. He loaded the stereo with some of his father's favorite music, Hank Williams Jr. and Steve Earl and Bob Dylan. He dug out an old Folgers can full of rusted, handmade nails they'd found over the years while plowing the fields, relics from past generations of hardscrabble farmers. He sharpened them with a file, and pre-drilled holes in the sycamore boards using a hand-crank drill his father had always cherished. With a plane he carved the boards into a traditional coffin shape. Then, with dawn approaching, it was time to come up with a plan for sealing off the ends. Jack had assumed some kind of vision would come to him while working, but nothing had.

Pacing out behind the barn, bathed in the pink glow of a sunrise that contradicted his somber mood, Jack was drawn to the pond, the little body of water that had been the source of such a crisis so many years ago. He walked over to it, and bent down along the bank. He reached in and scooped out a handful of the wet clay that made a natural lining, holding in the spring water since his grandfather had dug it out during another era. Struck by an idea, Jack hurried back into the barn. Up in the hay loft he found some chicken wire, which he cut and stapled to the ends of the coffin. Then Javier showed up. Marvin emerged from the house, where he'd slept, to help with the milking. Jack began trucking in wheelbarrow loads of clay, which he smeared across the chicken wire on both ends of the coffin. When he was finished the three men hauled it out into the sun so the clay could dry. Jack had left the top open. He'd prepared enough nails and prepped corresponding holes so it could be secured down once their father was inside.

"Good work, Jack," Marvin said as he bent down to inspect the homemade casket. "So long to grandpa sycamore, huh."

It was the name they'd given the great tree as little boys.

"Yeah," Jack said. "I think he was happy to be sacrificed for this purpose. Besides, I noticed another one in the woods just behind it, already a hundred feet tall."

Marvin slapped one of the rough boards. "Must be one of his offspring."

"For sure. That's why it felt okay to take him down. He's going to live on."

In the loaded silence that followed, the brothers pondered Jack's symbolic analogy. They each felt the undeniable significance of their father's passing, the burden of one generation giving way to the next. Suddenly the concept of the future no longer existed. The here and the now was upon them. The present was begging to be seized.

THIRTY-TWO

IF it could be called such a thing, the funeral was a success. The pact made by Susan and her two sons on the eve of the first day of the week was largely upheld. What they'd vowed was to all try their best to make the three days as upbeat and optimistic as they could. A stream of guests began the following morning and flowed straight through the day after and into the evening hours, forcing Javier to speed into town for an emergency pickup of Tiki Torches. By the end all three hundred gallons of milk had been passed out to grateful mourners. The same bluegrass band that played at Marvin's wedding, The Rattlin' Fiddle Boys, graced the farm with happy tunes on both afternoons. People danced. Susan and Margarat kept the food flowing out of the kitchen and onto tables under the tent.

Over the course of the wake, conferring with one another during brief moments of privacy, the three Browns shared their collective opinion that the atmosphere, although helped by the bluegrass and Susan's home-cooking, was made possible in large part by the lack of a coffin on display. Jack had tucked it into a dark corner of the hayloft. All three had to dodge the question of the location of Ed's body, agreeing to stick with the story that he was being held at a local funeral home in preparation for being cremated. They also didn't share the fact that the cremation ceremony was going to be held in the roasting pit behind the barn. When a few guests wandered back there and inquired about the giant pyre, the brothers passed it off as just an above average brush pile, for which they were awaiting a permit to burn.

Then came the morning of the cremation itself. All the food was eaten. The guests and the band were gone. Bouquets of flowers and gifts of cheese plates and fruit baskets lined the back patio. Javier arrived at dawn to help the brothers. The three of them stood behind the barn, assessing the situation.

"So I assume it's also my job to get dad into the coffin," Jack said to Marvin, who was already shaking his head.

"I'll help you, Jack. Just like I did getting him in the tank. These aren't jobs to tackle alone."

"True."

Moving in silent, genetically choreographed fluidity the brothers locked up the barn and left only the lights in the storage tank room on. Jack knotted the climbing rope they'd used two days earlier, climbed the metal ladder up the side of the tank, and released the cover, which rose on a hydraulic hinge. With Marvin harnessed to the opposite end of rope Jack was able to rappel down into the depths of the tank. Retrieving his rigid father, cloaked in the brown and white wool afghan that had kept him warm on his death bed, he jerked the rope twice. Marvin pulled the two of them back up to the top. Jack climbed down with his father balanced over a shoulder.

They had the coffin open and waiting in a corner of the room. Without saying it, they agreed to unwrap their father and bid him a farewell, to take in the physical sight of him one more time. They hadn't seen his body after death had claimed him. Susan had bundled him in the blanket right after coming downstairs to tell Jack the news that morning. And, when loading Ed into the cooler tank, they'd been too consumed with grief to even contemplate the notion. But now they felt ready. So Jack laid the corpse down on the painted concrete floor and slowly unwrapped the chilled body. Dressed in flannel pajamas, Ed's ribcage was visible pressing into the button-down shirt. The hollow sockets around his eyes were dark blue, contrasting sharply with the smooth and shining bald head.

Marvin chose to focus on his father's face. Aside from the morbid eye sockets it was set in an expression of calm repose, as if Ed was just sleeping. This view gave Marvin a certain amount of peace interlaced with the heavy sadness of saying goodbye. Jack let his attention settle on his father's hands crossed atop his chest. Ed's hands were unchanged by the disease that had ravaged the rest of his body from the inside out, as if he'd died before the cancer had been able to make it down his arms. They were strong hands, criss-crossed by thick veins, rippled with bulging tendons. His fingers were long but not slender, ending in fingernails that were uncharacteristically short. Jack thought his mother must have cut them the morning his father had passed. If she had, she'd decided to leave the dirt underneath them. These little impactions of soil had always been present under Ed's fingernails for as long as Jack's memory went back. He shrugged off the oddity that the dirt had survived his father being marooned for months on his deathbed. He simply took in the sight of those hard-working hands, unchanged even in death. Jack kept his eyes on his father's hands right until he and his brother had Ed wrapped back up in the afghan, knowing he'd need to remember the sight of them many times over the rest of his life.

The brothers carried the coffin out to the back of the barn on their shoulders, where they set it down beside the giant pyre.

The next task was to somehow lift the sycamore box containing Ed Brown up on top of the tee-pee of interlocking limbs. Jack, admiring his handiwork on the coffin, was at a loss.

"Can't you figure something out?" he asked Marvin.

"Oh, so The Boss is stumped," Marvin mocked.

Jack held his tongue as his brother paced in a giant circle around the pit. Jack watched him closely. After two trips around he stopped beside the men.

"See that big oak limb up there?" Marvin said, pointing up at the huge limb of a towering oak that extended directly over the pyre.

Jack nodded. "I see where you're going," he said.

"We need two cows, dad's old yoke, that climbing rope, and a hitch put on the coffin."

"I get cows," Javier volunteered, wasting no time to go off and round up two of the Angus bulls.

"I've got the rope and the yoke," Marvin said, nodding at the coffin. "Just needs one more addition, Jack. Then it'll be perfect."

Jack bent down to search out the right spot for screwing in a strong enough hitch to lift two hundred pounds fifty feet into the air.

By mid-morning the pyre was blazing. Flames shot up higher than the tallest trees on the property. Two steers were harnessed with the yoke originally meant for the two five-hundred pound bulls Ed used to keep around. He'd originally envisioned using them to plow his fields in the spring, but after enduring a horn thrust four inches into his thigh he'd gone straight from the hospital to a farm equipment supply store, where he purchased the tractor he would use for thirty years. Attached to the yoke apparatus was the long, thick rope looped over a limb high above the fire. The other end draped down and was fastened to the metal bolt on the coffin. Jack was behind the cows, a whip in one hand and his worn bible, a book he'd read through twice and had used as a pillow on so many boxcar nights, in the other. Marvin and Javier had the coffin lifted up on their shoulders. Susan and Margarat stood close together, hands shielding their faces from both the scorching heat and the abstract sight of the ritual before them.

Jack and Marvin exchanged a look. Neither wanted to speak above the roar of the flames and the crackling wood. For both of them the act itself, what they were choreographing for their father according to his exact wishes, was a perfect obituary. Neither man was good with words. But it seemed like one would have to speak up and say something on Ed's behalf. Marvin gestured at Jack with his free hand to imply that the one with a prop like The Bible had to step up. Jack accepted this obligation, but before he could get a word out Susan's voice boomed from behind them. All three men spun around. The cows almost bolted before Jack's quick reaction with the whip halted them in their tracks. Susan held her focus on the blazing tower of logs as she spoke, her voice optimistically mournful, grounded in the necessity of grief.

"We are gathered here on this perfect spring morning, the kind of morning my husband most loved. He measured the worthiness of a day like this by the number of birds awake before he rose. In carrying out his wish today, we are ensuring that Ed's death won't be an ending, that his spirit will always live on this land, that his heart will beat on inside his sons as they work this farm together."

Susan came close to choking before her next words. Margaret moved to hand her a scarf but she waved it away, fixing her gaze on the homemade coffin, her voice softening slightly.

"It's just like my husband to die in the spring. And how fitting it is, given that this has felt less like a funeral and more like a celebration of the full circle of a great man's life, a man who was the best farmer, the best father, and the most wonderful husband this world, and this woman, could ever expect to find."

She closed her eyes. The rest of them bowed their heads for a minute of silence punctuated only by the snorting cattle and the crackling, hissing bonfire.

The moment ended on its own. Jack moved the cattle forward. The rope stretched taught and squeaked along the limb high above. The coffin lifted slowly off Javier and Marvin's shoulders, rising phoenix-like beside the blaze. Once the cows had it pulled higher than the fire, the wooden box dangling vertically in the air, Javier and Martin guided it into position using long metal poles. As the flames licked the box Jack pulled the machete out of its holster at his waist and sliced though the rope. The coffin fell into the fire with an explosion of showering sparks. The steers clamored off towards the barn, mooing like banshees. The women gasped and huddled up tight. The men dashed out of the way of flying embers and partially burned logs. Everyone gathered in a circle to watch the fire rage, consuming the sycamore casket in no time. At the first sight of color from the afghan cloaking Ed's body they all turned abruptly and headed for the house. Jack instructed Javier to stay behind and monitor the blaze.

That evening the two brothers stood beside the pit surveying the mound of ash and embers, a huge pile of black and gray.

"We shouldn't have used so much wood," Jack muttered.

"Mmm," agreed Marvin. "Whole lot of ashes, huh?"

"Yup."

Marvin lifted his gaze to the upper pasture. "So, boss, how're we going to spread this out? I was picturing each of us with a bucket and a shovel up there just tossing it around. But that'd take us a week!"

"Sure would," Jack said, hands on his hips. "Don't worry, bro, this one I already thought out. The solution is two words – manure spreader."

A few minutes later they had the four-sided cart, capable of spreading a ton of manure over ten acres of land, hitched to the John Deere and positioned next to the huge pile of ashes. Using snow shovels they set to work, heaving the dusty ashes and smoking coals into the steel holding chamber on the cart.

"We should have had Javier stay," Jack grunted at one point, wondering if the shovelful he was throwing over his shoulder contained any ashes of his father.

"I think this is something only you and I were meant to do," Marvin said.

"I think you're right."

An hour later Jack was piloting the tractor on a bumpy course through the upper pasture. Marvin stood on the cart and monitored the functioning of the spreader as they worked their way down the field, moving from one side to the other. They finished just before darkness enveloped the farm. Idling beside the creek below the brothers strained to take in the scene of what remained of their father spread out across his favorite pasture. A crack of thunder interrupted their reflection, followed by a steady shower of large raindrops.

"A storm! Yee-haw!" Jack shouted as they rumbled through the creek and back towards the barn.

"It'll soak him right into the ground!" Marvin hollered. "Man never did like to waste time, did he?"

Rather than shout out a response above the roar of the tractor Jack just closed his eyes, took in the smell of the wet earth, and smiled through his tears.

THIRTY-THREE

A WEEK after the funeral Marvin sat in the chair at his father's desk in what used to be his childhood bedroom. He placed his mug of green tea on the desk's surface. It was the early afternoon, what Jack had been declaring siesta time of late. The biggest change around the farm, when it came to the rhythm of things, was that lunch and dinner now existed as separate entities instead of being combined into a great mid-afternoon supper. But with lunch done by one o'clock there was a gap of time before the late afternoon rounding up of the cows and subsequent milking. Javier and the Colombians didn't stop for any siestas, choosing instead to work off the clock on various side projects, while Jack curled up on his bed for what was usually an hour long nap. The only thing differentiating today from other days of late was that Marvin had slid his wedding ring on that morning before coming to the farm. He and Katie had decided it was time.

Marvin was taking these days to get to know his father's office. Today he was going through the drawers of the wooden desk, pulling out piles of paperwork he guessed might take a week to sort through. Marvin liked this side of his new job. He helped with most everything outside, but it didn't come to him naturally like it did for Jack. Taking care of the business end of things was his niche. Jack had been making it clear that he essentially wanted nothing to do with the accounting part of farm management responsibilities, as long as he had access to a relatively unlimited budget. Marvin had agreed to these conditions with the intent of working out a specific budget with Jack for the upcoming year. He knew any important financial documents would be saved on the desktop computer, but he was also certain his father would have filed back up hard copies of everything.

After flipping through some mundane receipts and annual reports Marvin stumbled on a one page card stock with bold print and the title Summary Of Accounts. As he scanned down the page, reading the sum totals in a column on the far right of the page, his hands started shaking. Their father had died a broke man. As he intensified his scrutiny of the desk papers that afternoon, Marvin found out more. He'd been doing fairly well, right up until the final days of his life, when he'd paid off every the debt the farm owed. There was nothing leftover in the account except a few hundred dollars.

Frozen with disbelief, Marvin stared out the window at the farm, the long red barn humming with fans, the giant blue silos towering behind, fluffy white clouds drifting above. He couldn't see any beauty in the scene, only the heavy burden of it all. Unable to stand the view he let his forehead come down onto the desk. He stayed in that position for some time, taking in long, slow breaths. He didn't move again until Jack's voice came from the doorway.

"Hey man, what's up? I think I overslept. What the hell are you doing?"

Marvin spoke into the desk, his voice muffled by the wood. "According to dad's accounts the farm is basically broke."

"What do you mean?" Jack asked, stepping up to the desk.

Without lifting his head Marvin held up a pile of papers. Jack took them out of his hand and sat down on the foot of the bed. He read through the pages one at a time, tossing them to the floor as he went, a slow smile spreading across his face.

"Marv, he paid off every single bill. The farm is out of debt!" Jack's voice lifted higher with every word.

"But there's no money in the account."

"Exactly. Most farms operate in permanent, large-scale debt. To be even is to be a success. Now all we have to do is maintain this position dad put us in. That fuckin' guy!"

"I guess I still have a lot to learn," Marvin said quietly.

"You do. That's why I'm the boss around here."

Marvin nodded slowly. Jack bent down and gathered the papers up off the floor. He handed them back to Marvin. But when his brother clasped them in his hand Jack held on tight. His eyes were locked on the solid gold ring around Marvin's fourth finger.

"What?" Marvin asked, tracing Jack's line of sight, discovering the source of his brother's outraged expression. Now that it had finally come, Marvin still wasn't ready for this moment.

"You're married?"

Marvin nodded once, sharply, trying to delay the necessity of using words.

"What's her name? Where has she been? You didn't invite her to the funeral?"

Marvin coughed into his fist. He stared at the floor. "Her name is Katie."

"Katie? Now that's a coincidence, eh? I've had her on my mind ever since I got back. Was thinkin' about trying to track-"

"It's no coincidence, Jack."

"What? You married my Katie? Katie Smignatelli?"

"She's my Katie now, Jack," Marvin said, curling up into a ball on the chair, expecting to be pummeled by a shower of fists, or worse.

Jack paced back and forth across the small room. He stopped the pacing and stared down at his brother. "I can't stay here. If I did I might kill you. Good luck running our farm."

He pounded across the room and out the door.

"Jack, we thought, it just happened, Jack. Don't be crazy!" Marvin shouted into the hallway.

"I am crazy!" Jack yelled back from his bedroom downstairs, where he was gathering up his banjo and his old worn out Bible, before heading for the back door.

"Guys? Is there something wrong?" came Susan's voice from somewhere in the house.

The back door slammed, shaking the walls.

"Yes, Mom," Marvin said, too softly for her to hear. "Something is wrong." He slumped down off the chair and lay there on the floor, his carefully constructed world crashing to pieces around him. He suddenly realized that even though he and Katie had formed a tight bond over the last few years it was nothing compared to the connection he shared with Jack. Blood ran thick, and would always trump any romantic union. Marvin shivered with the chill created by this rift finally surfacing. The shivers spread into goosebumps and a pounding heart as he tried to envision the inevitable crash of Jack's next return. He knew his brother would be back soon in the same certain way a shoreline expected the next high tide.

That night Marvin and Susan sat in the dimly lit kitchen. The cordless phone rested on the table between them. They'd been debating whether or not to call the police.

"He ran away, just like last time. Except he didn't break any windows. Maybe this time he won't be coming back home," Marvin said.

"He'll be back," Susan countered. "This isn't like last time. He doesn't have any more need to run. He has more important things to do now."

"Yeah, like murdering his brother," Marvin said.

Susan gasped. "Marvin, please. Your brother has changed. Trust me."

They held off on any discussion of how to move forward, sharing a dinner during which neither one spoke a word. Before going to bed Susan made sure the back door was open, that the light was on above the patio. But in the morning Jack had not returned.

Running through the night Jack felt liked he'd relapsed into the dark throes of an old habit, like a waking, recurrent nightmare. At first his goal was the same as last time, to run until his body became so exhausted that his brain shut down. But the further he ran the more his mind whirled. It was nothing like the last time, when he'd embarked on an adventure of the spirit. Then he'd been a man leaping into the unknown, severing his ties to childhood. This time he carried a heavy guilt on his shoulders. His pace slowed under this burden. He reached the rail line on the outskirts of town. Scraped, cut, and bruised he crouched beside the track. Less than an hour had passed when he heard the thunder of an approaching train.

As the train chugged past him Jack stood up, his eyes scanning the sides of the cars for a ladder to grab. When one passed by he sprinted after it. But when the moment came to grab on he veered away at the last second, an instinctual reaction his body made without input from his mind.

He wandered into town feeling like a stranger lost in a place he once knew so well, eventually settling down on a bench by the little creek that flowed under Main Street, the same stream that still carried the runoff from their pond at the farm. There he dozed in and out of sleep on the hard wooden slats. When morning came he roamed the streets of Springtown, hoping he wouldn't bump into anyone he knew, killing enough time until his brother would be leaving his house in town to head to the farm.

THIRTY-FOUR

At a pay phone in town, after a shave and a haircut at his old barbershop, Jack got Marvin's home number from information. After the fourth ring he almost hung up.

"Hello?"

The last six years were erased by that one word, by the light, bubbling voice unchanged by time.

"Katie."

He knew his own voice had been altered by experience, roughed up around the edges, more scratchy than smooth. Yet still he wanted her to recognize it.

"Who is this?"

"Guess."

"I'm going to hang up unless you tell me your name right now."

"My name is Jack. My last name is the same as yours."

There was no response, not even the sound of her breathing. Jack wondered if she'd dropped the phone.

"Jack . . .I'm sorry."

"Are you?"

He hadn't expected an apology so soon, thought he'd have to squeeze it out of her over time. "I am. You didn't deserve to come home to this. I don't know what I was thinking. I wasn't thinking. But, you know, I was so alone, a single mother. All I wanted was security. A stable kind of love. Marvin offered me both. I guess neither of us thought you were ever coming back, so we figured it would be okay. We were wrong."

"Maybe you were. But it's too late now, right?"

Katie didn't answer him. She didn't have to.

"Life moves, and you have to move with it," Jack continued. "On top of my dad dying, hearing about you and my brother was so hard. I almost ran away again last night. But I can't do that this time. I have to stay."

"I understand, Jack. Where are you now?"

"Springtown. I have to see you. Then I'll be able to go back home. I hope."

"Okay, Jack."

She told him how to get to their house.

Jack stepped through the great white pillars lining the front porch. He lifted the knocker on the solid black door, let it fall with a thud. The door opened immediately. They stood face to face for some time. Katie's mouth was twitching, as if she wanted to smile in order to break through the heightened tension of this reunion, but couldn't produce one.

"Do I look the same?" she asked shyly.

"You look like a woman. When I left you were just a girl."

She finally let the smile bloom across her face. "Babies will do that," she said, cupping her enormous belly, a swelling Jack hadn't even noticed. He'd been focused entirely on her eyes, even though she was mostly averting them.

"Congratulations."

"Thank you. Please, come in."

She stepped back, ushering him into the carpeted hallway. He followed her to the back of the house, into the great open space beneath a cathedral ceiling garnished by a skylight and a fan. The kitchen was on one side, a dining room on the other. Katie moved into the kitchen.

"Wow," Jack said. "My brother must be loaded."

Katie flushed. "Oh, he put everything he had into this house. It's his baby." She glanced at her belly. "Well, you know what I mean. Can I get you something?"

"Coffee would be great."

"Sure."

Jack dropped his backpack and banjo to the floor. He took a seat at a barstool in front of an open counter that divided the room in half. He twinged at the sight of Katie looking so at home in his brother's fancy kitchen. This was harder than he'd imagined it was going to be. But it had to be done, like a job to be completed so life could move on to where it had to go. After grinding some beans and starting up the coffee pot, she stood across from him.

"Do I look the same?" he asked.

She squinted her eyes and leaned towards him. "You look mostly the same, Jack. Except your eyes. They're not so blue anymore. I see some yellow, I think, that wasn't there before."

Jack smiled. "That makes sense."

"Why?"

"'Cause I was hanging out with wolves."

The coffee maker gurgled to a finish. Katie turned to pour some coffee into their mugs.

"Oh," she said, returning to the island with their coffee. "Milk and sugar?"

"No thanks."

She was acting more nervous all of a sudden. Her hand shook slightly while she added sugar to her coffee. She glanced at her watch, trying her best to avoid Jack's fixated gaze.

"What's wrong, Katie?"

"Oh, nothing. I mean, I guess that topic makes me unsettled. Brings back memories of a certain time. You know."

Jack nodded slowly, cupping his mug, breathing in deep the rich aroma. He let out a long sigh. "That makes sense. But the reason I'm able to sit here right now, and look you in the eyes without going crazy, is because of the last place I went before coming home."

"Where was that?" she said weakly, as if she didn't really want to know.

"A place called the Boundary Waters, in Minnesota. There are wolves there."

She took a step back. "I see."

"They're nothing to be scared of, Katie. They accepted me like a brother. They showed me their god. With this new faith I learned from the wolves I'm ready for anything life has to dish out. Like sitting here, right now."

"That's good, Jack. You seem at peace."

"I am."

As if on cue they both looked out the back windows at the fenced-in, manicured yard, with a swing set and a sand box.

"No wolves out there," Katie said.

"My brother and I are so different," Jack observed.

"What were you doing all the other years you've been gone?" Katie asked quickly, changing the subject.

"Sit down and I'll tell you."

Jack didn't sensor the details of his five years of wandering like he'd done for his father. He told her everything. He
accounted for every lover possessed, every bottle of whiskey
consumed, every boss abandoned. Katie took it all in without
seeming fazed in the least bit. At times she had a quizzical
look, as if trying hard to assess what had changed about him,
and what hadn't. Jack had certainly lost his innocence, but
he'd replaced it with the kind of wisdom that can only come
through wide-ranging experiences. He was treating the long
rambling monologue like a kind of confession, spilling the
darker sides of where he'd been and what he'd done, shedding
some of the guilt that had followed him back home. When
he got to the part about his debt to the Russian thugs Katie
stopped him abruptly.

"Jack! Do you think they might find you someday?" she
asked, thrusting her hands on her hips.

"No. Not unless I relapse and jump another train to
California. That world is entirely separate from this one.
From the farm, I mean."

"That's good," Katie said. "No more train-hopping for you,
Jack Brown."

"Yes, Katie."

He was happy to see how much she still cared about his
well-being. It made the situation easier to bear, knowing that
some piece of her love for him lived on, would always be
there.

"Thank you, Jack."

He thought he saw a tear forming in the corner of her eye.
"What about you? You must have some stories to tell."

"Oh," Katie said, looking down, her neck flushing red.
"They're pretty boring compared to yours."

"If you say so."

"I think you have to go now," she said without looking at him.

"Yeah, I think you're right. We'll have to take this whole thing one day at a time."

She nodded, her face tight in an effort to hold the tears back.

"I know where the door is," Jack said.

He collected his things and slipped back out into the day.

THIRTY-FIVE

JACK walked back towards the farm. When he passed Katie's old house he glanced at the black tar rooftop furtively, half-expecting to see their former selves basking in vernal love like some kind of museum installment. Around dusk, as he was nearing the farm, Marvin passed him on his way home after a day of work. The dark sedan came to an abrupt stop, then backed up along the shoulder to where Jack was standing. Marvin's window came down. Jack stood straight up, tall, so his brother had to stick his head out and crane his neck to confirm it was actually Jack Brown, and not some kind of apparition.

"You came back," Marvin said.

"Did you think I wouldn't?"

"Maybe for a second." Marvin nodded in the direction of the farm. "But I figured you know how much there is do right now, with haying season coming up and all."

Jack smiled.

"You're the boss, man," Marvin continued. "Mom and I would have been totally lost without you."

"Yeah, probably. Well, I've got big ideas for the farm, Marv, little visions that came to me in Minnesota."

"What were you doing up there anyway?"

Jack wondered how many times he was going to have to recount that portion of his adventures. "Hanging out with the wolves."

Marvin lifted his eyebrows in curious surprise.

"Yeah, they taught me everything I needed to learn," Jack continued. "There's nowhere left for me to run, Marv. I was just at your house, talking with Katie. Nice place you've got."

Marvin coughed out his surprise. "Um, thanks. So how did that go?"

"As well as it could have, I guess. Time will tell."

"It will, won't it."

Jack turned to look up the road.

"Need a ride?" Marvin asked.

"I do. My feet are startin' to ache."

Marvin pulled the car to a stop in the driveway. The brothers sat there for some time, their conversation focused entirely on the future. They knew by then that the past could be like quicksand, a place they might easily get hopelessly stuck in. Marvin explained how he thought it was going to be very difficult maintaining the status quo at the farm. A few bills were already starting to mount since the funeral.

"Debt is not an option," Jack stated, "especially after where dad left us, free and clear, with all the infrastructure you could ask for."

"So what's the plan boss? I'm at your command."

There was no hint of sarcasm in Marvin's voice. The stakes had become too high for petty emotions. They had a farm to keep alive.

"It's time to expand, Marv. Diversify, to keep up with the times. We're going to do maple syrup, and take the tourism stuff dad tried to start to the next level, hay rides and pick-your-own berries and, call me crazy, a baby animal petting zoo."

"I love it," Marvin hooted.

"And, when the time is right, I want mom to consider the idea of running a B & B out of the house. Think she'll go for it?"

Marvin slapped his bother on the knee. "If we both tell her to she will. Mom knows what's at stake."

"All right, then, Marv. Tomorrow the games will begin."

"Yes they will. Welcome home again, Jack."

"Eh. I've never really left."

"I know."

THIRTY-SIX

SUSAN was not surprised by Jack's immediate return, but it did little to assuage her enduring grief. She attempted to deal with the loss of her husband by crawling into the hole that was her office. She tried to bury her sadness under layers of desk work, beneath one hundred pages of emails, hiding it behind a half dozen new volunteer projects. Nearing sixty, she tricked herself for brief moments there in the windowless study, transported by her framed diploma to a time when books contained everything there was to know about life. She'd actually graduated college three years late, after many secret, all-night sessions in that same office. It was something she'd kept to herself, hoarding the accomplishment like a secret treasure, stashing her diploma in a drawer. Now she was hiding in there once again, half convincing herself that it was possible to go back in time and choose a different path forward.

It was a season of hibernation, one that might have become a string of seasons if her sons hadn't intervened. There was only one lamp in the office, with a dim yellow bulb and dusty plastic shade. The shade never used to be dusty. Susan's cleaning self, and all her other selves, mother and sister, nurturer, cook, gardener, were lying dormant. Only the intellectual side of her was awakening when all else had gone to sleep. The dim light felt good on her skin. The sound of shuffling papers calmed her. The little electronic song when she powered up her lap-top was the only music she heard, and she liked it that way. Susan indulged in this emotional cocoon, a dead-zone of her heart, for almost too long. She was jolted out of it just in time, one rainy afternoon a few months after Ed's funeral, when Marvin flung open the door to her office without asking, allowing the light and air from the kitchen to penetrate the vacuum of isolation she'd created inside. She turned around to face him, straddling the back of her desk chair.

"Mom," he stated forcefully, breathing hard from the exertion of another long day.

"Yes Jack?"

She heard the impatient distance in her own voice, as if she'd given up on life for awhile, and didn't like being dragged back into it. She would emerge when the time felt right.

"Jack and I need your help."

Susan's face softened. "But Marvin, I'm no spring chicken you know."

"I know." He glanced at her framed certificate in Portuguese from a series of classes she'd taken at the local community college. "But we were thinking you could at least help us translate some things for Javier – there are some complicated jobs we just can't explain to him in a way he can understand. What do you think? It might be good to get out of this office a little, you know?"

Susan took in a long, slow breath. She understood this request of Marvin's had arisen less from his need for a transla-

tor but more as a way to coax her back to the surface, a gentle
tug towards the light, and the living.

"You're right, Marvin. I can't hide in here forever, even
though I fear that life is beginning to take more from me than
it has left to give. But never mind that. We've got a farm to
run, don't we."

"We do," Marvin said. "And a damn fine farm at that."

Jack's first priority, now that he was back to stay, before running
maple syrup lines or fixing up the hay wagon or converting the
farmhouse into a B & B, was to build himself a house. He knew
right away where it had to be, along the top of the upper pasture,
right above where his father's ashes were slowly percolating
into the soil. He was certain the act itself, pouring concrete into
the ground and raising beams hewn from the family forest,
would root him permanently to the place, could become the
anchor weight of his soul that ensured another escape was not
an option no matter how hard staying ever became.

"Why do you want to live way up here in the upper pasture, so far from the road?" his mother asked him when he
asked her permission.

"Because someone has to keep an eye on dad," Jack said.

"But I'll be dead soon enough, and then you can have the
whole farmhouse," Susan argued.

"Oh Mom, please don't say that. One of the reasons I'm
building it is because I know you're gonna be living a whole
lot longer."

"We'll see," Susan said. "I hope you're right, because I'm
sure not ready to go."

Jack's house-raising was an Amish kind of event, grassroots
and local. After laying a foundation, along with Javier's help

working overtime, he was able to erect the entire frame and the roof over the course of two weekends. Everybody pitched in a helping hand. Javier and the Colombians did most of the heavy lifting. Marvin helped Jack calculate angles and pitches and slopes that were new to him. Neighbors showed up, most of them second home transplants intrigued by the concept of a house-raising party. And there was a crew of Ed's friends, including many former farmers, who wielded hammers and screw guns, fastened sheet rock and positioned panels of tin roofing. And Susan and Katie brought waves of food and drinks from the bottom of the hill, providing the nourishment the group required to make it through the twelve-hour days of building. After the second weekend Jack had all the makings of a beautiful two-story post-and-beam house. Now he could gradually chip away at the interior work, the electric and plumbing and insulation, while turning most of his attention back to the farm. But before anything else Jack had to build himself a shrine.

He carved the little altar, more like a miniature cave, into the ground where the upper pasture met the woods, above and beyond his house. He dug the arching dome into the soil using only his pocket knife and bare hands. He used mud from the banks of the pond down below to solidify the walls, and to form a small floor where offerings could be made. There he placed the only souvenir he'd emerged with from the Minnesota wilderness, the wolf's tooth, bright white against the dark earth. He said a short prayer thanking the animal it had come from. Down on his knees, his forehead resting on the moist ground, Jack went out on a spiritual limb, crossing into uncharted religious territory.

He asked the spirits of the wolves to unite with the soul of his father and, together, to watch over the farm and bring it prosperity. He vowed to return every week with an offering for both, promising bones and coffee beans respectively. Walking back to his house Jack was more confused about his definition of god than ever, and more clear at the same time. He chuckled out loud over his prayer at the shrine, finding humorous irony in his plan to join his father's spirit with those of the wolves, animals Ed had so fiercely shunned while alive. But Jack knew his father would have no choice but to participate in his pagan, one-man religion. Ed Brown had held deep animosity but also a solid respect for the predator Jack had grown so connected to. In the after life all bets were off. His father's spirit would do what Jack demanded of it, because the underlying purpose was the land. And the coffee beans would never fail to lure him in for a listen.

That November, when the woods were open and the ground dry, determined to be the owners of a profitable small farm, something that was no less than a miracle in America those days, the brothers tapped hundreds of maple trees. They ran lines of plastic tubes in synaptic patterns from one tree to another, each line culminating in one of the steel holding tanks they scattered along the base of the sloping forest. They enjoyed the work, trading the drilling and the tap hammering duties back and forth. It was something Jack had always wanted to do, even as a kid, but had never found the time. With Javier and the Colombians holding down operations in the barn they now had the kind of freedom to explore new money-making endeavors, a freedom Jack and his father had never had. While traipsing through the woods on those afternoons the brothers didn't talk much. Words only seemed to get in the way of the new relationship they were trying to form. Simply working together on a project, however, helped solidify their bond not only to each other, but to the farm as well. During one of these afternoons in the woods Marvin hesitated, the gold drill bit pressing into the smooth gray bark of a medium sized sugar maple. Jack stood behind him with a steel tap in one hand and a hammer in the other.

"Whatcha waitin' for, bro?"

"Just thinking, Jack."

"You've been doin' a lot of thinkin' lately. Best thing for thinking too much is workin' too much. That's what I've found, anyway."

Marvin began squeezing the drill trigger, then stopped his finger and turned to face Jack. "Well, the truth is I traded my career for this farm, because I thought I couldn't have both. Only one or the other." He waved the drill in the air with frustration.

"You did the right thing, Marv. Because you love this place more than anything else. Just like I do. Although you probably don't realize it yet."

Marvin cocked his head. "Maybe you're right," he said, looking past the tree he was drilling, peering into the open forest he'd spent countless hours in as a boy.

"Of course I'm right," Jack said. "Now drill the goddamn tree."

The tension underlying their adolescent and young adult days had by no means vanished. If anything it had morphed into something deeper, becoming a permanent part of their relationship. This allowed them to finally accept it, to let the forest absorb its overflow, allowing their hard work to silence it all over again each day. And Katie helped out by largely staying away from the farm.

THIRTY-SEVEN

STICKING with their pact to boost the farm's income through profit-generating activities on the land, Jack and Marvin focused themselves into becoming businessmen first and farmers second. With their maple operation ready to go for next spring, complete with a sugar shack stocked with five cords of wood and a used evaporator from Vermont, as winter approached they spent much of their time inside preparing for the future. Marvin holed himself up in the office upstairs, where he drafted complex, color-coded land use plans and rotational grazing systems for their three hundred acres of property. He produced sheets of colored squares and patterns of dots, graphs and charts, soil composition analyses and planting schedules corresponding to a variety of crops. Jack used the kitchen table as a makeshift desk, where he sat and read any literature on sustainable farming he could get his hands on, highlighting important passages and taking notes on key concepts and specific practices. One of his primary focal points was a search for a new market to tap into, a niche that might be less well known than cattle. His research was nudging him more and more in the direction of meat goats, but until he could learn more he just kept that idea to himself.

Once the holidays were over, as dysfunctional family moments during Katie's appearances at the farm slowly became the past, Marvin and Jack lobbied for their mother to convert the farmhouse into an upscale bed and breakfast. At first Susan flat out refused to consider the idea.

"I don't want strangers spending the weekend in my house," she protested one frigid January afternoon, a day so cold even Javier was taking frequent breaks to come in and warm up by the wood stove.

"Mom," Marvin countered. "You have to think about the money we could bring in. For two couples to spend the weekend here we could charge close to a grand, and all we'd have to do is feed them some eggs and change the sheets."

"You mean all I'd have to do," Susan said.

"Yeah, you're right." Marvin showed her a puppy dog face.

"C'mon, Mom," Jack piped in. "I want to show you the carpentry skills I picked up along my journeys."

Susan brightened a little. Marvin gave his brother a thumbs up behind his back. Susan looked around the kitchen. "I wouldn't mind lightening this room up a bit. Put a few more windows in. Maybe a skylight or two. What do you guys think?"

"Sounds great," Marvin said.

"We should get to work on this right away," Jack added. "Like now."

"I'll go print out our plans so mom can approve," Marvin said, dashing up the stairs to the office.

"We're gonna need a website, Mom. Marvin probably knows how to do that too."

"But what should we call the place, Jack?"

"Hmm," Jack said. "I hadn't thought about it. Seems like your department, anyway. Why don't you ponder it for a while."

"I already know," Susan declared.

Marvin stopped on his way back down the stairs. "You already know what?"

"The name of our B & B," Susan bubbled.

"Oh yeah? What's that?" Marvin asked.

Both brothers hung intently on her words.

"Spirit Hollow Farm."

Jack and Marvin connected eyes.

Susan looked back and forth between them. "Well, what do you guys think?"

"It's great, Mom," Marvin said.

"Yeah. Beautiful," Jack added in a hushed voice.

Marvin carefully spread out a series of blue prints on the kitchen table as the weight of the name settled in silence around them. Future guests would have no trouble figuring out the source of half the title, given the farm was perched towards the end of a narrowing valley. The other half would be mysterious to the outsider, perhaps arousing images of a Native American chief, some ancient soul benevolently haunting the fields and forests. But the brothers immediately understood what their mother meant by the word spirit. There was rarely a day that passed when at least one of them didn't feel the substantial soul of Ed Brown lingering in shadows and sunbeams alike. He was the farm, and the farm was him.

As Marvin and Katie were drawn even closer together thanks to the birth of a son they named Edward, things at Spirit Hollow settled into a natural rhythm. The brothers worked together in relative harmony. Javier and the Colombians adjusted to their one boss being replaced by his two sons. The brothers' new projects became largely successful, generating the kind of additional income they needed to pay themselves decent salaries. Marvin proved himself to be an adept accountant, cutting costs and making wise investments, activities that paid off almost immediately. Although he didn't shirk his role with the labor intensive activities such as haying, he spent many daytime hours in their father's former office, powering himself on Diet Coke while working up spreadsheets and land use plans.

In order to get himself through the haunted hay rides, Uncle Jack took to carrying a flask of whiskey in his coat pocket. Otherwise, aside from a once-a-month poker night with Javier and the Colombians, he largely steered clear of his train-hopping ways. But by the time next summer rolled around, having been back for over a year, a restlessness began to settle in his bones. It would hit him during the late afternoon, when Marvin went home to Katie and their three employees headed to their shared apartment, leaving Jack alone with Susan. He enjoyed his mother's company, and her fine cooking always eased the transition from day to night. But the restlessness would return after dinner as a tingle in his belly, a particular hunger no amount of his mother's shepherd's pie could satiate. Awaiting sleep in his unfinished bedroom, the sweet smell of summer washing over him, his mind drifted regularly to memories of Katie, and their rooftop romance forever lost in the past.

THIRTY-EIGHT

JACK had tried to let go of her the day he left, but his heart had never really forgotten what loving Katie had felt like. After having had enough lovers to cut notches around an entire belt, his heart always circled back to Katie Smignatelli, to her dirty blond hair and freckles, Van Morrison mixes and their late-night, roof-top picnics. Lonely for the first time in his life, Jack craved another Katie. The layer of ice that had formed around his heart, the protective coating which had allowed him to stay away for that many years, was beginning to melt in tiny increments. He knew the right girl, all soft and warm and sweet, could thaw it out, completing the job Mariela had started. At thirty-two years old, Jack was trying hard to cultivate an ability to transcend his need for sex. He was hoping to avoid further complications from romantic love, which had begun to strike him as a false utopia better left for others to pursue. He'd tasted bodily freedom while his spirit had been in chains. His suffering was past him now, which brought a deeper kind of freedom than riding trains and roaming the country had ever given him. Free at last, the true work of his life was just beginning. Jack Brown was becoming the Farmer of Spirit Hollow. But there was so much other work to be done, the work of a husband, and a father, tasks he had yet to undertake.

Jack started visiting his earthen shrine more frequently. He prayed there feverishly, twice a day, asking the god he'd never stopped believing in, the force he credited with keeping him alive during his wild years of train-hopping, for another Katie to come into his life. That's all he asked for, aware that faith only worked when not too much was expected. The Katie he knew and loved before was gone, just as he'd become a new person since their honeymoon youth. He struggled to forget their talk of being soul mates, confirmed over and over by all the shooting stars, halfheartedly trying to convince himself their relationship had simply been a false dream encouraged by the euphoria of youth. He didn't mention this notion in his prayers, but if he was able to find a similar connection with someone else, being beside the right woman could supplement the one-way conversations with his god, comforting dialogs that had helped him survive the years away from home. With his heart blanketed by the presence of this woman, he would be able to focus his prayers solely towards the purpose of supporting the farm.

Early one afternoon Jack found his mother at the kitchen table writing out one of her characteristic lists. He sat down across from her. She looked up at him and smiled. Jack realized for the first time that his mother's hair was going from gray to white, and had been for the past year, right before his eyes.

"You look worried, dear," she said, reaching out to firmly squeeze his calloused, dirt-caked hand.

"Oh, no, everything's fine. I think I'm just a little nervous, that's all."

"Nervous about what?"

Jack shuffled his feet under the table. "Well, that's what I came to you to talk about."

Susan leaned back, folding her hands across her lap, settling into her listening pose.

"I hope it's a girl that's making you nervous," she said.

Jack's eyes widened. "It is. How'd you know?"

Susan once again took her son's hand in her own. "Because, Jack, a mother can see when her son is lonely, in need of feminine company, if you know what I mean."

Jack smiled. "Can't get anything past you, Mom."

"No you can't. Now, what's going on?" Susan slapped the back of the hand she'd been squeezing.

"I can't stop thinking about Katie. I mean, I never really stopped thinking about her while I was gone. But now it's all the time. I'm trying to force myself to accept that she and Marvin are happy, because it's true. But I can't stop my mind from asking what if, over and over. What if I never went away for all those years?"

"That question is irrelevant, and you know it, Jack. You were supposed to go away. Marvin was supposed to be with Katie. Things work out the way there were meant to. You know that."

"I do."

Susan smiled. Her face radiated motherly concern. "Do you still pray, Jack?"

"Yes," Jack said, slightly startled by the question.

"Then you should pray for a nice woman to come to you. It might just work."

"I have been, Mom."

"Then pray harder," Susan said firmly. "And in between praying, ask Javier if he has any advice."

"Javier? Why?"

"You never know. I've been getting to know him quite well lately. We've been having some conversations in Portuguese. I'm just saying he might be able to help."

"Okay," Jack said doubtfully, leaning over to hug his mother tight. "Thanks, Mom."

"For what?"

"For being a mom."

That night Jack prayed hard, for over an hour, wearing the skin off his knees where they pressed into the ground in front of his shrine. By the end of the session he was a beggar, pleading with his ancestors, the wolves, and the stars, begging them all for one more shot at love.

The next morning, after the first milking, Jack asked Javier to meet him out behind the barn. The little Brazilian had the nervous look of a man about to be reprimanded for a mistake he didn't know he'd made.

"Relax, amigo. I only want to ask your advice about something."

Javier's tension receded slightly, but he remained on guard. He wasn't used to being sought after for counsel by his employers. "Yes, senhor?"

"Well, I know you've been talking a lot with my mother."

His face brightened at the mention of Susan. "Sim, much talking, me and the senhora."

"Last night, when I told my mom that I think I need to find a woman, and very soon at that, she suggested I speak to you about it."

Finally the little man's overflowing, gap-toothed smile returned in full force. "Yes, senhor, I agree. You need the amor."

Jack laughed. "Okay, so we all agree on that, then. But why does she think you can help?"

Javier pulled on his pony tail, looking pensive. Jack wondered if this pose of deep thought was only for show, since the Brazilian must have known right away what Susan had been thinking. Javier sat down on the stone wall that extended out from the barn. He placed both hands on his knees. Jack paced back and forth in front of him.

"You know I have three daughters. Two are married. The most young, a very beautiful girl, Fluorinha, she not married, senhor. I know she very much wish to come visit her father. She live in Salvador. Bahia state, to the north. I go there, and bring her back with me, senhor. And then she can live here, in your new house. If you like her."

Javier seemed exhausted after this outpouring of sentences, more than Jack usually heard him speak during an entire week. Jack stopped pacing. He stood facing the little man, contemplating the idea. During their all-night poker matches he'd been privy to many arguments about who were the most beautiful women in the world, Colombians or Brazilians. Of course he vividly remembered the sensual charms of Mariela, his voracious Brazilian lover in Portland. The two men shook hands, hard and long, looking deep into each other's eyes, acknowledging the significance of the ancient human tradition of two families arranging the possibility of being joined through wedlock. Jack wondered if he was agreeing to this scenario so readily because it struck him as a fantasy that might satiate his longing in the short term, a daydream with little possibility of actually coming true. Javier reached into his pocket and pulled out his thin wallet. He lifted a small, bent photo from inside, and held it up for Jack to inspect. It was a black and white photo of a young girl exuding a beauty both exotic and earthy at the same time. Her eyes were wide open, bright. Jack handed the photo back.

"Javier, she's beautiful."

"Obrigado, amigo. She send me this. From the graduation." He tucked the little photo back into the wallet with great care.

"So," Jack said, "how much will it be for the trip, for you to bring her back here?"

"Three thousand dollars. Have to pay boat man. He pays others."

Jack frowned.

"Too much?" Javier asked nervously.

"It's not the money, Javier. Isn't it a dangerous trip? Is there a chance you won't make it back?"

Javier raised his thumb and forefinger, almost touching. "Small chance. But we make it. No problema."

Jack was starting to doubt the whole idea. But he trusted the Brazilian's confidence. All he had to do was tell Marvin. He thanked Javier and went inside the house. He found his brother in the upstairs office. A spreadsheet was displayed on the desk top monitor.

"Hey bro."

"Hi Jack."

"Wanna take a walk?"

"Sure. Let me just save this."

"Watcha' working on?"

"The budget for next year."

"Ahh."

Jack was glad he didn't have to sit in front of a computer screen figuring out a budget. Marvin would present him with a printed copy for his approval when he was finished. They walked together through the house, out the back door, down the driveway. When they reached the road Jack turned left, then stopped abruptly.

"Maybe we want to go the other way," he said.

"Yeah. I agree," Marvin said.

They turned and walked south down the road, heading away from the half-finished development that loomed in the opposite direction, its unseen presence a constant reminder of the potential fate of a failed farm. They walked in silence for some time. After they passed the former Smignatelli house Jack finally spoke up.

"I need a woman, Marv. It's as simple as that."

"I understand, Jack. Completely."

"And there sure ain't no prospects around here."

Marvin nodded. They let the notion that he'd snatched up the only one who could have been a prospect remain unspoken.

"So I had a little chat about the subject with Javier," Jack continued. "It was mom's suggestion. Turns out the guy has an unmarried daughter. She's twenty years old. And gorgeous. He thinks she'd jump at the chance to come here and meet me."

"That's great news, Jack." Marvin slapped his brother on the back. "I'm so happy for you."

"Yeah. Javier could make the trip in February. He says it will cost three grand to get them back safely, using a mule."

Marvin stopped abruptly.

"What? We don't have the money?" Jack asked.

"It's not the money, Jack. It's Javier. You know there would be at least a fifty percent chance he doesn't make it back. At least. We can't afford to lose him. He knows everything about the farm, down to the last bolt on the tractor. There's no way to replace him and keep up with our new ventures at the same time."

Jack kicked at the ground.

"Why don't you make the trip?" Marvin asked him.

"So you're saying I'm more expendable than Javier?"

Marvin passed his hands through his hair in frustration. "You're not expendable, Jack. Unless you did something very stupid down there you'll be back. You're a U.S. citizen. You can take a plane. Javier and his daughter will have to be smuggled into the country like drugs."

"Fine. I'll go myself then. As soon as possible." Jack spun on his heel and started walking briskly back towards the farm.

"Jack?" Marvin called out.

"What?" Jack yelled back without turning around.

"Wait up. Please."

He stopped and waited for his brother. They walked back together. Neither one said a word.

That night Jack took a break from packing. He climbed the spiral staircase to the recently completed third story of his house. It was a final addition he'd added on a whim, an octagonal cupola with glass walls that emulated the widows' walks common on the New England coast, in which the worrying wives of lost sailors used to pace through the nights. He thought of his version as a bachelor's walk, where he could sit in the evenings scanning the undulating horizons, wondering from which direction love might come to him, trying to envision a country-girl princess on horseback riding in to rescue his stranded heart. This night he was focusing his attention higher, on the star-splattered sky, the exact pattern of constellations he'd come to know so intimately on Katie's rooftop all those years ago. He was asking his god for a shooting star kind of sign telling him what to do.

Earlier, while packing his bags and trying to visualize this trip to Brazil in the name of finding a wife, Jack had been consumed by dread. It was hard to take in a full breath. He was rushing through something that should have been savored. So he'd climbed up into the cupola to assess his state of mind. To breathe. The question he was asking the stars was whether he should go on this trip, a journey that, regardless of its goal, was producing so much anxiety inside of him. While building his house he'd been consumed with a steady mantra, an over-and-over voice telling him he was here to stay, that to leave again would be his death, in one form or another. Yet here he was, driven by loneliness, preparing to fly off to another continent. What he was asking god, by way of the stars, was whether he needed to accept the losses that his erratic youth had cost him, and to hunker down in this house, on the farm he loved, even if it meant being alone for the rest of his days.

Jack was on his back, the top of his head pressed into the base of a cool pane of glass, the stars splayed out in a master-piece above. "Is that what you're asking of me, God, Dad, the wolf, whatever you are? That in order to become the Farmer, to fulfill my destiny in your eyes, I have to never leave this place again? That I must stay here and look my fate square in the eye every day, alone?"

Jack let his question, and that last heavy word, drift out into the cosmos for a long time. A shooting star, one heading north to south, would have told him to go. But the sky was silent, indifferent. In the stationary stars he found god's answer. He had to stay still, face-to-face with his karma. Eye-to-eye with Katie Brown during every holiday, birthday, graduation. It was time to let go of the ecstasy-inducing god of his youth, and the wild god of the wolves, in exchange for the gritty, earthbound deity that defined the life of a farmer. In this way he'd never be alone. He had the stars, his family, the cows. He had the farm. And the farm had him.

THIRTY-NINE

WHEN Jack informed Javier of their decision not to let him go to Brazil, and that he himself wouldn't be going either, Javier asked if Jack would write a letter to his daughter explaining the situation. He told him she'd been so looking forward to meeting him, and having a chance to come to America. Jack agreed, and so began a regular correspondence between them. After eating dinner with his mother every night, Jack would make the climb to his empty house at the top of the hill, where the first thing he did, before studying Portuguese or finishing off another detail of the interior, was add an installment to his next letter to Fluorinha. He wrote about the details of his days, sharing his inner thoughts about the littlest of events, always making sure to ask her a few questions about her own life. Javier helped him translate the letters, and they mailed one off to Salvador every week. A week later, without fail, her next letter would arrive smelling like coconut, with graceful words painted across the sun-worn paper in purple ink. Before long Jack didn't need

Javier's translations, and could savor the mystery of their air-mail relationship all to himself.

So Jack stayed, and the farm began to flourish. The waves of tourists from the cities grew larger every season. They filled the house on weekends, and all summer long. The hordes with sweaters tied around their shoulders came to buy Christmas trees in November. The people, many from New York City and Boston, bought maple syrup and meat, milk and cheese, eggs and wool sweaters, all the time ogling over the Spirit Hollow label and gushing about how great it felt to support a real family farm. The ones with little kids brought them to pet the baby sheep, ride the hay wagon though a maze of corn, or even just to play in the creek while their parents toured the sugar shack and the milking system. They came year after year, and Spirit Hollow Farm became a thriving business. Jack developed a secret belief that their father had left them with no money in the bank as a kind of postmortem challenge to adapt in order to survive, his statement that a farm, like any business, should not operate in debt. Jack would never let go of this theory, maybe because it pushed him through humiliating moments as the farmer-on-display for rich city folks. But motivating himself to work hard was never an issue. Hard work kept him alive, and climbing on the haunted hay wagon no longer required a medicinal flask of whiskey to ease his shame. All he had to do was think about his father's hands. His memory of them, his duty to honor those hands, gave him all the motivation he needed.

Jack knew without his father's lingering spirit watching over him, while his memories of that summer with the wolves receded further into the past, he might have run off to Brazil at any moment. But his father's undeniable presence, intertwined with the land and the house he'd built with his own hands, kept him on the farm day after long day. Jack understood that if he left home again his only destination would be death, if not a physical one than a spiritual demise from which he would never be able to recover. Most days around the farm were pleasant ones. He studied Portuguese at night in his house on top of the hill, and his relationship with Javier strengthened considerably. The two men were soon able to work with harmonious efficiency on any project they decided to tackle, while the two Colombians provided just the right amount of support. Marvin flourished with his role as manager, spending long stretches of time in the office upstairs working on budgets and pasture data and pricing trends. He would escape from time to time and lend his hand on a project, enjoying a break from being inside. Jack would tease him about wearing sunscreen, warning him to be careful not to harm his soft hands.

And Jack was comforted by the sight of his mother aging so gracefully. She was doing the same things she always did, keeping up the wood stove and preparing great Sunday feasts, maintaining the fruit trees, planting and harvesting the one-acre vegetable garden, spinning her wool, and engaging in the various side projects she had going on in her office room. Even though her pace had slowed she somehow got the same amount of work done as she always had, as if she'd learned how to make little dams in the river of time, had cultivated some kind of shaman's skill and could elongate a moment. Stretching seconds into longer minutes, she was able to accomplish as much in a day as she had thirty years ago. Jack loved watching her slow and steady strength as she completed a task. And he knew she watched him out of the corner of her perception, making sure he wasn't forgetting the wisdom he'd returned imbued with from his time in Minnesota. Susan knew, as well as he did, that he needed every ounce of this deep understanding he'd cultivated in order to handle Katie's visits to the farm.

Marvin's family came over once a month for Sunday dinner, on Thanksgiving day, and Christmas Eve. These visits were the hardest things Jack had ever endured in his life. They were more difficult than living on an inner city park bench or being shot at by Russian gangsters or sweating in front of bread ovens at four in the morning. He had to show up for these large dinners, feeling like his loneliness was tattooed across his forehead. He forced himself to endure Katie and his mother cooking together once again, the same sight he used to take for granted during the Sundays of another time, when Katie was his. Jack succumbed to Edward's persistent requests to play games, trying to avoid the role of the creepy bachelor uncle, straining to smile while organizing whiffle ball matches pitting Marvin and his stepson Greg against Jack and his nephew.

But what tortured him most of all about these gatherings was how Edward hardly resembled Marvin at all. Jack could see traces of Katie in the boy. He had her freckled cheeks and round nose. But almost everything else about him, his big hands and stocky torso and over-sized shoulders, was a carbon copy of his namesake Ed Brown. As this realization crept up over time, Jack struggled to swallow it down while remaining aware of the sickening kind of dread it created inside him, a feeling that severely complicated his thoughts about his future on the family farm.

FORTY

SUSAN had been aware of the Rising Moon Yoga Center ever since her belated honeymoon to a nearby bungalow, when she'd been inexorably drawn in by the butterfly sign and long, tunnel-like driveway. She first went there the winter after Ed's death, for the twenty-one day intensive class called Yoga And The Process Of Mourning. She went more in the spirit of work, knowing her grief for Ed was a task she had to accomplish by whatever means necessary, a job to slog through no matter how long it took. She was guilty about spending any of the life insurance money on herself, even though the entire family and all her friends had encouraged her to do so. Each year Susan found herself craving the little seaside village that had come to be like a second home, always choosing the month of March to get away as a reward for surviving another New England winter. Her body relished the chance to unfurl itself from the constrictions imposed on it by the endless cold. The warm breezy air would caress her spirit, rejuvenating it. And, best of all, better than the early morning dips in the ocean or the ecstasy-inducing yoga positions, was the fact that she wouldn't have to cook a single thing for an entire month.

Once her years of intense grieving for Ed had passed, Susan reached a place she sometimes thought to be more beautiful than anything heaven could promise. Not that she spent too much time pondering the concept of life after death. She'd never been one for the idea of heaven, or hell, for that matter. But she'd always been fond of the simple saying Heaven On Earth. Where else would it be? There was hell on earth too, and everything in between. Lately Susan was starting to realize that everyone had his or her own little piece of heaven to find in this world, and that was the primary task of living, no matter how long it took to get there. It had taken her seventy-one years, even after having been grounded in a moral code and strong work ethic her entire adult life. Now, beginning her eighth decade, she'd finally reached a plateau of gentle bliss. Even the darkest days of dead winter had a breezy lightness to them. And Ed's absence was no longer her first thought in the morning, as it had been for three years.

Her kitchen had transformed from a place of dutiful work, first with the daily task of filling her family's stomachs, then those of her weekend guests from the city, to a place of peace and solace. Constantly imbued with the smell of bread dough rising and classical music, Susan had a regular view of her two boys, grown men working the farm, through the window above her soapstone sink. It was on these specific occasions, kneading dough in rhythm with Mozart, watching Jack give his older brother a tutorial on some detail about the tractor, that Susan knew she'd made it to her version of paradise. The bliss was mixed with relief, a continuous bodily sigh that told her she'd finished all her jobs in life. The rest, her meals that still came in bountiful waves of made-from-scratch aromas, teaching her daughter-in-law how to spin wool, advising her middle-aged sons on life's difficult issues, were bonus activities. Susan was now living on borrowed time, dancing through a world that didn't need her like it once had, a garden for her still nimble mind to recreate each day, for her soul to feast on in the here and now of every season.

Following the initial period of years after Jack's return, while the brothers successfully instigated all the new tourism-based activities to supplement their milk revenues, things settled into a long stretch of continuity. The weather, seasons, animals, and tourists provided more than enough excitement around the farm. And then there was Katie. She was a country girl blossoming into a mother and a wife right before Susan's eyes, gleaning every new skill she taught her. In the long, drawn out hours following their ritual Sunday dinners, Katie mastered spinning wool, knitting, canning, and gardening. After becoming proficient at all of these, following her pregnancy with Edward, she began making forays throughout the region in order to pick up more advanced homesteading abilities, things like cheese-making and honey bee tending, eager to add whatever she could to the farm while also trying hard not to burden Jack with her presence.

Above all else Katie became a cook. During their once-a-month Sundays and holidays together Susan made a point to teach Katie hands-on lessons in her kitchen. After a couple years of mentoring she decided it was time to hand her daughter-in-law her bible of recipes, a three-ring binder filled with pages stuck with dried food and rippled from spilled liquids. Some were hand-written by relatives and friends, others cut from newspaper articles, and some photocopied from Susan's favorite cookbooks. The passing on of the recipe book was a ritual being born, a sacred moment in the family history witnessed only by the two women participating in it. Katie cherished the binder, and spent hundreds of hours trying to perfect the many varied dishes, carefully tucking the book in a fireproof safe hidden in the back of her pots and pans cabinet. Months later she called up Susan and nervously invited her over for dinner. She invited Jack too, but he politely declined. Although neither woman thought of it that way, the Sunday afternoon supper that Katie prepared entirely herself, using six different recipes from Susan's cooking bible, was an unspoken passing of the torch, a hand-off of responsibility from one matriarch to the next. But unlike her own supper preparations over the decades, solo endeavors of marathon proportions, Susan was happy to see Marvin actively engaged in helping his wife. He prepped veggies, preheated the oven, and cleaned the dishes as Katie progressed. Relaxing in a leather sofa under the cathedral living room ceiling, sipping fresh squeezed cider from that fall's apple harvest, Susan had to force herself to stay put. The smells of sliced onions and boiling potatoes and simmering meat, the building blocks of her legendary shepherd's pie, wafted across from the open kitchen, begging Susan to participate. But she sat still, pretending to read her book. She tried to remember that although her role was in the process of being taken over right before her eyes, yet another casualty in the forward steamroll of time, she still retained an even more crucial identity on the farm, one she wouldn't be relinquishing for some time.

Susan had planted and harvested every vegetable her daughter-in-law was using in the kitchen that Sunday afternoon. It would be a few more years before the task of raising her two young boys became anything less than a full-time job for Katie. Only then would Susan hand the reins of the one acre family vegetable garden entirely over to her daughter-in-law. This thought not only helped Susan relax, something that still didn't come easily to her, but also gave her a practical reason to keep on living. Susan Brown was by no means ready for death. It was just that she'd found living to be much more enjoyable when every day, week, and season contained a goal of some kind. Maintaining the garden, the soft rich soil that had been worked for over a century, provided more than enough goals, filling every year with the day-after-day challenges inherent to growing her family's food.

Their relationship grew stronger with time. Katie became the daughter-in-law Susan had always subconsciously craved. The calm and beautiful woman had returned so naturally into the family, and spent long hours with the grandmother of her youngest boy. When he grew older, Marvin and Katie decided Edward would be home schooled, while Greg would stay in the school system where he'd built up some solid friendships. Susan shared many of the teaching duties with her, often having an easier time getting the boy's attention than his own mother did. The three of them would take one field trip a month, traveling as far as New York City for a visit to the Natural History Museum. Edward taught Susan as much as she taught him. And that fierce look in his young eyes, his constant quest for the next challenge, brought warm memories of her husband flooding back in gentle waves.

One day, during a rare mid-week visit, showing her mother-in-law a new contra dance step in the living room, Katie went out on a limb. "I think I should sponsor a dance party at the senior center in town. You would be the star of the whole night! Maybe you could even bring a lucky man home."

Susan stopped dancing. She took a step back, her face stone serious. "Never," she said, fingering the cross under her

floral-patterned blouse. "For me, the commitment of marriage lasts beyond death."

Katie nodded. "I understand."

"You might understand, Katie, but do you agree?" Susan
asked, thinking about her son.

Katie hesitated before answering. "I do."

While making this strong assertion about her enduring
fidelity to Ed, Susan couldn't help wondering if, given the
opportunity, being romantic with another man would be a
proposition she'd definitely resist. Ed had been gone for three
years now, during which time the farm, and the land, had
substituted as her constant companion. But lately this hadn't
been enough to keep the urge for an amorous form of human
company, the only thing absent in her life, at bay.

FORTY-ONE

DAN Cook wasn't leaving his retreat in the jungles of Belize, the five-story tree house with an open air elevator, to resurrect Sunset Valley. He still owned the property up the road from the Brown farm. It sat there untouched, preserved like an archaeological record of a failure on the largest of scales, one of only two failures he'd ever experienced. While the unfinished development had been a business failure, the other had been a defeat of the heart. Beyond this general difference these two downfalls shared not only a geographic setting but, when contemplating both of them, Dan never wavered in his certainty that if he'd only had more time both projects would have been met with absolute success. Because everything else he'd ever done had. The regret produced by his persistent indulgence in hindsight prevented him from being able to lose himself completely in the magical new world he'd created in Belize.

Once he realized Susan could never be his for as along as Ed was alive, rather than wait for death to arrive at the Brown farm Dan had abandoned both pursuits at once, retreating for a jungle oasis. He owned ten square miles of rain forest, a tract that included two indigenous Mayan villages, an eco-lodge he'd constructed that employed most members of these villages, a butterfly sanctuary, and a resident population of three jaguars, all in addition to his towering tree house built of old growth bamboo and recycled sea glass. There were hydroponic gardens growing everything from coffee to mangoes, and a hunting reserve full of wild game. Dan Cook was the king of this miniature tropical empire. He had an array of locals at his beck and call. His every whim, once properly articulated and fully funded, was made into reality. His every need, both intellectual and physical, was satisfied without delay.

Of course this included his sexual desires. The young local women threw themselves at him, each one trying to outdo the next in a competition for his favor. They cooked him epic feasts, gave him hot oil massages, bathed every part of him, and gave him their brown bodily charms with great enthusiasm. For twenty years Dan had worked hard to have the opportunity to create this final masterpiece, the first place he could feel truly at home, while basking his senses in everything the little portion of paradise had to offer. The only thing tying him to the past, beyond his memory, was the weekly arrival of the Sunday edition of The Springtown Journal.

He would read the paper from cover to cover in his fifth-story library, where screen windows looked out above the jungle canopy, thoroughly enjoying his only palpable connection to life back in America. He read fast, since the humidity would wilt the newspaper in a few hours. One of his most ambitious endeavors in the jungle had been the lamination of all his books, tens of thousands of pages now immune to mildew and rain storms, stacked on the sea glass shelves of his open air library. One of these Sunday papers had stood out above the rest, an issue with a full-page obituary for Ed Brown. After reading the eloquent dedication, and seeing Susan pictured in black-and-white, standing with her family at the wake, Dan had made a pledge to wait three years. Now the time to make one last trip to Springtown had finally arrived.

It was Susan who saw him first. Spinning wool in the living room, her attention was distracted by a shiny car pulling over in front of the house. Unlike Jack's return in another, unrecognizable form, long-haired and ragged, Dan had been relatively unchanged by time, aside from having whiter hair and darker skin. Susan watched him dash across the road, heading for the front door, a formal entranceway the family never used. Even as he knocked repeatedly on the door she stayed seated at her spinning wheel, trying to strategize a reaction to this man once again intruding into her life. She waited one knock too long, the one that stirred Marvin from the upstairs office, his curiosity drawing him down into the living room.

"Aren't you going to answer it?" he asked his mother, still frozen in her wooden chair.

She nodded slowly, standing up.

"It's probably Jehovah's Witnesses or something," Marvin said as he stepped into the room.

"No," Susan said faintly. "It's much worse than that."

Or was it, she wondered. While reaching for the handle of the thick front door, Susan decided she had an obligation to invite Dan in, to hear whatever it was he had to say. The sight of him standing on the granite front step, deeply tanned, his green eyes shining bright, confirmed her decision.

"Mrs. Brown," Dan said, bowing slightly. "I came to give you my condolences, in person, for your loss."

"Well, Mr. Cook, I appreciate the gesture, but you are three years late."

Dan nodded his head slowly. "Yes, yes, I know. I live far away, and have many obligations. This was the first chance I got to make the trip."

Susan didn't believe this for a second, seeing past his graciousness into the likely motive behind his return. She stepped back, turning to wave him into the room. "Marvin, would you mind - " She stopped herself short. Marvin had left the room.

He was in the kitchen, on the intercom with Jack, whose shouting voice reverberated through the house for the guest to hear.

"I'm gonna kill him! I'm gonna fucking kill him!"

"Jack, easy," Marvin coached, his body recoiling with shock from this sudden emergence of the old, largely dormant Jack they all used to know so well.

"Easy my ass. Tell that shit head developer that I'm going to get Javier's gun, and then I'm coming in through the back door, and if he's still inside I'm going to shoot him. So can you please pass that message along?" Jack yelled through the intercom. "Do it politely if you want. Just do it."

Marvin turned around to see that Susan and Dan were now standing in the kitchen. "It's already been passed," he muttered before lifting his finger off the talk button. "Maybe you guys should take your little rendezvous off-site. I'll distract Jack for awhile, Mom. But Mr. Cook, I wouldn't recommend coming back. My brother doesn't joke about things like this."

Wide-eyed, Dan turned to Susan. "He would really shoot me? Murdering a wolf is one thing - "

"He didn't kill the wolf, Dan. But remember the pledge I gave you, about my husband shooting you if you came back to the farm?" Susan asked him.

Dan nodded sheepishly.

"My son would simply be acting on his father's behalf. That's what he does. Let's go. You can take me into town. We'll get a cup of tea, and catch up."

"Sounds good," Dan said, heading immediately towards the front door.

Susan gave Marvin a quick hug, and whispered into his ear. "Keep him calm, Marvin. I need to do this. For myself."

"I know, Mom. Go."

They didn't go to a tea house, or a coffee shop. They went to a bar. It was the seediest, smokiest bar around, all pool cue chalk and stale Bud. Two small, dusty T.V. sets played Fox News and a baseball game. They sat at the bar and drank shots of cheap tequila. Dripping with lime juice and salt they engaged in a kind of foreplay, flirting while pretending not to. They touched, at first accidentally amidst the bursting laughter of their conversation, and then intentionally. She traced his collarbone with a fingertip. He squeezed her wrist. She held onto his knee. Susan let herself go, like falling off a waterfall, and Dan was there to catch her. But even three tequila shots deep she had the presence of mind to define the rest of this rendezvous to her liking.

"You're going to take me to a hotel, someplace out of town," she whispered in his ear above the jukebox playing Guns & Roses. "We're going to stay up all night. Catching up. No sex. Then, in the morning, you'll bring me home. Actually, you'll drop me off a mile from the house. Any closer and my son will likely smell you."

"And then what?" Dan asked her, his emerald eyes sparkling with the question.

Susan shrugged her shoulders. "Then we'll take it one day at a time."

"Works for me!" Dan said, shouting out the words before composing himself a little. "I've just been learning how to live that way. The Indians in Belize have been showing me how."

"That's great, Dan. I've been living that way most of my life." Dan lifted his eyebrows playfully. "Who taught you? Your husband?"

Susan shook her head in slow motion.

"No sir. Ed had trouble taking it one year at a time. That man was always looking forward. No."

"Alcoholics anonymous?" Dan teased, lifting the beer he was chasing his tequila with.

"Buddhism," Susan stated, bringing her pint glass to touch his, letting a finger brush against the back of his hand.

"Cheers," Dan said.

"Cheers."

"To Buddhists."

"And Belizeans," Susan countered.

They laughed together.

"Are they even called that?" she asked.

"No. But it has a nice ring to it."

"It does."

Susan wasn't sure if it was very late that night or very early the next morning. She was walking the mile of country road towards the house she'd lived in for forty years. She shook her head, partly in an effort to clear out her hangover exacerbated by a lack of sleep, while also trying to come to terms with what she'd said to Dan in the bar. One day at a time? She was seventy-two years old. As her husband's death had shown her, all she could ask for from any given day was the good fortune to wake up, to have the strength to tend to her garden and take care of her house. Yet here she was opening the door of her heart for another man to step in. The night with Dan had been an act of rare spontaneity, one she didn't regret, at least not at first. Although he never brought it up, as the weeks went on she knew Jack was aware of her willing participation in Dan Cook's new round of courtship. She was missing so many of their previously shared dinners without a specific excuse that Jack was bound to have put two and two together. Susan only hoped her son's silence on the issue was another sign of his newfound maturity, and not some kind of volcanic eruption boiling just beneath the surface of his skin.

FORTY-TWO

Dan moved into the same motel he'd lived out of during the early days of Sunset Valley, before he converting his onsite trailer into a bedroom. He never ventured up to the old development, which he still owned, was still paying taxes on. And he was careful never to drive to the farm, instead picking Susan up down the road for their illicit dates. He let her set the pace, responding to her specific cues while cultivating a new degree of patience, reaching a deeper level of tolerance than even his project in the jungles of Belize had demanded. During this process he finally became aware of the fact that some women weren't to be conquered like victory prizes after sexual skirmishes, but instead could be complex creatures tuned in to what truly mattered. Women like Susan, the nurturers, the ones who sustained all life.

Dan couldn't help wondering what direction his life might have taken if he'd found a woman like Susan earlier. He asked her this once, while driving towards the farm after taking in a movie at the little theater in town.

"That's not relevant, Dan," she said. "You weren't ready for a woman like me. Until now."

He nodded, trying hard to keep his eyes on the curving road. He'd missed half the movie just staring at her face, her strong yet feminine features set in a peaceful expression, unchanged by the drama playing out on the screen. With the other women in his life he'd always been more focused on their bodies, distracted by hips and asses, breasts and bellies. Not that he wasn't attracted to Susan's body. He desired her fiercely. To him she looked closer to fifty than seventy. Her surprising libido also belied her age. After two months of dating they hadn't moved beyond long French kisses in his rental car parked along the side of the road. Dan knew he'd get to discover the treasures hidden beneath her clothes in due time, a time she would decide. So during dinner dates and Sunday walks, back road drives and town park picnics, he regularly found refuge in the details of her face, indulging in the view of her sun-darkened skin, her light blue eyes, the tiny golden hairs on her cheeks. At times, although he never told her, he felt like he could see the evolution of her beauty contained in her features, from teeny-bopper to twenty-something to young mother, through middle age to where she was now, perhaps more beautiful than ever. And when she held his hand he was as giddy as a high school kid on prom night.

Dan Cook couldn't help fantasizing about spiriting Susan away to his empire in Belize, to share his jungle kingdom for the rest of their days. But he also recognized that her attachment to the farm and her children ran deep, that he was no competition for those ties that defined her. Entering their third month of courtship, Dan was growing slightly urgent, as he was needed back in Belize to deal with some situations that had arisen since his departure. He decided to bring it up one Saturday afternoon while they were strolling through the park in town. He asked her to take a seat at a picnic table, because he had something important to say. He didn't bring up the fact that it was the same spot where Ed had almost choked him to death.

"What is it?" Susan asked, resting her chin on her hands, elbows propped up on the table.

Dan struggled to stay focused, to not lose himself in the blue of her eyes, a quality of color that always reminded him of his favorite swimming hole in his jungle oasis. "I want you to come to Belize with me. You don't have to stay forever."

"Don't worry. Forever is not an option."

"I didn't think it was. So how about a month or two? I know you'd love it there, and with winter coming . . ."

Susan closed her eyes, taking a moment to ponder the idea. She spoke without opening them. "I have been going to Hawaii in March every year since Ed passed, to a little yoga retreat I discovered on our honeymoon."

"I'll build you a yoga studio. And I'll import the best teacher I can find."

Susan smiled, opened her eyes. "I'll go. January to March, if you'll have me that long."

"Of course. You could stay even longer if you want."

Susan shook her head firmly. "No. I'll have to get back to plant my garden." A shadow of worry darkened her face.

"What is it?" Dan asked, trying to hold back his jubilation.

"Well, Jack's been very accepting, in his own silent way, about us. But when I tell him that I'm leaving with you for three months, I'm not sure what his reaction might be."

Dan looked away for the first time since they'd sat down. "What do you think he'll say?"

Susan clenched her jaw for a moment, then released it. "It's not what he'll say that worries me. It's what he'll do."

Even though it was only October, Susan didn't waste any time informing her sons about her plan. She called them both into the kitchen that afternoon, as soon as she got back to the house. Marvin and Jack sat down obediently at the kitchen table, hanging on her words. They'd never seen their mother nervous before, even during the days leading up to Ed's death. She procrastinated by putting some dishes away in the cabinets.

"Mom, spit it out," Jack muttered. "I've got work to do."

Susan turned to face them, resting her palms on the great wooden chopping block in the middle of the room. "First of all, Jack, in case you're not aware of it, I've been seeing Dan Cook for a couple months."

"I'm aware of it."

"Okay. I just didn't want you to get upset, to have to see it. So he's been picking me up down the road when we go out."

"I'm not upset," Jack muttered unconvincingly.

Marvin glared at him. "It's her own life, Jack. Does she have to stay faithful to dad forever?"

"It's not that," Jack countered. "I want you to be happy, Mom. But Dan Cook is an asshole. Simple as that. I just thought you had standards."

Susan brought up a hand. "Before you judge him, let me tell you, he's changed quite a bit. Trust me on this one, Jack."

Jack thrust his chair away from the table and stood up. "So what else do you have to say besides the fact that you've been secretly dating the developer who stole the Wilson tract from us? Like I said, I've got work to do."

"Wait, Jack. Sit back down. Please." Her voice was strong, unwavering.

Jack sat down. His eyes found the coffee maker in the corner behind her.

"Dan invited me to Belize, where he lives now," Susan continued. "I told him I'd go, for three months, January through March. I'll come back in time to get the garden going -"

Jack was up and out of the kitchen in a flash. The back door slammed closed behind him. Marvin stood up. He draped an arm around his mother's shoulders.

"Don't worry about him, Mom. He'll settle down. We both just want you to be happy."

Susan let her head fall into Marvin's chest. He rubbed her scalp. She closed her eyes, trying to envision Dan's tree house in the jungle. All she could see was a light shade of green.

FORTY-THREE

Susan went to Belize every winter for the next eight years, until Dan died of a sudden heart attack in her arms one tropical evening. After staying long enough to ensure his estate was forever preserved as an eco-lodge owned by the local villagers, she returned to Spirit Hollow fully aware that her last breath would be taken in the old farmhouse where she'd lived the majority of her life. Utterly content, her garden now fully passed on to Katie, Susan was content to watch the last of her Golden Years play themselves out. The tapestry of her time on earth unraveled slowly, the fabric of her life draping down across the farm. Rocking in her chair on the back porch, now screened in and her favorite resting spot during three seasons, Susan remembered all the times she'd listened to her husband speak of his bond with the land, the barn, the house. How the draining of their wells by Dan Cook's development felt like he'd been raped. Susan had always listened but never shared a similar connection, at least not one she'd been conscious of. Now, however, nearing eighty, her first grandchild already in high school, she was beginning to know exactly what Ed had been talking about.

Susan first noticed a palpable bond with the land upon acquiring a sudden ability to sense an upcoming shift in the weather. She knew a thunderstorm was on its way before the appearance of dark clouds or the sounds of rumblings. She could predict an early frost or a wave of Indian Summer. Sensing imminent blizzards and sunny skies alike, she began to understand the systems around her, how the grass and trees and soil interacted with the air. For most of her life, although she'd tried not to show it, her moods had been drastically affected by weather. Cloudy days made her melancholy, sunny ones lifted her spirits, while windy days made her nervous. From her new perspective, at one with the land, the weather was neither good nor bad, but a part of everything. Clouds provided the pasture grass with a rest from the sun in the same way the winter gave the soil a break from the plow.

Needing less and less sleep every year, Susan was spending long hours late into the nights on the back screen porch listening to the sounds, watching the stars appear above the ridge-line horizon. She understood now why Ed had chosen those specific burial procedures. At some point during her late-night, back-porch hours, Susan decided that she wanted her boys to do the same thing for her. So one morning she woke up early to catch Jack making a pot of coffee in the kitchen, a ritual he'd kept alive in his father's honor even after moving into his own house at the top of the hill. She caught him by surprise reading the front page of the newspaper at the kitchen table. He lurched in his chair, sloshing a bit of coffee out onto the paper.

"Mom! What are you doing down here so early?"

Susan glanced at the clock. It was quarter 'till five. She collected the back of her fleece nightgown in one hand and sat down beside her son. She admired the strong lines of his weathered face, his long, salt and pepper hair, his thickly veined hands. She wanted to tell him he reminded her of Ed at the same age, but kept the thought to herself. Jack didn't need to hear that from his mother. Besides, thanks to all the photos around the house, he likely already knew that he looked more and more like his father every year.

"I got up this early so I can ask a favor of you, before I'm gone."

"Mom, I told you I don't like that kind of talk."

Jack started to get up, eying the coffee pot and another cup to calm himself down. Susan put a hand on his leg, easing him back onto the chair.

"Jack, please. I'm eighty years old now. I just want to be prepared, if you know what I mean."

"Of course I know what you mean. You want us to cremate you just like we did for dad, and spread you out where he is. Now can I get another cup of coffee?" He gulped down the last of his coffee, flinching at the heat of the liquid.

She took her hand off his knee, releasing him. "So I guess that's a yes?"

"Yes, Mom."

Susan closed her eyes and listened to the sound of coffee being poured into a mug. Soon, my dear husband, she said inside her head. So soon.

Without Belize to go to in the winter Susan resumed her March pilgrimages to Rising Moon Yoga Center. After her stays there she would always return to the farm energized and ready for another eleven months of the daily struggles of grief and joy that still made her life worth living. A constant theme during these retreats now, surrounded by others in their final years, was the acceptance of death. Many came there to work on building a graceful approach to dying. But the concept was such a mystery, even in the minds of the teachers in their borderline state of enlightenment, that there was much discussion of the subject over the communal vegetarian dinners. Susan mostly kept to herself during these conversations. She was comfortable with death by that point in her life, could understand why it was so often humanized, given a character and a form. She knew death in the same way she knew a few passing acquaintances, people she wouldn't refer to as friends but who managed to show up in her life from time to time, lingering around just long enough to be more than strangers.

Her first experience had been the death of Ed's border collie Jill. Susan hadn't realized how close she'd been to that creature, the black and white dog always at her husband's heel. Jill's intense loyalty to Ed had not been the dog's choice. It was programmed into her border collie DNA. But still she'd managed to give Susan plenty of affection. The dog had proved herself, in Susan's mind, to be smarter than many humans she'd known. Jill had a most peaceful exit, cradled in the rocking body of her master, slipping into death's embrace from the complications of old age. Susan had been unexpectedly crippled with grief, realizing how much she'd loved the dog only after its death. Drowning in tears, trying to console her devastated husband, she didn't register death's presence in their living room that night. It was only looking back, after losing another border collie, seven sheep, three horses, five goats, countless chickens and cows, both parents, her sister, her husband of fifty-two years, and, finally, her lover, did she realize that death had been in the living room that day, had stayed for a few days afterwards, and had returned many times since. So Susan knew it was silly to be afraid of this entity that had just as much right to exist as anything else did. Her own ending didn't concern her one bit. She just couldn't bear to see another family member go. But she had a strong feeling that she wouldn't have to. The land would take care of her boys, and their children, long after she was gone.

FORTY-FOUR

SITTING on the front porch of his log cabin after a day of good work, looking out over the farm and beyond the mouth of the valley, Jack felt something close to contentment. Soon he would stroll off through his fields carrying a plate of steaming food for his mother. She didn't have much energy to cook anymore, but the last thing he and Marvin wanted was to put her into a nursing home. And, just like Ed, she desperately wanted to stay on the farm right through to the end. Jack was determined to make that possible. A big part of this goal was expressed in his nightly walks down the hill with her dinner, meals he enjoyed preparing, efforts that allowed him to cultivate a decent amount of confidence in the kitchen, another skill he could add to his list.

Jack was smiling to himself over the fact that he might have put one hot pepper too many into the spaghetti sauce for his mother's taste when he walked in through the back screen porch. What he saw in the kitchen stole his smile in an instant. His mother was draped over the table, her head resting on an unfinished scarf, her face serene and composed, eyes open. Jack didn't rush to her. He knew she was gone. Instead he just stood there in the doorway taking in the space that had been his ultimate sustenance, the source of life he always came back to, even now, with a kitchen of his own on top of the hill. There were hanging baskets of onions and fruit, glass jars of herbs and beans tucked into corners and lining windowsills, great cast-iron pans, counter top cutting boards with the scars from decades of his mother's knife work. The kitchen and Susan had been one. The sudden emptiness of the room was overwhelming him. He desperately wanted to shake his mother awake so the kitchen, and therefore everything else, would feel normal again.

Jack grabbed the cordless phone and stepped into the living room, purposefully averting his eyes from the table. He wasn't ready to deal with the sight of his dead mother. When he called Marvin's house Katie answered. He spilled the news to her, and was happy when she told him to cry, which he did, in long waves of sobbing that almost choked him.

"I can't remember the last time I cried," he said, wiping his tears off the receiver. "When Marvin and I spread dad's ashes on the pasture, I guess. But those were tears of relief, almost joy, because his suffering was over. These tears are different. They're hard."

"I know, Jack," Katie cooed. "What can I do?"

"I need to talk to Marvin."

In the living room Jack's eyes found his mother's Shaker spinning wheel in front of the quilted arm chair. Moonlight was striking one of the carved wooden spokes. He drifted towards it, drawn by the object that was so much a part of who his mother had been. Reaching down to turn the spool, half full of black and white wool, he wondered if he could mourn the loss of her through objects. He didn't want to see her ever again. He couldn't. Even though the task of building a coffin was destined to be his, and his presence at the funeral pyre would be required, he wanted nothing to do with what happened in between. Javier would have to help Marvin load her in and out of the milking tank.

"Hello?" Marvin said, startling Jack out of his trance beside the spinning wheel. He sat down in his mother's chair, letting the tips of his finger rest gently on the quilted arms, pinching the phone onto his shoulder with his cheek.

"Mom's dead, Marvin."

There was nothing on the other end except Marvin's long, heavy breathing. Jack listened to the breathing for some time. The sound relaxed him, as if his brother was sitting right there in the living room.

"I'll be right over, Jack."

"I think it's going to be a long night, so prepare yourself. Maybe you want to pick up Javier on your way."

"What? Why? Wait a second, did she -"

"Yeah, mom told me how she wants it done. The same way as dad."

"When did she tell you that?" There was an edge to Marvin's voice.

"A few months ago."

"And you didn't tell me?"

"I forgot about it, really."

"I see," Marvin said.

Jack got up out of the chair and started pacing around the living room. He wanted to go into the kitchen and brew a pot of coffee to calm his nerves, but that would mean walking past his dead mother. "Listen," Jack said sternly. "This is no time to be fighting about something that isn't important. She probably told me 'cause I'm the one who's always around, that's all. Now get your ass down here so I don't have to be alone with . . ."

He glanced down the hallway towards the kitchen.

"Yeah, I'm coming. And I'll bring Javier."

"Oh, and Marvin?"

"What?"

"Mom also told me, the same time she talked about her funeral, that she wanted you and your family to move into the farmhouse when she was gone."

It was a spontaneous lie that surprised Jack even while he was uttering it.

"Oh really? Well, of course she wouldn't tell me her other dying wish."

"She was always consistent," Jack said weakly.

"Yes she was. All of us Browns are."

"Just please come soon, Marv. I need a cup of coffee."

"Why can't you make it?"

"I can't go in the kitchen."

"Why not?

"Mom's in there."

Jack left the phone in the living room and went out through the front door that hadn't been used since the day Dan Cook had showed up. He looped around to the back of the house and sat down in the grass. He just wanted to be alone with the stars. Leaning back on his palms in the dew-soaked grass, he stared up at the clear sky. His eyes quickly found Orion. The familiar pattern of stars gave him a kind of comfort, a constant he needed now that the most permanent person in his life was gone forever. He let himself fall back in the grass. His view became the star-splattered sky and nothing else. He thought about his mother, wondering if her spirit would linger like his father's had been for all these years. If it didn't, where would it go? And would his father's soul follow her? It was deep stuff even for Jack to be contemplating. He shuddered in the cool, wet grass. A shooting star shot across the entire sky, north to south, answering the first question. Free at last, his mother was finally leaving the farm. He didn't wait for another comet to signal his father's departure as well. Jack knew it wasn't time for him to go. He sat up and clasped his knees in his arms. His dad was the same as he was. They were both there to stay. He had to believe in this before believing in anything else, god or love, heaven or hell. The land had a claim on him that it didn't have on anyone else but Ed Brown. Not even his mother had been bound to the farm in the end, evidenced by the dramatic shooting star. The blue headlights of his brother's car creeping up the driveway abruptly ended his meditations, jolting him back to the here and now of all that he'd just lost.

By the time Jack made it up to his house there was barely enough of the night left for a quick nap before the morning milk. Marvin was asleep in the house while Javier rested on some hay bales in the barn. They'd been able to drain an entire holding tank of milk into gallon bottles. Javier and Martin had gotten Susan's body, cleaned and dressed by Katie, in without a glitch utilizing their technique from the time the brothers had done the same with Ed. Once inside his snug house, Jack climbed the spiral staircase to his bedroom with heavy legs. Exhausted, his body was looking forward to the chance to lie down for a few minutes. In bed Jack thought about his lie to Marvin. He had no idea where it had come from. Maybe he'd grown so used to Katie being his sister-in-law that the notion of her replacing his mother's presence in the farmhouse kitchen would be a good thing for everyone. If he could make it work it would be his proof that he'd truly let go, had attained a state of being that might resemble something close to enlightenment.

With both of their parents now gone there was no need to hold on to the irrational belief that the farm was more his than Marvin's. His once ferocious competition with his brother had been softening steadily every year. Jack needed Marvin to be as close as possible now. The only question was whether his brother would make that leap. Jack figured that, given the way he'd expressed his mother's postmortem desire, Marvin would have no choice. Because if he didn't make the move back into the house he would think that he risked the chance of being haunted by what would be a serious ghost. Sensing dawn's approach, Jack got up and put his work boots back on, strengthened by the knowledge that while his mother had left, his brother was coming closer. Jack needed everybody around him now. Even Katie. He wanted to sit on his porch in the evenings watching his nephew play in the fields. He could picture Katie below in the farmhouse knitting hats for the winter just as Susan had always done, could see his brother and Javier chatting in the driveway. Right then, walking down through the fields, Jack decided he would build Javier an apartment off the back of the barn.

The old Brazilian, now in his seventies, had become like a grandfather to both Marvin and Jack. Although he fiercely vowed in his still-broken English that he'd never retire, Jack thought he should do something to make the old man's life just a little easier. He'd had a harder lot than most, and possessed an undeniable toughness to show for it. Javier deserved a commute of a few feet in his twilight years of handling the cattle. Jack knew his mother would have approved. Once past her initial wariness of the man, and the experience with the dead wolf, she'd warmed up to him considerably over the years. After much persistence she'd been able to figure out how to make a few of his favorite Brazilian dishes, steaming, lime-scented platters she'd bring out to the barn to lure him in for supper.

When Jack reached the barn he found Javier getting the pumping machines ready for the milking session. Jack slapped him on the back. "I just decided that I want to build you an apartment off the back of the barn, with a kitchen and everything. How's that sound?"

Javier focused on his task of lubricating the suction pads. His face was heavy with sorrow. His normally quick, wide smile was nowhere to be found in the wake of Susan's death. He nodded in somber acceptance. "I take that, senhor. Obrigado."

"No problema, my friend."

"I help build," he said, looking up at Jack, his eyes full of water.

"All right, then. But first we have another funeral to get through."

Susan's wake was different than Ed's. Not nearly as many people showed up. But Marvin and Jack didn't care about their mother's popularity with the locals. Ed had been like a celebrity across the county. He'd not only been the sole survivor of plunging milk prices, but had also defeated the developer who'd threatened their small town atmosphere, the only collective asset they really had left. The unfinished subdivision was like a ghost town without any ghosts, since no one had ever lived there. Susan had nurtured a few close friendships among some local women, most of them knitters and spinners. But her primary focus had always been on family time. The only problem with the low attendance at her wake was that it left them with over fifty gallons of bottled raw milk and a lot of the food Katie had prepared. The brothers decided there could have been much worse things to deal with, and set about eating the food and drinking the milk with their families.

If she could have, Susan would have told people it was the yoga that allowed her to experience her own death as it was happening, to realize she could treat it the same way she had life, as a series of jobs, little tasks to be taken up and completed. She also would have pointed out her long-held theory that the Tibetans were right about the nature of dying. It was a long and arduous journey, a dark path through a constant barrage of fire-breathing demons trying to scare her from continuing forward, strange beings with hate in their eyes boring down on her. She quieted her fear with the intuition that the soft white glow in the distance was a much better destination than anything that lay behind. When she offered these demons love and understanding they moved aside one by one. Next she was confronted by a steady flow of relatives emerging from the darkness all around her, family members from the past and present and future, all of them with a need, coming at her with giant mouths begging for her help, for her motherly attention they weren't getting anywhere else. She knew they were on a mission to distract her, so she focused on continuing forward to the light that resembled a full moon behind a thin veil of clouds. Except this white glow had a subtle warmth to it, like the gentle sun of an Indian Summer day. When this stream of relatives finally abated, she'd seen everyone except her husband.

Then came the animals. First there were larger, more ferocious versions of creatures she'd seen on the the farm over the years, a black bear the size of a grizzly, coyotes bigger than any wolf. Unlike the previous attackers she knew these beasts were not a threat to her soul. Her body, the only thing they could possibly have harmed, she'd left far behind. So she made it past them easily, and found herself in a meadow of grasses softer than silk, surrounded by the gentle animals she'd always loved, swallows and rabbits and deer. They told her with their eyes to wait there. She did, floating in a warm sea of light.

At some point a voice, soft and female, made ripples across the white bath she was suspended in, answering the only question of her unanchored spirit. "Yes, you can stay here as long as you want. Here there is no such thing as time. At some point you will want to go back. Then I will come to get you."

Susan would wait there until she saw her husband.

FORTY-FIVE

THE day after Jack and Javier completed the apartment off the back of the barn the little Brazilian vanished. The Colombians wouldn't say a word about it when Jack pressed them. All he wanted was confirmation of what he suspected. Still a hard worker by all means of the definition, Javier had likely noticed his declining capacity for putting in a full day. Aware the brothers would be fine without him, knowing they would have tried to stop him from going if he'd informed them of his plan, he'd left for Brazil in the middle of the night. Jack was certain Javier had been receiving letters of his own from Fluorinha. She had recently turned twenty-eight, by no means a young woman in Brazilian standards. It was now or never, and Javier had made his move.

Ever since Marvin and Katie had moved into the farmhouse Jack had been declining Katie's persistent invitations to join them for dinner. He'd usually been working with Javier on the apartment well into the evening, and the little man often accompanied him up to his house, where Jack would

whip them up something simple to eat. On the first night of
Javier's absence Jack didn't feel like eating at all. Instead he
made a small fire in his wood stove, even though the fall night
lacked any chill, and curled up on his futon with the shoe box
full of weekly letters from Fluorinha. He stayed up all night
re-reading every one. There had been a few phone calls as
well, so he tried to remember her soft voice, using his imagination to hear her speaking the words he was reading.

Jack loved her descriptions of daily life. She seemed to
thrive on taking care of things; her aging mother, her sisters'
little children, the stray dogs in her neighborhood that no one
seemed to feed or shelter. Little things made her happy. Her
words jumped off the page when she wrote about a soft breeze
easing the heat of a summer afternoon, or the smell of farofa
being sauteed in butter on her street corner, an aroma she
couldn't describe to him even in Portuguese. All she could do
was offer to make it for him if they were ever lucky enough
to spend time together. Jack smiled when he read that line
for the second time. It was nearing two in the morning. He
remembered when Javier had translated it for him, how his
black eyes had lit up with delight.

"She wants cook farofa for you, senhor Jack. Muito bem!"
he'd said, obviously taking this desire of his daughter as a
major step forward in their pen pal romance.

Energized by the letters, and the hope that soon this
woman would be there to replace them, Jack stayed up right
through the time for the morning milk. He got dressed in the
gray light before dawn, put the fire to bed, and strode down
the hill to meet his brother, who would hopefully be waiting
for him in the barn.

FORTY-SIX

STICKING with a Brown family tradition, while settling into the farmhouse Marvin and Katie left Susan's office untouched, treating it the same way the brothers' childhood bedrooms had been handled by their parents. But following a little ceremony Jack had led from his shrine in the upper pasture on the one-year anniversary of their mother's death, Marvin decided the time was right to clean out the little room off the kitchen. Javier had yet to return, although he'd made contact from Brazil a few months back to announce he'd at least made it there safely, so the brothers sought out many diversions to keep their minds off his precarious return trip with his daughter.

A couple days into the project, overwhelmed by the amount of intellectual pursuits he was trying to compartmentalize, Marvin came across back-to-back discoveries that shocked him. First was her diploma from Wellesley, framed and polished but tucked away in the depths of a bottom drawer of the desk. No one in the family had known, until that moment, of Susan's late-night, off-campus effort to finish her undergraduate degree. The brothers would never figure out why she wanted it to be a secret. Jack guessed their father wouldn't have supported her wasting valuable energy on a degree that a farmer's wife had no practical need to obtain. Marvin had to agree. The very next night he stumbled upon an even more dramatic artifact. It was a letter addressed to both her sons. Marvin couldn't stop his eyes from reading the whole thing. He wished he'd been able to hold off, because when he finished he had no choice but to go up to his brother's house and show him what he'd found.

Marvin sat at Jack's hand-hewn maple table while Jack fired up Ed's old coffee maker, which had finally migrated up the hill after Susan's passing. When the machine started gurgling to life he joined his brother at the table.

"So, what'd you find?"

"A letter. To us. From mom."

"Weird."

The folded letter sat on the table between them.

"What's it about?" Jack asked.

"Sunset Valley."

"No way! You know, I've been wondering lately why we never asked mom what Dan had done with it, I mean the guy didn't have any children, or even siblings as far as I can remember."

"You're right," Marvin said.

Jack's eyes lit up. Adhering to an out-of-sight, out-of-mind philosophy, neither of them had ventured up the road to the old development during all these years.

"Did he sign it over to her?" Jack asked eagerly.

"He did." Marvin reached out and slid the letter over to Jack.

"Oh, man, we can more than double the size of our farm! How great is that?"

"Read it before you get all excited."
Jack snapped the paper open. He read the words out loud.

Dear boys,
    You will be reading this letter after I'm gone,
    but don't be sad, I'm in a good place. Dan
    confessed to me what he did to obtain the
    Wilson farm. I chose to forgive him for this,
    as I hope you boys can forgive me. Before
    he passed on, as a kind of retribution, he
    signed the title over to me. I decided to put
    the land into a conservation easement. That
    land can never be touched again, except by
    the footprints of people taking walks, or the
    paw prints of the animals that call it home.
    I do hope you'll respect my decision.

Jack locked eyes with his brother. "Was she going crazy!?
What would dad have said about this? I can't believe her."
    "Read the rest," Marvin said solemnly.
Jack took a deep breath before continuing.

    I know you boys are likely upset with me.
    And your father, bless his heart, would
    never have approved of what I've done.
    But it was my decision to make, and I
    made it because I firmly believe there
    is great danger in things getting too
    big. Especially farms. I didn't want
    you boys to lose perspective. Our
    farm is big enough to keep the both
    of you busy for the rest of your lives.
    And nature, wild things, need places

to call home too. So I wanted to do something for the plants and animals that are such a part of this place we love. I've named you both as the caretakers. The first thing you'll need to do is make a nice sign. I hope you boys understand me. I love you both so dearly. Goodbye.

Each brother was too busy trying not to cry in front of the other to be upset with their mother about what she'd done. Marvin, consumed as he was by bottom lines thanks to his position as manager, would hold on to the belief that his mother had done the wrong thing for years to follow. Jack, however, clearly saw the wisdom of her decision by the end of the following day, after he and Marvin made a visit to see what had become Sunset Valley Sanctuary.

The next evening, as Marvin and Jack drove north up their road, they both expected to see the mini-suburbia in a relatively similar state to what it had been around the time of the lawsuit. Jack stopped his truck where the old welcome sign had been, the colorful scene of rural harmony on top of which he'd draped the wolf carcass on that fateful night. But the only evidence of the sign was a pile of rotting, painted wood lost in towering weeds. The neighborhood roads, formerly smooth black asphalt, were now impassable. Sumacs and oak saplings had burst through the pavement, creating gaping cracks. Field grasses had filled in these cracks, and the surrounding tar was beginning to crumble.

The brothers wandered down these broken streets in hushed amazement, taking in the sight of a powerful man's abandoned vision being so boldly reclaimed by nature. The concrete foundations that once defined the landscape had buckled and fallen, filling in the basements with piles of rubble one step away from dust. Most were hidden from sight by towering brambles, vines, and young trees reaching for the sky. Amidst the vegetation stood the noble water pumps, their red paint chipping off, their rusted handles twisted into odd shapes. Light posts lay fallen beside street signs, both swallowed by the all-consuming vegetation. What rose up above everything, shining silver in the sun, was the old Wilson silo. It was largely unaffected aside from a few daring vines clinging to its smooth rounded sides.

"Looks like nature's taking the place back for herself," Jack said, breaking their silence. "In the end, maybe neither farms or developments will survive. Just the earth, in all it's crazy random glory."

Marvin shifted his attention to the top of the surrounding ridge line. "I really hope mom put in a clause that allows us to use the power from those things down at Spirit Hollow," he said, nodding at the towering turbines still standing, spinning earnestly in wind currents the brothers couldn't feel where they stood.

Jack smiled at his brother's persistent fiscal practicality. But he was still in a state of rapture over this surreal scene they were standing in the midst of, and didn't want to be distracted by any more words. He left his older brother standing on a crumbled street and started hacking his way through the brush, heading towards the silo. He came upon a swampy marsh, what had formerly been the Wilson's pond for their herd of cows. The giant white boulders Dan Cook had lined the shore with were barely visible through thick stands of cat-tails. His beach of imported sand was now a mud flat. Jack skirted around the mud, still aiming for the silo now only a few hundred feet away. While crashing through the five foot tall grasses and pricker bushes something in the mud stopped him short. He bent down to one knee. The large paw print was unmistakable, another version of the same ones he'd seen in the farm's driveway all those years ago.

The claws made clear marks in the soft wet earth, telling him the wolf had been there just recently. Jack placed a palm on the print, barely covering it with his hand. He looked up at the silo, then the ridge, and then the sky. His mind wove a connection between the farm and the wild. He saw how his mother, in preserving Sunset Valley, had shown anyone who happened to be looking that these two worlds, although sepa-rate, depended on one another to exist. Farms grew food so people didn't have to venture into the wilderness to kill some-thing to eat, thus forcing wolves onto farms to do the same. Jack tipped back his head, closed his eyes, and let out a long, deep howl that emerged from the bottom of his lungs and echoed back and forth across the valley. Afterwards, while catching his breath and considering saying a quick prayer, his howl was answered by another. Jack stood up. All his senses were on alert. The hair on the back of his neck stood up. Goosebumps popped out on his skin. The wolf had answered him, one final confirmation that his god existed, that his mother had done the right thing in preserving this place. Jack never suspected it had been his brother howling. And Marvin never told him it was.

FORTY-SEVEN

YEARS later, Jack woke up with a start. He knew right away that a substantial change had happened, something beyond the gradual alterations to his world that he'd been watching take shape over the last decade. To begin with he'd recently turned sixty-five, crossing into the realm of an official senior citizen. Dwarfing this personal threshold were the shifts in the normal cycle of things lately, strange weather patterns that he found deeply disturbing. In August they'd had twenty days over a hundred degrees and now, in early October, a snowstorm. Every other year there was no maple sap run. There were droughts and floods from one season to the next. Haying time became impossible to predict, and one cut a year was being lost to the unpredictable elements. The only things that held steady were the Christmas trees he and his father had planted, and the tourists he and his brother continued to woo. Marvin had opened a new law office in town, and had been taking on a few cases to supplement the farm's income. Beyond these local effects the world as a whole was imploding on itself. The Chinese, having poisoned their own country, were flooding the U.S. in waves, forcing the government to close the borders. Jack had already evicted a few Chinese nomads from the hay loft in the barn. India and Brazil were now the two largest superpowers, but even they were struggling to maintain their prosperity in the midst of a global ecological crisis spiraling in a rapid descent.

Following his birthday, now that their daughter was old enough to travel, Fluorinha had taken her to Salvador to visit her Brazilian relatives for the first time. So Jack had been sleeping in the glass-walled cupola perched atop his house ever since they'd left. Rising to his knees he pressed his palms into the cool, frosted glass. He was trying to hone his mind in on what exactly had shifted, the specific change he'd felt immediately upon waking, something beyond all these other changes that had been going on for years now. He pressed his forehead into the glass. His warm breath melted a circle into the frost, like the tiny window of a ship's cabin. Looking out through this peephole his view was only the upper pasture, the still-green grass poking up through a layer of fresh snow. And then it struck him like a fist in the gut. His father's spirit had left the farm. This is what had changed in the night.

The first thing Jack did upon leaving his house was to head for the shrine at the top of the hill. There he would ask his god what to do next. He wondered who, or what, would be listening to his prayer now. Not only had his father's soul departed, but Jack hadn't heard the howl of a wolf in a decade. He had to fight the notion that he was simply using one part of his mind to address another, because he didn't want to open up the possibility that this was all that praying ever was, a two-way conversation with oneself. So this time Jack chose to focus his attention on the ground. He spoke to the soil that made up the shrine. Without a cow bone or coffee bean offering to distract him it was an easy thing to do. He dug his hands into the rich earth while he prayed, feeling filaments of his energy course out and into the ground, before returning to him stronger, enriched with substance. His voice was low, rhythmic, strong.

"Please, good earth, I ask you to give me clarity, to tell me what you need from me. As always, I am your servant. I have given to you as much as you have given back to me, fine soil. So please, hear my prayer, and when the time is right, allow me to see your answer."

It didn't take long for Jack to witness the soil's answer. His wife and daughter had recently returned from Brazil. Now more than ever his daughter, whom they'd named Javia in honor of her grandfather, with her perfectly smooth skin deepened into a darker shade of brown, her long black hair cascading in whirls across her shoulders, was striking Jack as a symbol of what the future might hold. Not for a moment did he ever regret not having a son. Beyond the issue of her gender his daughter seemed destined to flee for Brazil rather than stay in America and eventually settle down on the farm, appeasing Jack's half of her ancestors. He could see this glimmer in her eyes after the trip south, a tropical twinkle in the corner of her brown eyes that spoke of an easy familiarity with a place he knew only through his wife's descriptions. Jack had yet to make a pilgrimage to Fluorinha's homeland, as he was still holding onto the belief that to leave the farm a third time would be his death, spiritually, physically, or both.

So Jack was thinking about his daughter as well as his still unanswered prayer while he ventured up into the woods above his house with a chainsaw, embarking on the first of many tree-felling expeditions required by what was already prom-

ising to be another long and hard winter. His first selection
was a medium-sized oak with a splintered trunk. He kneeled
beside the tree and said a quick little prayer, thanking the tree
for giving up the last few years of its life to keep him and his
family warm that winter. He pulled the cord on the saw. The
engine sputtered to life. Jack stood up and brought the spinning blade into the thick, grooved bark. His arms shook as
the saw ate its way into the trunk. Jack smiled. He loved this
annual task, a job independent of milk prices and tourists, a
task of pure self-preservation.

Nearing the middle of the trunk, with his second angled
cut about to meet his first, the saw hit a giant knot and kicked
back. It spun out of Jack's hands. The whirling blade sliced
deep into his thigh. Jack's entire body went numb as he stood
watching his blood spill out onto the forest floor. The hot red
blood melted quickly through the thin layer of snow, soaked
up eagerly by the unfrozen ground. He thought about dropping to his knees right there, to give in and let himself be taken
by the land. But even within his state of shock he was able to
resist this first instinct, to see it wasn't the right path to take.
Staring down at his blood being absorbed by the forest floor
he saw in perfect clarity the answer to his prayer at the shrine.
The land was warning him to leave, telling him that contrary
to his long-held belief, to stay on the farm would now be his
death. Standing there on a precipice between the worlds of
the living and the dead, Jack heard the land speak. The place
he'd given most of his life to wanted to be left alone, to enter
a period of many winters, an era of darkness and rest until a
new dawn arrived to awaken its fertility all over again.

Jack turned and hobbled his way out of the woods. When
he reached the pasture the pain finally hit in a sharp, gut-
twisting surge. He screamed out, then fell to the ground.

While he struggled to cinch his flannel shirt around his thigh in a makeshift tourniquet he heard the door of his house slam, and the urgent voice of his wife calling out to him.

"Jack!? Where are you, Jack?"

"Over here," he shouted back, using up the last of his energy. "We have to go," he said to himself, just before passing out.